The Last Best Resort

John Standridge

Cover art: "Sea Breeze" by
Claudia León Shapiro
USED BY PERMISSION

To Lynna Ruth Standridge,
the one love of my life

Disclaimer

~~~~~~

This book is a work of fiction. Names, characters, places, and incidents either are products of the author's imagination or are used fictitiously. Any resemblance to actual events or persons living or dead is entirely coincidental. The futuristic scenarios described are not a prediction, but rather a fantasy; and any that may transpire are not of the author's doing. For perspective, this book was written during the time period from October, 2009, to March, 2010, during which time the DJIA advanced from 9,750 to 10,900, with the general expectation that the recession was over and the stock market would continue to rise.

Acknowledgements

It is with a great sense of pleasure, honest humility, and personal freedom that I acknowledge a lifetime of teachers, friends, and above all, family. Winston Churchill could have been referring to me when he derisively remarked, "He is a humble man with much to be humble about."

From a time when I was very young, my mother, the consummate English teacher, read *with* me, at least one book per day, honing my love for literature and literacy. I remember all of my teachers, but she was the best.

Friends nourish and nurture the spirit and soul. Their friendship is an act of grace: it cannot be bought or obtained by any willful means. I cherish those whose giving and nurturing spirit has called upon them to bestow upon me that greatest of gifts – friendship. It is life affirming and validating like no other dynamic.

I am blessed with a loving wife and two sons who daily give me cause to be proud of them. I have written rather extensively of my nuclear and extended families in a previous work of non-fiction, *The Delaney Kids~ Bought and Paid For*, so I won't go into details here. But it is my wife and lifetime partner, Lynna Ruth Standridge, who makes all things possible. Women are empowering that way. Not only has she supported my efforts and activities for over forty years, she is my coach and spiritual mentor, my compass and my stability. That she would read, edit, and offer suggestions for this current work of fiction is merely icing on the cake.

It was, however, the proof-reading by my son, Aaron, which thrilled and amazed me. It should not have come as such a surprise how incredibly literate and erudite Aaron has become. I am nonetheless exceedingly grateful for his last minute renderings and advice.

Lastly, I would return to another of Winston Churchill's quotations. It fits so clearly the process of writing and publishing a book.

> *Writing a book is an adventure. To begin
> with, it is a toy and an amusement; then it
> becomes a mistress, and then it becomes a
> master, and then a tyrant. The last phase
> is that just as you are about to be
> reconciled to your servitude, you kill the
> monster, and fling him out to the public.*

Turning and turning in the widening gyre
The falcon cannot hear the falconer;
Things fall apart; the centre cannot hold;
Mere anarchy is loosed upon the world.

– **William Butler Yeats**
Irish poet and Nobel laureate

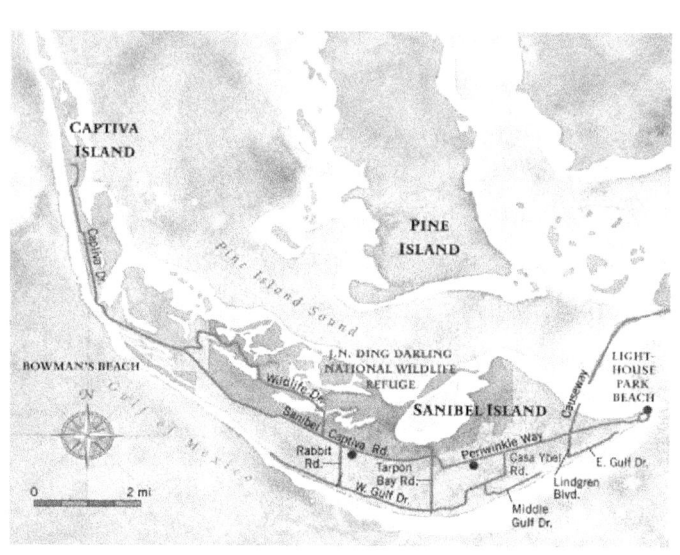

PREFACE

Sanibel Island, 2023 – the world has changed after a decade of widespread anarchy. Scattered small religious wars continue in Iraq/Iran, Syria/Palestine, Pakistan/India, Indonesia, and throughout Africa. A global economic collapse, a decade previous, has produced widespread unemployment and a loss of state services ranging from police protection to government checks to infrastructure, such as road repairs, dependable electricity, and sanitation. The wealthy and privileged individuals have found relatively safe enclaves such as Sanibel Island, although the causeway had to be demolished and the beaches must be patrolled. Satellite services and cell phones still provide service to those fortunate enough to have working devices, and the Internet is partially functional. Water, gasoline, food, and medicine are at a premium, however. With no means of enforcing its laws and with looting by roving bands of ethnically similar ideologues being widespread, the US government functions in name only. Cottage industries and peaceful communities of back-to-the-earth types survive through self-sufficiency.

Law and order is enforced locally to the extent possible. Regional military factions constitute a type of citizens' militia, forming *laissez faire* governance. Ten years into the process of sweeping away the old order, the world struggles to find its new direction and purpose.

Life on Sanibel Island is an anomaly – an artificial attempt to live the life that went before. Most people on the island are not deluded, just determined to preserve some semblance of "civilization." This former resort island now becomes their last best resort in an attempt to resist the changes sweeping over the planet. For some, the island is a base of operations; for others, the better of poor choices for hanging on to a vanishing lifestyle. Still others have found a hideout from a world that was seeking to punish them – a world that now no longer cares what they had done that was deemed wrong when the societies functioned. Some of these characters will grow, becoming wiser, more mature, self confident, change agents, and simple decent people. Some will leave; some will die.

Book One

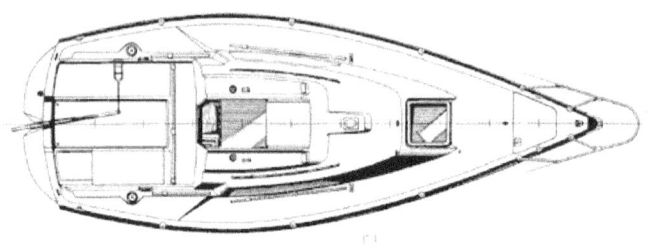

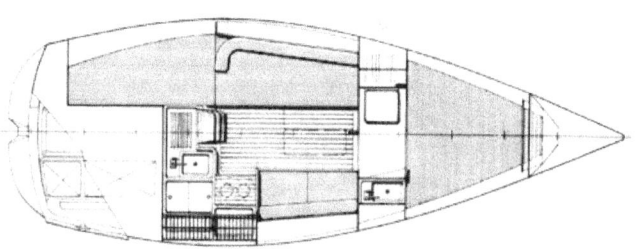

2

Chapter One

The blast caused Jesse to bolt upright out of a sound sleep. It was close, maybe a mile away. It was sabotage, not terrorism. Jesse O'Connell's first thought, later to be confirmed, was that the Captiva crew followed through on their plans to blow up the small bridge linking Sanibel and Captiva Islands. The citizens of Sanibel had set the example two years ago when they hired professional demolition experts to permanently scuttle a section of the long causeway linking Sanibel to the Florida mainland. Clearly the small population of multi-millionaires on Captiva wanted one more layer of security. Despite the patrols, some paranoia persisted. Some of the necessary workers on

Sanibel were undesirables at some level on Captiva. It had always been like that – one-upsmanship in the exclusive society game. But this game was about more than just survival, it was about surviving in style, survival with amenities.

Jesse's cell phone pinged. *Give me a ping, Vasili. One ping only, please,* thought O'Connell, summoning the obscure reference to a favorite movie. One ping only – just enough to get his attention if he wanted to be found. One ping only – just enough for plausible deniability if someone complained that their call was ignored.

The caller ID told Jesse that the caller was Sheriff John Cochran. "OK, I'm awake. He heard it, too," Jesse said to no one there. Jesse pushed the green phone icon but did not talk. He never spoke first.

"Jesse, it's me," said the sheriff.

"Hello, John. It's a little early for fireworks, isn't it?"

"Or anything else. Can you meet me at the pass?"

"It will take a few, but I'll be there soon enough."

"By land or by sea?"

"Not much moon. I think I'll walk. Be there in about twenty minutes."

What Jesse left unsaid was that it was too much trouble to motor a twenty-seven foot sailboat along the island coast when a brisk walk would get him there just as quickly and do a far better job of waking him up.

"Take your time," said Cochran. "I wouldn't want you to get there first. There's no telling who might be hanging around." Cochran was warning his friend about the perpetrators being in the crowd of the curious. Of course they would want to watch the investigation, would want to see if anything was noticed that would point to them, and would want to see how upset the Sanibel crowd would be.

Jesse arrived first despite Cochran's warnings. The walk from Tween Waters' marina to Blind Pass was short and brisk. Only a handful of Captiva residents were standing around looking at the damaged bridge. Some had gone back to their beds already. They probably knew this was coming. The serious conversations could wait until daylight, over coffee. The few that *were* there all knew each other. Everybody knew everybody else on the islands. Hushed conversations were happening in groups of two or three or four.

The bridge was a mess. Far more explosive force was used than was necessary. The job was amateurish and even sloppy. Someone with more C4 than sense had probably parked a jon boat or some similar small boat against the pylon and let 'er rip. An entire section of roadway was missing.

Mangled rebar and concrete stood as testament to the structure that stood there less than an hour ago. The bridge was no good even as a footbridge now. Was this necessary? Some paranoid fool (or fools) just created a massive inconvenience. What was the damn point?

John called out from across the water of blind pass, "See any bodies?"

Jesse glanced at the onlookers. "No dead ones. You?"

"No. I'll look around and come back in the daylight. Call if you find anything."

"Depends." Jesse was sending several messages at once with that reply. Loyalties were complicated. He docked his boat on Captiva and didn't want to take sides too quickly and certainly not so publicly. Besides, John Cochran should not make such easy presumptions on his time. "I'm headed back to bed." *We found what we came to find,* he thought. There were no surprises here. "See you at breakfast."

"Alright," said Cochran. "See you then. I'm still going to look around."

"Well, that *is* your job, now then, isn't it?"

"Suppose so, Asshole," Cochran muttered under his breath, envying his friend's freedom.

O'Connell walked the distance back to the marina, back to *Serenity,* a twenty-seven foot C&C Mark V sailboat. He swung over the steel cables and landed lightly in the cockpit. The wooden door was in place but not locked. What was the point? If someone wanted in, he would rather keep his door intact; there was no ordering a new one. Jesse removed the doors and tossed them, one then the other into the cabin. They bounced on the bed cushions and he climbed down after them. He tucked them aft, under the cockpit, and settled himself under the light blanket. *Damn*, he thought. *What a wanton and exorbitant nuisance.* He fell asleep a moment later.

.   .   .   .   .

The next morning Jesse awakened slowly. He got up without lighting the alcohol stove, left the boat and walked the short distance to the showers that were a welcome amenity at the resort marina. Back on *Serenity* he traded his robe for the trademark shorts and pull-over shirt – three buttons and a collar – that would serve socially for yachting or tennis, or in this case, breakfast. His slip-on boat shoes gripped well as he quickly hopped around the top deck, tossing his mooring lines onto the wooden dock. He hand-pumped the bulb on the gas line to prime the Mercury outboard, fired the ignition once, and slowly slipped out away from the marina. He would circumnavigate Captiva counterclockwise to meet

Cochran for breakfast on Sanibel. The wind was easterly so the sail would do quite nicely. He hoisted the mainsail smoothly and let her fill with air, billowing with a graceful taught curve. Jesse killed the engine. Twenty minutes later he was tacking into the wind as he rounded the northern tip of Captiva Island and navigated Redfish Pass. He waved back to a familiar figure on the beach and looked away toward North Captiva, then scanned for other craft. The coast was clear, so to speak.

Out on the gulf *Serenity* picked up speed as the wind billowed the mainsail aggressively. Jesse raised the jib and you would have thought the silver trophy was a siren's call, urging the captain toward insanity. *Serenity* listed all she dared. The waves lapped the gunwales as an incautious skipper alternately skimmed and plied the waves. "Holy Mother of God," said Jesse to no one there.

·   ·   ·   ·   ·

Jesse docked *Serenity* at Casa Ybel's new facilities. State of the art accommodations included a cleaning crew to pressure wash the exterior and a maid to freshen and straighten the cabin. Gas and water were topped off and the battery was given a trickle charge. Jesse was thinking he could get used to this, but he valued his independence and privacy too much to change marinas.

John Cochran was sitting at a corner table. There was coffee service on the white linen tablecloth, and Cochran was leaning back in his chair caressing a large cup in both hands and staring off at who knows what. Jesse could tell he hadn't been here for long.

"What kept you?" chirped Cochran, looking up at Jesse.

"Traffic."

"Sit down. Drink up."

Jesse sat, poured a solid cup of coffee, and made eye contact. "What's the word?" He looked around for wait staff and, seeing none, gave them credit for discretion.

"Don't tell me you didn't see this coming."

"Everything but the timing. Now what?"

"Captiva wants to meet. They want everything to stay as it has been: same arrangements and the same shared 'investment' in infrastructure."

"That's not going to happen. They have changed the balance, haven't they?" Jesse wasn't asking so much as confirming that Cochran understood.

"Damn straight." Cochran flared. "They have changed the balance big time. This is not just about hubris. This is distrust."

Jesse spotted a waiter and jerked his head back in a summons. An obsequious Hispanic man appeared tableside. "May I take your order?"

"Eggs Benedict."

"Make it two."

"Very good, sirs."

A satisfied, uncomplicated, anticipatory silence was broken by Jesse. "So when is the meeting?"

"Tomorrow."

"So soon?"

"Nobody has any illusions here. We know they blew the bridge and why. They know we know. They could have brought in a crew and done the thing in broad daylight a small piece at a time. They just didn't want to debate the issue. Nobody's admitting anything, but we know and they know we know."

"Losing the bridge is damned inconvenient. They owe us."

"Aren't you one of them?"

"Stow the drama, mate. I can dock *Serenity* anywhere. You know I don't run in those circles."

"Yeah, well, come to the meeting."

"Wouldn't miss it."

Two waiters brought trays of breakfast feastings. They sat the domed plates in place with disciplined choreography. Then with panache they handled the knobs on the stainless steel domes and lifted them in mirrored arches. "Will there be anything else at the moment? More coffee?"

"Yes, please."

"Right away, sir."

.   .   .   .   .

The Sanibel library was chosen as a meeting site. Island Security, a private paramilitary force, had established a presence and secured the perimeter hours before the meeting was scheduled to begin. Composed of seasoned ex-military personnel, Island Security was respected for their dispassionate efficiency and their ability to anticipate trouble. They were incredibly high tech with a computerized command center filled with the latest holographic computer monitors. Thanks to a Homeland Security grant acquired by Sanibel's own U.S. Senator, Island Security had continuous real time access to a geosynchronous satellite that could track the infrared images of each individual on the island or within miles of Sanibel's beautiful beaches, making beach patrols a thing of the past. They got the job done and the islanders realized that they earned the small fortune they commanded for their services. People clearly felt safe on Sanibel; as well they should for that kind of money.

Robert Mills and Sandeep Patel were the first to arrive. Their boat trip from Captiva was short and the bicycle taxi from the bayside marina in Tarpon Bay roughly three blocks to the Sanibel Library was quick as well. The principal players from Sanibel were early as well, thanks to the heads-up from Island Security that tracked the pair every step of the way from their Captiva homes. The bicycle taxi was an unnecessary luxury for such a short distance thought Mills, but Patel recognized it for what it really was: a guard and an escort. The bicyclist in front of the rickshaw device was an undisguised Island Security corporal, well-muscled and sporting a clear military bearing. He unloaded the two beside the silver, modern sculpture – titled, *Keystone* – outside the library entrance. Mills and Patel were shown to Meeting Room 4, just behind the elevator that separated the room from the library's ground floor foyer.

Headed by Sanibel Mayor Henry Farber and Ron Weber, the island's treasurer, the dignitaries also included Jeffrey Rodgers, Sheriff Cochran, and Dr. Wilson. They had gathered at Farber's office in City Hall then walked across the parking lot as a group. When Jesse O'Connell came in, the room was starting to feel crowded.

"I invited Jesse," said Cochran. "He helped me look around at the bridge bombing night before last."

12

"On which side of the table is he going to sit?" asked Weber.

"Put him at the head," said the mayor. "Maybe he can referee."

"Not bloody likely," Jesse shot back. "I'm no diplomat, Henry. You know that."

The atmosphere was tense but not threatening. These men had known each other for many years. They had worked and played together. They and their wives had worked shoulder to shoulder on the same charity organizations before the collapse. Afterwards, they had organized the island's defenses, beefed up the desalinization facility, established the luxury goods trade, ensured a steady supply of electricity and day laborers, and attended to all the sundry details of keeping Sanibel the resort community that people of considerable means expected.

Still and all, these were passionate men, and proud, and pissed.

"Damn it, Bob. Are you so paranoid? What did you think – that we were going to drive a battalion of tanks across our little bridge and invade your garden party?" Henry said with a quiet and dramatic disappointment.

"It is mightily inconvenient for me and every other bicyclist on both islands; and it was unnecessary." Jesse had spoken his piece.

"I am sorry, Jesse. Henry. Gentlemen, I do apologize," said Mills. "Our people have gotten fed up with the thefts and property damage. Most of it is minor, I know, but that is part of the problem. Island Security won't crack down on your day labor people. They sneak over to Captiva and grab what is not chained down. You Sanies just look the other way because you are afraid your favorite mechanic will get exiled. Security got that message and won't pursue the small stuff. Well, we have had enough."

"Christ, Robert. You did not have to blow the bridge," said Ron.

"It's done."

"You really had no right, Bob," Henry said coolly.

"It's done."

Mills had said his rehearsed speech. Now he was playing broken record. He had anticipated the objection, but he was not here to negotiate the fate of the bridge. The deed was done.

"You owe us big time, Bob." Henry was regaining control. "The bridge was as much ours as it was yours. You owe us for a new bridge."

"We'll see," said Mills.

"Furthermore, you want something or you wouldn't be here. I know you, Bob," said Farber. "You want something today."

14

"I just want to stay friends, Henry. I want to continue to work together, to share resources and 'promote the mutual defense'."

"You have a sorry ass way of showing it."

"Still, that is what I want. That and to reassure you that the bridge was not an opening salvo of hostilities."

"I never suspected that it was. You and Sandeep and George and Phil have been talking about taking down the bridge for some time now. You have your own live-in staff and island residents so that you don't need our day workers, but Jesus, Bob, did you have to go all Hollywood on us? The world has drama enough."

"We had talked until we thought that the cooperation angle wasn't going to happen. We were tired of the debate and you know the people on Captiva. They didn't get to their places in life by compromising. These are take charge guys. Parking a cherry bomb under a bridge is poor sublimation for a corporate take-over, but you get your juices flowing when and however you can if you're this bunch."

"Forget that shit!" said Ron. "You had no damn right, and that is as sorry an excuse as you could have come up with."

"It's done," said the broken record.

"You owe us," said the other broken record.

"It's done."

15

"You want a peace treaty? You want to negotiate some cooperation going forward? You will pay us for the bridge," said Henry Farber, the mayor of Sanibel.

"I am prepared to negotiate," said Robert Mills, the mayor of Captiva.

"We will have to have the replacement cost of the bridge. We will need the settlement in gold. We have citizens to placate, or rather *you* have our citizens to placate," said Ron Weber, the island's treasurer.

"Half the replacement cost of the bridge," countered Mills. "The bridge was half ours to do with what we wished."

"Three-quarters of the replacement cost of the bridge, Robert," demanded Henry. "This is not a *prospective* negotiation. You destroyed our property and usurped our property rights. You were an aggressor and saboteur. You will now make restitution. Three-quarters of the replacement cost of the bridge, Robert, or go to hell."

"Three-quarters of the cost of the bridge, Henry. It is agreed. Ron can get the numbers together and Island Security can oversee the transfer of bullion," said Robert.

Over the next hour the leaders arranged to set up a diplomatic town meeting to establish understanding with the Sanibel population, reviewed and revised local rules, discussed what services are shared, which are exclusive, and reinforced their mutual defense pact. They tabled discussion as to whether to include North Captiva in the defense pact, but thought the northern crew might appreciate being included at the next gathering in one month. North Captiva could bring additional money to the table, but hell, everybody here had money. No, what North Captiva could bring to the table was a sense of community, a little outreach for the sake of brotherly love, a little solidarity; and right now the southern islanders could use more of those commodities.

.　　　.　　　.　　　.　　　.

Three miles away Beverly was walking home along one of the many bicycle paths. The day was beautiful and the temperature was perfect. She had finished a small job washing and waxing an electric Maserati convertible, and had been paid two baby Krugers. The popular trinket coins weighed exactly one-tenth ounce and were pure gold, *putus aurum*. Her afternoon take home was about $250 at today's rates, she thought. Not bad. Gold had fallen sharply from its peak of $10,000 an ounce just a few years ago. Still it was better than nothing.

Beverly thought to herself, *This is not noble. There is no nobility in being here, among the privileged.*

Still, she had to be somewhere. As long as there was electricity to air-condition the condo that she called home, and to run the desalinization plant toward the north end of the island, there were worse places she could be. She could make a living here – here where the gold is, as Willie Sutton would have noted. She was in great demand tending flower beds and vegetable gardens for the well-to-do. She could work at her own pace and in the cooler evening hours if she wanted. Those people with more money than God were generous enough with those who served a purpose and who could be trusted.

Today was beautiful with clear blue skies, a warm breeze from off the gulf, and gorgeous tropical landscaping in all directions. How could she even think to doubt her decisions to stay on Sanibel Island and make that decision work for her? She had friends; she had safety; she had food and water. If this was survival, she had chosen wisely. Still, the masses were having it hard and this was not noble. "OK, Old Kinderhook," she said aloud to no-one within hearing range. "If I have chosen a comfortable survival over nobility, so be it."

Chapter Two

The explosion rocked Belfast like none the
city had ever known. Those who were not thrown
from their footprints were either closer and dead,
or further and stunned. A hushed silence followed
as the citizenry checked themselves, then their
surroundings. Everyone had wide eyes and
furrowed brows. People went from looking at each
other to looking at familiar structures – still
standing but almost appearing to be trembling in
the aftermath, each surrounded by a haze of dust
that shook loose everywhere at once, some with
shattered windows. Then with hope desiccated
anew, these denizens directed their collective gaze

to the ash and smoke now rising from town center. The warm red glow at the base of the city's own cloud was anything but cheery.

Some gathered now to talk, but softly; some did a slow pirouette as they turned in their doorways to return to the diminishing safety of their homes, to catch the report on television. Others began moving toward the scene of the blast. All were ghostly quiet and seemed to be *willing* themselves to move, but softly, so as not to attract the attention of the terrorists or of those terrified. There *would be* retaliation.

The blast was the result of at least six car bombs, a euphemistic term for six large paneled vans filled with modern explosives and positioned strategically around British military headquarters. The solitary tattoo, unlike the rat-a-tat-tat of a drum phrase, indicated that each was under the same control of a single wireless trigger. Oliver Cromwell Nielson, the conservative Tory member of the House of Lords, was the distinguished guest of honor this day. The papers were well full of his much anticipated visit. He was promising the people of Belfast and all of Northern Ireland more political and military support. He was promising security; and his unflinching presence among the people was evidence of his sincerity, his grit and determination, and indeed his inestimable courage. If the bombing was intended to send his lordship a message, it was not a message he was expected to repeat to parliament.

Hundreds lay dead; hundreds more lay writhing in fear and agony. Tens of thousands were rendered massively dispirited. Several city blocks, some with fine old architecture, lay in ruin. The military high command and its communication infrastructure were gone. The police suspected that they could be next. The insurrection was not the one of gentle potshots and the on-again off-again negotiations of the previous century. This civil war was a thorough bitch-slapping intended to destroy the enemy once and for all. This time like the last time, there were no front lines. It's just that this time there was financing and organization.

An encrypted Internet had replaced rallies and gatherings where people got up on their soap box. Only the Orangemen still gathered, but not to instill conviction, more of a show of bravado. Reveling in centuries of sanctimony, they now more closely resembled their brown-shirted counterparts than crusaders for a lost cause. Either way, they were on a descending trajectory; and already apologists were popping up to smooth over a rewritten history. The Irish might be indisputably a subhuman race of drunkards and fools, but after twelve millennia of invasions, plunder and genocide, these sinners, saints, and

21

scholars were warriors, too, and intent on reclaiming their island.

.   .   .   .   .

At the Thistle and Shamrock Pub, a Catholic bastion in a protestant city, Seamus was holding court.

"He would win hands down if the election was today. The last bombing saw to that! It was a sure get-out-the-vote move on their part."

"I doubt the fools would go so far as to blow up two or three fookin' city blocks, now Seamus," said Sean. "No, it was our boys fer sure, an' more power to 'em."

"Ahh, ye'r right, Sean, but it was so very foolish this close to the election. We're all fools. McMasters will take it fer sure, an' he'll reinstate the Penal laws if he gets his way about it. We're fools an' we're fooked."

"Damn him. He's all piss an' hate when he riles up the crowds. I wouldn't cross the fookin' street ta piss on 'im if he was on fire, that's fer sure."

"I'll drink ta that, Sean." Seamus looks into the mirror and sees a friend in the dimly lit barroom. "Jimmy! Jimmy, me boy, come over here an' have a bit of the Guinness wif us."

Jimmy joined the pair. "I am afraid that I'm not in much of a mood today, Seamus."

"What is it that's weighin' on ya, Jimmy?"

"'What's not?' would be an easier list." The three paused for a moment of personal reflection. "My sister's hungry, Seamus. She's got kids to feed. The church helps some. There's charity from friends, but it only goes so far. Everybody I know is stretched to the breaking point. The IRA's widows and orphans funds ran out years ago, not that they couldn't divert a little from the war chest, if they had a mind ta."

"How long's it been now since 'the accident'?" Seamus still referred to Billy's death as an 'accident'. Jimmy's brother-in-law was caught by British troops planting I.E.D.s – improvised explosive devices – and rather than surrender, Billy took the whole British squadron with him. He had not intended to be a martyr, a suicide bomber, but the opportunity presented itself and he took it. Witnesses said the young hero positioned the device so that the blast pattern was directed at the British, then he triggered it before they could tell what he was doing. No time to think; no time to act.

"Three years," answered Jimmy. "It seems like an eternity." Jimmy had known Billy for a year before Billy met and married Jimmy's sister, Ann. They were close friends before they were in-laws.

The three fell silent again. Eventually, Sean pulled a long draught off of his Guinness and sat the glass tankard down with a thud. He got their attention. "Enough of this, ya morose fools! Let's have a story!"

"Have you heard about John and Mary?" Jimmy-boy began as he perked up his body posture.

"No," Seamus lied. "Tell us."

Jimmy squinted at the two and decided to proceed. "John was havin' a pint at the pub, ya see, an' he says to the lads, he says, 'Let's have a contest.' He says, 'Let's see who can have the best toast.' The lads like this idea, an' Sean was there," said Jimmy, glancing over at his smiling friend. "An' Sean says, he says ahh, 'May you be through Saint Peter's pearly gates a full hour before the devil even knows ye'r dead.' An' the lads like that. They say, 'Ahh, very nice Sean.' An' it comes 'round to John, ya see, an' John lifts his glass an' he says, 'May I spend the *rest* of me life...between the *legs* of me wife!'" Jimmy raised his voice for emphasis. He grinned at Seamus and Sean as he glanced at them, bringing them further into the story. "An' the lads liked that one. They had not heard it before an' John won the contest. When he got home, Mary was still waiting up. So to placate her he says, 'Mary, me darlin', I won the contest. I had the best toast, an' it was all about *you*, me luv.'

An' Mary says, she says, 'Oh? Now what would you be sayin' to the lads about me now?' An' John says, 'Ah, yes, then.' He says, 'I said may I spend the rest of me life...in *church* with me wife!' 'Oh, did ya now, John?' teased Mary. 'Come on ta bed, ya old fool.' So the next day, Mary runs into Sean at the market. Sean grins an' leans over to her an' he says, 'Ahh, Mary. John won the contest. He had the best toast an' it was all about you, me darlin'.' 'Yes, he told me,' she says. 'An' ya know, I thought it was very strange.' 'How so?' asks Sean. 'Well,' she says, 'You *know* he's only been there *twice*!' 'No!' says Sean, all wide-eyed an' all. 'Yes!' Mary assured him. 'An' the first time, he fell *asleep*! ... An' t'other time I had to pull him by his ear ta get 'im ta come!'"

All three men roared with laughter, and half the pub either laughed or grinned with them, depending on how many times they had heard the joke or some variation of it.

One man in a booth kept his composure too well. No one paid the dour man any attention. There were plenty of reasons in this world to be disengaged from frivolity. Economic and political chaos had rekindled anarchy and the animal spirits of the IRA. The tenuous peace of the last two decades had faded and calls for a united island nation battled with devolution toward regional tribal war lord chieftains. Ireland's future was as uncertain as ever, and that was pretty damned uncertain. One thing the locals knew for sure: if McMasters was voted in as Northern Ireland's Prime Minister, it would be the British and the North that would lead the charge to unite the island in a conquest of the new forces of the regional chieftains; not the South and the Republic of Ireland as one might have suspected a decade ago. Ireland *would* unite or splinter. The question remained, if Ireland did manage to unite as one island nation: "Under whom?"

Chapter Three

The explosion was little more than a firecracker in volume, but it was sufficient to destroy the hinges on the gate. Behind this erstwhile protection lay one of Atlanta's wealthiest residential communities. These residents had to know on some level that this was coming sooner or later. It had been a few years since the last one. Choreographed community invasions had been going on for years, getting bolder and more efficient with the learning experiences of repeated execution.

When the economy collapsed, and collapse it did, there was anarchy. At first it took the form of rioting and protests centered on the disappearance of government programs and particularly those all-important federally-issued checks. Money to pay for healthcare, schools, police and fire protection, roads and bridges, disability income and welfare, and even politicians' salaries, all of it and everything else, stopped during a span of about one year, nearly a decade previously. The state and federal flows of money had not resumed. For a few months in those early days of the collapse, the more dedicated public servants, especially teachers and policemen, worked without salaries hoping for a reinstatement of salary and benefits. Most knew that there would be no reinstatement. Many simply had nothing else to turn to but their work, their profession. This was certainly true of doctors and nurses. Their healing arts were what defined them, made them who they were. They had no choice but to continue working with the ill and injured. It gave their lives purpose amidst the chaos.

Barter systems developed and the rule of law became local – sometimes very local with neighborhoods creating vigilante organizations. Offenses might be governed differently from one cluster of dwellings to another. But just as a single homeowner, even if well-armed, would be no match for a home invasion by a disciplined gang; neighborhood defenses would be inadequate against an army of gangs organized by a warlord.

The dominant warlord in the Atlanta region was without question Major Kipling Alderman. "Kip" had been a sergeant major in the U.S. Army, but his leadership skills had consistently surpassed the officers to whom he reported. Some of his former Army commanders resented his input, but most valued his tactical expertise. Major Alderman's current self-promotion was largely tongue-in-cheek with regard to rank but was totally deserved on the basis of merit and respect. He was among the first in the country to bring together various gang leaders, show them the advantages of cooperation and synergy, and bring to them a military style of organization and discipline. As the mega-gang evolved into a formidable warlord army, treaties were negotiated with neighboring regional organizations to form the Southeastern Alliance; and Major Alderman's soldiers' fortunes grew. His men would walk through fire for him.

It was one of Alderman's divisions that now moved tactically through the smooth asphalt streets lined with pristine concrete sidewalks, manicured landscaping, and the ubiquitous McMansions. The C.E.O.s, C.I.O.s, C.F.O.s, accountants, stock brokers, and power brokers who lived in such privileged digs were not bad people. Many were no longer particularly rich. Some would have been foreclosed upon and evicted from their nice homes if the system still functioned.

Alderman's division, led this night by Captain Damien Lincoln, rolled through the subdivision streets in the new Humvees that sported decent armor. Accompanying the lead vehicles were troop carriers plus one temporarily empty 18-wheeler, and one urban tank. Fuel was being refined once more now that gold was circulating as currency, and no organization currently controlled more gold than the Southeastern Alliance, headed by Major Alderman. After tonight, the Army of the Alliance would have even more gold under their control.

The urban tank was a new addition and mostly used as a show of force: big time force was a solid deterrent. The cannons and machine guns were more maneuverable and the treads on the urban tank had been replaced by four-wheel drive and four-wheel turning. The additional maneuverability gained by having rear wheels that turned counter to the front was a dramatic feature.

After spreading out geographically, the troops dismounted on cue in squads of seven men, each squad assigned to four houses. At fifteen minutes per dwelling, the gated community was allotted only one hour for clean-out operations.

Neighbors could only peek out of windows as two Hummers stopped mid-street and seven paramilitary men sporting automatic rifles, utility belts, and Kevlar vests converged rapidly on the

Silverman's house. They could only stare in stunned silence as the troops *rang the doorbell* and waited politely for someone to answer the door. A steel battering ram was ready if needed, and after two minutes the troops used it, almost gently, to open the door. The Silvermans were in hiding if they were at home.

Inside the opulent dwelling the experienced troops fanned out to secure the environment. A frightened teenager or elderly individual could be behind any structure, shotgun cocked and loaded, and Kevlar did not shield the face.

"Clear!" came the call from the library.

"Clear!" came the call from the kitchen and other rooms.

"Clear!" came the call from the basement.

"Family!" came the call from the bedroom. "Four in the closet."

The frightened foursome was guided under guard to the living room and allowed to sit comfortably in the conversation pit – the sectional sofa.

"You didn't answer your door," said Jackman, the squad leader. "Next time we call, save us some trouble and open the door."

Next time? thought Leo Silverman, but he answered, "Yes, sir."

"Good. Now, is this everyone? If you lie, everyone dies – the truth and everyone lives."

"This is all of us, everyone."

"Good. Where are you valuables? If you lie, everyone dies – the truth and everyone lives," Jackman repeated in a rote catechism.

"We keep what we have in a safe. I can open it for you."

"Good," said Jackman. "Now is good."

As Jackman and Leo Silverman climbed the stairs to the bedroom safe, Jackman's men were efficiently choosing items with market value, from art to silver, but not necessarily electronics. The world now had more flat screen TVs than it did people who could afford service. The newer holographic TVs and computer displays were a different matter, however, and the Silvermans had both. *Had* both.

Jackman's squad was leaving the front door with select items and returning empty-handed for the next batch with the measured discipline of a line of ants. Jackman descended the stairs, flanked by Silverman and one of Jackman's squadron. The soldier was muscular and he needed his physical gifts to manage the bulk, more so than the weight, of this particular trove. Not all scores were this lucrative, but this lush neighborhood was replenished, and ripe for the picking.

In the alcove Jackman looked at his watch. It had been twelve minutes and forty seconds since the door had been breached.

"Time!" he yelled, and the squad filed out. Those with items deposited them in the troop carrier trucks to be transported to the eighteen-wheeler. Forty-five minutes later these vehicles would again serve to carry troops.

The Silverman's neighbors were all waiting at the door for their timed visits. There was no running, no hiding, and no calls to be made. The plundering was efficient, orderly, and franchised according to the playbook of the new civilized order; but there were also no rapes, murders, or torture. Who needs violence when you can instill learned helplessness, and the playbook of the new civilized order had accomplished that for Lincoln's division on this night.

One hour later, as Lincoln's army rolled out of the still-beautiful Atlanta neighborhood, neighbors who had not mingled for months stood in small groups in their cul-de-sacs and driveways, talking in hushed tones. Had it really only been two years since the last time they were last here? It was three or four years between invasions prior to this. Was the cycle getting shorter? The neighbors were comparing stories, seeking reassurance that no one was injured, reviewing anemic contingencies against future invasions, taking stock of food supplies and sources, and reawakening as human survivors. Backyard gardens needed to get bigger. Life had taken another turn, and it was probably not the last. It was decided to have the gate reattached.

.   .   .   .   .

Life had taken many turns since the economic implosion occurred in earnest. In rapid succession the brokerages, banks, and their insurers melted down as they proved totally inadequate to service the enormous gambles they had undertaken – from Dubai architectural behemoths to the credit default swaps. These credit default swaps were little more than a pyramid of leverage to the extent that undesirable crumbling real estate was capitalized worldwide in an amount that was tens if not hundreds of thousand times its true value. It was like extending a million dollar loan capitalized by a five dollar bill by the time the loans were repackaged time and again. Thank goodness the risk was spread around so widely: that way all could share in the benefits of the confidence game.

When the fifty-some trillion in credit default swaps exceeded the fifty-some trillion of U.S. debt and obligations – over one hundred trillion total in liabilities because the U.S. government assumed the liabilities of the insurance company that insured the credit default swaps – someone finally did the math and discovered that there were only fifty-eight million Americans in the work force; and with an unemployment rate of 10.2% and growing, that amounted to over two million dollars per U.S. taxpayer. Since ninety percent of these had no disposable income, living paycheck to paycheck, those with any spare change owed approximately twenty million dollars each. Ouch. The unsustainable debacle did not improve for long when the government took on massive amounts of taxpayer liability to bail out other wayward institutions. That temporary hope was dashed by an even greater malaise as the next, and larger, wave of collapse occurred. It mattered not the skill of the Captain if he or she took the helm after the damage to the ship was done; that sucker was going down.

And sink she did. A credit-based economy cannot function without the availability of credit. Toward the end of the "uh-oh" decade as it came to be called (and not just for the two zeros in the year or in the White House) not only did the stock markets crash, but also bonds, metals, and every other traded vehicle. Some banks stayed open, but only because the FDIC had exhausted the means for closing them; not that it mattered because there was no money to return to the depositors in their long lines, much less was there any money to lend. Debt supersaturated the society like moisture in a heavy cloud, and the laws of nature demanded precipitation. Debts were defaulted on at all levels, the money supply imploded, and capitalism itself went on strike. Without tax revenues, governments at all levels became immediately unable to service their debt; interest rates soared and every government service failed to function. The survivors of the food riots and famine soon learned to grow their own food. Efforts toward self-sufficiency were hampered, however, by a spoiled environment and creeping desertification. Chaos became the new order.

Subprime mortgages were one thing, but they were nothing compared to the fiasco of the *sovereign debt defaults*. Sovereign nations have only other sovereign nations to bail them out. So it was with Dubai's rescue by the United Arab Emirates: so it was with Greece's rescue by Germany. Even as early as this second rescue attempt, the German taxpayers protested in the streets over being asked to pay for Greek citizens' profligacy and socialist largess. The deprived Greeks rioted in response to the *Nazi's* (as the Greeks were beginning to call the Germans) parsimony and resistance to coming to Greece's aid. Soon, however there was no country willing or able to bail out another bankruptcy of even one more sovereign nation. Sovereign debt imploded, and with failed credit, government functionality everywhere disappeared.

Things had gotten really bad all over. Unemployment exceeded fifty percent. Society withdrew like a turtle into its shell. Trade restrictions, import taxes, and other protectionist measures contributed to widespread failures among manufacturing. The Middle East wars progressed from a quagmire to a financial disaster to a political and public relations nightmare. Separatist movements evolved into geopolitical powerhouses; venomous media bloggers became their leaders. Terrorist attacks restricted domestic freedoms more than anyone could have predicted, with internal travel papers and encrypted identification cards being required at multiple checkpoints. Banks failed on a grand scale when congress finally cried, "Enough!", and failed to raise the debt ceiling for the umpteenth time to bail out the FDIC. The chairman of the Federal Reserve was labeled a "great fool" and barely escaped the beheading that many called for. The United Nations, the World Bank, and the IMF each became powerless, ineffectual, and bankrupt, and ceased to exist. The "rich" (anyone with property) became vilified, heavily taxed, and eventually had their assets seized. The "poor" (individuals and countries) did not materially benefit from "debt forgiveness".

There was no money to pay the hundred thousand troops abroad, and no money to bring them home. Treasury obligations were not able to be met by rolling over the old debt into new debt as in years past. Local law enforcement officials were suddenly disposed toward growing gardens, chopping wood for the home fires, and defending the homestead against the steady increase in roving, starving gangs. Neighborhood associations quickly armed themselves as the only defense against increasingly well-armed and organized mega-gangs that eventually formed allegiances to regional warlords. Federal and state militias proved inadequate in number and frequently were outmatched in the sophistication of weaponry, motivation, and training as well. Some of the newer maps were beginning to move the border with Mexico north to more accurately reflect the political and demographic realities.

Elections became a thing of the past. There was no money for the balloting process, and even if there had been, the campaign stops were a potential killing field. Assassinations were common but so increasingly were indiscriminate attacks on the civic minded audiences. One could be dissuaded of those proclivities rapidly. Senators and congresspersons at state and federal levels were "elected" in the "smoke filled back rooms" just as they always had been. The citizens were mercifully spared the expense and charade of the ballot box: that was the main difference. The

Democratic Party disappeared: that was another difference. Since there was no longer any semblance of democracy, that seemed only fitting. The republic was served by angry confused individuals who did not have a clear plan, and if they could have developed one, they did not have the means or resources to put it into effect. That much at least had not changed.

Squatters moved large family groups into abandoned homes. The countless difficulties visited upon a citizenry whose scientific and mathematics literacy skills had been replaced by pop culture and celebrity hero worship cannot be enumerated. Having no clue as to the forces that shaped their destinies, the foolish and ignorant became even more helpless and depressed. Many gave up, became angry and critical, or lapsed into magical thinking. Suicides became commonplace. The more savvy individuals used cunning and insight to become safe and powerful. A few used their relative safety and power to gradually develop cunning and insight.

The economy by 2023 was sputtering towards a rebound, trying to find some new set point – some equilibrium. After the markets collapsed in a freefall, cash money had value as it always did after a spiraling deflation – it's just that there wasn't any to go around. The federal government's attempt to "crank up the printing presses" a decade previously had been met with contempt by the global bond market, whose electronic world-wide repudiation of the obvious ploy was instantaneous. There was no level of interest rate high enough to stem the implosion of the availability of credit from all sources. The velocity of money hit zero. The U. S. government was dealt the most severe of a series of blows that called in its debt and cancelled its ability to function – no federal employees: no bureaucracy. Even the fabled printing presses of the U. S. Treasury fell silent.

Gold, the *inflation* hedge, was now the only real money for the *deflation*. The golden rule went into effect: *he who has the gold makes the rules*. Once gold began to circulate as currency, oil refineries began to produce gasoline, private utility companies generated electricity, satellite services resumed operations, even cell phones and the Internet were back on line, eventually there were limited airline services, resort hotels, fine restaurants, and high-end concierge availability of nearly any specialty service or product – if and only if a person was wealthy enough. The über-rich were protected: the poorer masses became like the serfs of the middle ages. It was not as extreme as the fall of Rome. It just felt like it to some.

Chapter Four

Sharon Welker was gently awakened from her afternoon nap by the cries of a red-shouldered hawk. *"Keeyer...keeyer...keeyer...keeyer...keeyer...keeyer...keeyer...keeyer,"* whistled the hawk in a series of cries with their descending pitch. Sharon slept with her windows open to take advantage of the cross breezes that come off the gulf. She was, like most Sanibel natives, a squatter in one of the many abandoned condos that overpopulated the resort community. Locals referred to this quick-claim phenomenon as *"movin' on up"*. Sharon's condo was in the Coquina Beach grouping on Nerita Street. What she especially liked about the location was the proximity to the beach – perfect for a professional beachcomber – and the easy walk along East Gulf Drive took her to Tuttle's Sea Horse Shell Shop, where three or four days a week she worked selling sea shells, gold and silver coins and jewelry, pirate paraphernalia, and nautical décor items.

At fifty-two years, Sharon was still a free spirit. As a native she shared a special privilege with Jesse O'Connell, Beverly McMahon, John Cochran, Liz Forbes and a few others, including Tuttle himself. In the last ten years the island population had been cut in half, from roughly six-thousand to about three-thousand, and the tourist crowd of nearly ten-thousand was totally gone. Visitation was by permission of the Council – no exception. Occupation, permission to live on Sanibel, was at the pleasure of the Council. The Council chose the leaders and approved negotiated details. The members of the Council were billionaires – with a "B". It was good that they trusted the natives. It was very good that they valued the natives as being as essential to the ecosystem as the sea grapes and gopher tortoises. The natives contained the institutional memory. The natives were produced by the island, its history and *zeitgeist*, and Sanibel, its beaches and its cocktail parties, would not be Sanibel without its natives. The Council was wise to value them.

Alison Swanson was sitting at the table beneath a slowly turning ceiling fan with oversized woven blades in Sharon's screened-in porch. Sharon slid the glass door and stepped into the area.

"Sit down, girlfriend. You were sleeping when I got here, so I helped myself to the bar and tried to keep quiet. That last part was not easy," Alison said.

"Hey, Ali. So what do we have in mind for the evening?"

"We have choices."

"Name three." Sharon lit two cigarettes and handed one to Alison. "Wait! Let me fix a drink and pee; not necessarily in that order."

"I'll fix you one, honey. What's your pleasure?" said Alison who was already sliding the door to the living room on her way to the kitchen while Sharon opened the sliding glass door on the perpendicular wall that led through the bedroom to the bath.

"Time flies when you're having rum," called Sharon from the bathroom. "But whatever is in there will be fine."

As they gathered back around the cabana table, Alison said, "You're in luck – some light rum, some dark rum, some spiced rum, a little coconut and mango – some no name concoction."

"It needs a name. Damn, that's *good*!"

"Call it a *tango-mango* or some such.

"There's probably already a *tango-mango*.

"Like I care."

"Me neither." Sharon lifted her glass in a toast, "Happy Cuban Independence Day!"

"Girl, this isn't July 26th."

"Every day is Cuban Independence Day!"

"You are so weird."

"I'll drink to that."

"Me, too."

"So... Three choices for tonight."

"Thing one: Clyde's playing at Ellington's."

"Clyde's always playing at Ellington's."

"Clyde's good; and Liz will be there."

"Clyde is very good, but he was there last night and he will be there tomorrow night."

"Thing two: Jesse's moving his sail boat to Castaway's marina. The whole place will be a party."

"Don't even tell me thing three."

"I thought so."

"How will we get there? It will be midnight before we could walk to that end of the island."

"There is a Trolley Bus; believe it!"

"No!" Sharon squealed and rocked backward spilling some rum and flicking ashes on her blouse.

"Believe it! Beverly's driving. It leaves from Pinocchio's at five."

"It's five o'clock somewhere all the time, isn't it?"

.　　.　　.　　.　　.

There was no enforcement of drug laws on Sanibel. "What drug laws?" locals would ask. Pinocchio's was as well known for its fine choice of chemicals as for its original ice cream recipes. Panama Red was an available marijuana choice – and it *was* choice – as well as one of the ice cream flavors. There was also the *Hope Springs Eternal*: a vanilla ice cream with morphine sprinkles on a waffle cone.

By the time Beverly pulled into the parking lot with the Sanibel Trolley, more than a few party goers had gotten a head start at Pinocchio's. Eight people climbed onboard, including Sharon and Alison. Two couples, including Bob and Pauline, joined the mostly singles gathering. Beverly would stop for others at the marked Trolley Stops, until the vehicle was full. Then she would just "Smile and wave, Boys. Smile and wave."

Bob had the group's attention with a story from the old days about directing some "tourists" to 800 Dunlop Road, the police station, after they came into his store and asked where they could score some drugs. Then Sharon told stories about skinny-dipping as a teenager in some condo complex's pool and another one about meeting Danny Devito and how charismatic he was. The group actually broke into song along Sanibel-Captive Road. *What do you do with a drunken sailor* ran fourteen verses. The verse where you "lock him in the closet with the captain's daughter" was particularly boisterous. The group arrived about sunset.

Approaching the end of Sanibel, the end of the road now that the bridge over Blind Pass was gone, the Trolley unexpectedly turned left, commandeering the parking lot of the Mad Hatter, a damn good little restaurant and defiantly different. Passengers unloaded into the restaurant to visit the facilities and/or the bar. There was Jesse, grinning, saying "What kept you? Sun's going *down!*" Drinks freshened and in hand, everybody went to the beach. *Magical moment happening!* The sunset was glorious. The sunset was not always glorious. Sometimes twilight just happened. Sometimes it just got greyer and darker with minimal color. Tonight was spectacular. *Thanks, God*, thought Jesse. *Thanks for validating my move.* The sky was orange and purple, mostly, with a deep rose glow and brightly lined clouds with pink, red, and yellow highlights – cumulous clouds. The glow was so intense it was breath-taking and was reflected by the opposite horizon. Damn.

Damn, damn, damn.

Damnation.

Man!

Kurt, the chef from the Mad Hatter, had prepared the *hors d'oevres*. How special was that? The favorite seemed to be small plates of the Duck'n'Berry – a slice of roasted duck with a raspberry sauce and side items of grilled asparagus and diced beets. The conversation, the dancing, the embraces were ongoing. The circle of friends was *knowing*, in that special way of knowing, in regards to each other; they were caring, and full of fun. Grateful for a life of warm comforts and cool jazz, they chased the sunset for the perfect martini. Yet they could run deep, silent, and true. Friends! Forever! And for as long as it lasts.

Across the island, a mere eight miles east-southeast from the marina, the Sanibel Think Tank was holding forth in the bar of the Jacaranda.

"Check," said Cochran, and he took a sip of scotch – Johnny Walker Black.

"Check," said Wilson, and he took a sip of Irish whiskey – Michael Collins. He would ordinarily have ordered Jameson but on the way to the bar, in the patio dining area, he noticed a mirror with the Michael Collins logo. He thought he would try something different. He liked the Jameson better, he decided.

"Raise," declared Rogers, and he slid a heavy clay blue chip to the center of the table. The small number of chips already gathered seemed to ignore the newcomer.

"See you and raise twenty," said Farber, and he slid the additional blue chips.

"I'm out."

"Me, too."

"Call," said Rodgers, gently topping his previous blue chip with two others. "Let's see them."

Henry Farber turned over three cards. With the four that were already face up on the table, the best he could make was a pair of queens, king high. It was a pretty hand but not potent.

"You disrespected the game, Farber," needled Rogers, showing his winning hand. "You are going down." He reached for a cigar that was in a proper marble ashtray, leaned back and brought the cigar to his mouth. The tip glowed round and orange for a number of seconds. Rogers replaced it in its tray and grinned as he raked his spoils to his section of the table. He exhaled the cigar smoke, not at Henry Farber, exactly; not away from him either, though.

Mayor Farber looked chagrinned.

John Cochran was sorting the cards, preparing to deal the next hand. He said, "Jesse's probably moving his boat tonight, from Tween Waters to Castaways."

"Don't let him hear you call her a *boat*," warned Farber.

"You got that right," grinned Rogers, cigar in teeth now, and removing it he sipped from his glass of Ketel One.

Only Henry did not drink during the regular gatherings of the Think Tank. He drank his share in a previous life. These days he told them: "One drink was too many and a thousand was not enough." He apparently didn't mind his friends imbibing, though. To be sociable, he would sometimes order a Clyburn whiskey, a fictitious whiskey from an old Batman movie, and the bartender would knowingly bring him apple juice.

Cochran dealt two cards face down to each player and one common card face up. The men in turn examined their cards, their potentials, and one then the other tapped their holdings sharply with their middle finger. Cochran turned over another card.

The Sanibel Think Tank used to be a morning coffee sipping gathering near where East Gulf Drive meets Periwinkle. As members exited Rosie's Island Market and Deli with their coffee, Republicans would sit on the benches to their right, and Democrats would move and sit left. Get it? The core group of opinionated retirees would discuss local and international politics, sports, pop culture, and any other subject that might arise. No problems were fixed however. That stipulation was apparently in their charter.

The partisans had plenty of intellectual ammunition with which to criticize the other. There was blame-o-plenty to go around. The founding principles of the United States had been relentlessly destroyed in a one-two knockout punch. The first blow came from the left with decades of expensive social engineering; the deadly blow, however, came from the right, with an onslaught of deficits and debt from wars and tax cuts, protectionism, polarizing hubris, freedom-curtailing legislation beginning with the Patriot Act, and the destruction of our global image as terrible secret activities and other misdeeds became known.

That group disbanded years ago, however, when things were getting untenable in the country – not just the waves of market crashes, but the beginnings of the genuine anarchy to come. For one thing, a tax insurrectionist movement took control of the right wing branch. Their "my way or the highway" attitude included assassination of the president or a military coup. Impeachment as a course of action was too mild. The Democrats accused the insurrectionists of being so far to the right that they should sit at the bench in front of Pinocchio's, further to the right down the walkway.

Just before this original group stopped meeting, someone had recorded a cacophonous discussion on Fox news, where everyone was talking, trying to raise their voice over everyone else; and he or she recorded a similar show off of MSNBC. Whoever it was then placed an old cathode ray tube television on each bench and set timers to play the Fox recording on the right bench and the MSNBC recording on the left. The programs started playing precisely at seven a.m. when the first of the Think Tank started to arrive. This "performance art" went off without a hitch, and everyone thought it was the funniest thing that had happened on Sanibel in years – well, everyone except the Sanibel Think Tank. They were probably getting tired of each other anyway.

"I will see you, and raise," said Farber, sliding a stack of chips toward the middle of the table.

"There you go, disrespecting the game again," said Rogers. The former NSA intelligence agent was feeling the pressure this time. He might have to bluff.

"Says you," said Farber. "Put up or shut up."

.   .   .   .   .

The next day was gorgeous – highs in the eighties, not at all humid thanks to the off-shore breezes that prevailed. Beverly was walking to Chapman's to help him with some landscaping. Well, not so much to "help him" as to *do* some landscaping for him. Brady Chapman was clearly rich – not Council member rich, more like *new* money, first generation stuff. He did enjoy tending his orchids, but he left the *work* work to others. Beverly had never minded getting her hands dirty and getting her exercise at the same time. On days like this one, it seemed a privilege to simply be here. More than "seemed", it *was* a privilege.

Jesse O'Connell was rich, too, she was thinking, but you would never know it. Of course he was *here*, on Sanibel. That was a clue. And he did not work at a job. There's another clue. But he was always helping people, doing things like minor repairs or pitching in whenever there was a clean-up after a storm. He could work all day with a chain saw. She would have to give him that. And his body showed it. She would have to give him that, too. And Ph.D. smart – philosophy, it was rumored. He never discussed himself. Truth was: Beverly was having trouble getting last night out of her mind. She and Jesse had exchanged looks more than once. But Jesse was not a showy kind of person. In fact he was as quiet and private as anyone she had ever known. If he was seeing anyone special, you would not learn that information from him.

Still the party at the marina last night was *fun*. They had built a large bonfire on the beach, gulf side, in full view of the destroyed bridge that spanned Blind Pass. They had toasted the locals who had already erected a swinging foot bridge, from one concrete mass to another, in order to restore foot traffic between Sanibel and Captiva. They had lifted their glasses more than once to conservation causes, to the capitalistic success of Che Guevara T-shirts, to Poseidon and the minor gods of the west wind, to Mrs. Cavendish, wherever she is, and sundry other eclectic issues. Last night was fun and Beverly couldn't get it out of her head; not that she wanted to.

Beverly had turned off Middle Gulf Drive and was about to start down East Gulf Drive when she realized that she was near Sharon's condo. *She would not be awake yet,* thought Beverly. *Not after the night she had.* She and a few intrepid others had exited the Trolley at McT's. "I'll let her sleep."

She found Brady Chapman, where else, in his greenhouse tending some rare orchid species.

"Good morning," she greeted cheerily. "You must teach me to grow orchids someday."

"Good morning, Beverly. I would be delighted. How is your day going?" Brady matched her cheerfulness. He was always pleasant and unassuming. He also seemed to treasure the supportive and unassuming relationship that he enjoyed with Beverly. Handsome and athletic, but unmarried, many wondered if he was gay or just particular. He was dressed in white and could have just come from a "Great Gatsby" movie production. His white fedora served the purpose of a necessary sun screen.

"What is today's agenda?" asked the eager worker. "The front gardens look like they could use a little weeding and some mulch."

"Yes. That would be good. Why don't you start with that and I will look about for other issues."

"Right, then. May I borrow the Gator to go get some mulch?"

"Certainly, the keys are in it."

Beverly turned and was off about her chores. It was indeed a beautiful day.

.   .   .   .   .

June Weber was ready for the garden party she was hosting. The house was immaculate with rich woods, silver and porcelain accoutrements, and fresh cut flowers. The party was outside in the garden, of course, but the couples would come through the front door and would negotiate their way through the house, gathering plates and drinks along the course.

June would just run upstairs to "powder her nose" before her guests arrived. Then she would be ready.

Upstairs she did a line of coke at her dresser. Through an open door she saw her husband in his bedroom, getting ready. She went in softly and hugged him silently, resting her head against his chest and shoulder. They stood like that for minutes.

"Hello, lover," Ron said at last, contentedly.

"Hello, darling," said June, and she meant it.

"How's the time?" asked Ron.

"It's close to three. People are coming at five."

"Mmmm," said Ron and he smiled.

"Mmm-hm-hm-hm," laughed June, as he pulled her by her arm towards the bed.

.   .   .   .   .

Captain Rodriguez walked to the wall, punched both fists toward the wall, coming within inches of it, and spread his fingers and arms simultaneously. The motion brought to life a holographic display of the island. Even without the infrared image display activated, Rodriguez could discern individuals and their real time movements. The clarity from the optics available on the geosynchronous satellite stationed over the Florida gulf coast was unbelievable. When he reported the season's first sea turtle nesting to the local conservation society, they were thrilled and impressed. It was an easy PR gesture. *They think we are a nice troop of 'serve and protect' types*, thought the Afghanistan veteran to himself. *They have no idea*.

The islanders also knew little about how much privacy they had surrendered to obtain security. Headquartered in the old Sundial condominiums, Island Security had everything in one well-sealed enclave. Barracks and infrastructure were taken care of easily; the grounds contained over four hundred condos, a restaurant (mess), training facilities that included four pools, twelve tennis courts, and a gym, officers club (the former bar), rooms for electronic surveillance, vehicle storage and a motor pool, and even a beach on which to drill. Bandannas, the former gift shop, was commandeered by the quartermaster. The burnt orange Spanish Hacienda across from the main entrance was made into the general's private dwelling. The Sundial's structure was also the tallest in the vicinity, a tactical plus if local firepower was needed. The only real concern is that the men might begin to lose their hard edge and even their discipline when surrounded by amenities such as these. The men, some 250-300 combatants at any given time, certainly were in better spirits than those he left behind in the Middle East. That conflict had spread from Afghanistan to Pakistan to Syria, and was now approaching its eighteenth year with no end in sight. *Give it a rest, President Pollard,* he thought. *Declare victory and come back home (what's left of home, anyway).*

There was a group gathered around one of the high-def flat screen monitors still in use. It was touch sensitive and a corporal was honing in on an area of Turner Beach by touching the screen and spreading his fingers. "Idiot alert," mused the corporal. "These two are rutting."

"Whoo-hoo," said the crowd. They were rooting for the home team.

"Let up on them," said the captain. "You're about to read his tattoos."

The corporal moved his hands from the outer corners of the screen toward the middle and the image of the lovers shrank as the observed area widened.

"What if they are terrorists, Cap'n?" said a disappointed private. "What if this activity is just a diversion to make us look the other way?"

"Good point, Markowitz," said Captain Rodriguez with apparent sincerity. "Track them for another hour or so. See where they go."

He returned to surveilling areas on the holographic display, moving his arms broadly, grabbing sections of real estate with a claw-shaped hand and zooming in with a finger-spreading motion. Unauthorized watercraft within miles of the island was his first priority. It might be his imagination but there may have been a change in the boating traffic pattern. If some group from the mainland was starting to take interest in Sanibel, he needed to know it sooner rather than later. There had never been a flotilla launched, but groups of three and four boats had strayed from the usual fishing lanes. These activities were no longer tracked by military or civilian marine navigation outfits, so there would be no co-ordination or sharing of information. The priorities and resources were no longer there, and "Homeland Security" had functioned in name only for years now, as did the rest of the country. *No,* thought Captain Rodriguez. *We are on our own here.* He moved a few more surveillance areas into view, and then he thought another thought. *Better here than there.*

.   .   .   .   .

Towards twilight, Beverly approached Chapman on his back patio. He was sipping sun tea. There was a fresh container, a large glass jar, on the adjacent table.

"Want some tea?" he asked as she came onto the flagstone.

"Sounds great," she smiled back at him. "What's next on the list?"

"Oh, I think we've done plenty enough for one day," he said, knowing full well that it was she, not "we", who had done the "plenty" part.

He dug into his pocket and retrieved a gold coin. He offered it to her without getting up.

Beverly looked at the one ounce coin held lightly between his thumb and index finger but did not reach to meet up with his outstretched hand.

"That is too much," she said matter-of-factly.

"I know but it's all I have. There are more one ounce coins than there are the fractions. Call it an advance. I'll 'pay it forward' for a week's work, and then I'll give you another one until you find time to do another thirty or forty hours work. And then another and so on. My yard really likes you. See how lush and pretty everything is?"

"OK, then," said Beverly, and she reached for the coin, palm up. "Thank you."

"No. Thank *you*," said Chapman; and he meant it.

On her walk home, Beverly reflected on the scenes she passed, and with them the reflections these observations prompted. A bicyclist smiles at you. People are walking in groups after some time on the beach. Pleasant conversations and peaceful scenes of everyday life are the norm on Sanibel. Beaches, gardens, cocktail parties, humor and intelligent conversation were the rule in dramatic contrast to much of the world. Cars were hybrids or electric, with the exception of Dr. Wilson's old Jeep and the occasional Island Security military vehicle. Most transportation was done on foot or bicycle anyway.

The island was not returning to the way it was before the causeway was built, however. Anyone who expected a return to those halcyon days had simply not thought it through. Sanibel certainly had a period of time when island life was isolated and idyllic. This period was probably best represented by the pioneering generation that took advantage of the Homestead Act nearly one hundred years previously. Imagine getting one hundred and sixty acres of Sanibel property just for living on the land and growing some tomatoes. The four dollar ferry ride was just expensive enough to keep you home for a month before going over to the mainland for provisions or to see a doctor. Land developers ruined that sense of isolation and freedom when they built the causeway; but just because the causeway was no longer there was no reason to believe that things would ever be the way they were. There were fundamental differences now. Then it took free land to attract people to the sweltering barrier island; now it took untold resources to keep them away. Then it was subtle greed; now it was blatant fear – polar opposite expressions of optimism and pessimism.

.   .   .   .   .

The guests began arriving at the Weber's house. The brick driveway was congested with smart cars, hybrids, sports cars, Vespas, and Mopeds, but surprising few bicycles on an island where the bicycles outnumbered the people. Some of the guests were paired off, committed couples, but most were singles, not yet, or rather no longer, committed to just one person. Entanglements were complicated on Sanibel. There were many beautiful people here. Island demographics ran contrary to this party's mix: there were more married couples than singles. It was just that comfortable married individuals were not always up for the high energy revelry that the singles seemed to crave.

Beyond the lush semi-tropical vegetation, past the portico, stood June Weber, welcoming her guests, steering them through the small mansion towards the garden in back. There was the pool, the landscaped paths to the beach, the chef carving beef tenderloin, the bars in tiki-hut styling, the statuary, the lanterns, and the band. There were people reminiscing and people listening open-hearted. There were tender-hearted victims of wounded relationships and broken-hearted victims of a life-long love lost. There were seekers and searchers, and there were users and fools. There were drug addicted sycophants and power-addicted arrogant ones. In other words, this was your typical party. Nearly every guest, on some level, resented the Webers for what they had, who they were, and how they could show themselves and their home to others so honestly and naïvely. And the Webers *were* being naïve. They were just having fun. Well, yes, they were doing coke, too. But they offered it around generously.

Chapter Five

The good doctor knocked on the door hard, knuckles against wood, trying to be heard above the pulsating music and cacophonous din inside. An attractive woman opened the door and smiled broadly.

"I am with the Mimosa Witnesses," announced Michael Wilson, "and I am here to give testimony."

"Come in Michael." said the woman flirtatiously, spinning her body and pulling him into the room with unseen eddy currents. "The bar is in the corner if you can work your way to it."

"I suspect it is there whether I can get to it or not," he said but she was not listening and was already being separated from this encounter by the throng of friends alternately laughing, talking, drinking and dancing through the night.

The room was cavernous with shoulders rubbing and heads bobbing everywhere except for a large rectangular space in the middle of the room. He couldn't see what was there so he decided to investigate by climbing one of the two stairways leading to the balcony to his left. It meant postponing his drink, but he had all night for drinks and conversations and who knows what might transpire.

The twin staircases framed the rectangular void; one straight-edged against the front wall, the other against the back, both curving in a gentle arch of railing toward the center of the room while ascending to the balcony to the left of the room. Wilson climbed the closer of the two, to his left against the front wall. Half way up he couldn't believe what he was seeing. The rectangular space was a swimming pool in the middle of the main room of this very strange house – this party house. In the center of the balcony railing there was a break in the railing overlooking this room. In that spot was a small platform. The only reason for the structure that Wilson could imagine is that it was a diving platform. Was the pool really deep enough for a second story dive? *Somebody has way more money than sense,* he thought.

Michael followed the balcony to the back wall where another walkway, the size of a hallway, stretched along the back wall to the right. He took it because it took him away from the crowd of revelers. Now he walked along a railing that overlooked the pool and party below. Someone waved happily and Michael waved back. He came to a hallway of sorts at the far corner of the room – no doors, and it sloped down gently. *Probably wheelchair safe,* the doctor in him thought. He took the passageway and the sound of the party faded quickly.

To his right were storage rooms, each twelve feet by twelve feet, one after another. They were separated from the passageway by steel folding security gates, whose large diamond shaped gaps would fold to nothing when opened. One room contained musical instruments: an accordion, two trumpets, many guitars and keyboards, a drum set, and more. Another had quilts and blankets, antique furniture, and oriental rugs. Another had wine, improperly stored but adequate for short term purposes. The next room was filled with wooden boxes, arranged so that a person could get to most of them easily. This went on for nearly ten more rooms, each with some sort of organizational theme; then the passageway came

65

to a level landing. The slope had probably brought Wilson to the main level. The area was well lit but starting to feel closed in. He could turn back and go up to the balcony or he could turn to his left and follow the passageway down further. He chose the latter.

The second downward slope paralleled the first, separated initially by a wall, then by a vertical distance as well. There were no storage rooms this time, but there *was* art on the wall. It was very good art of an extremely eclectic mixture – moderns, classics, primitive, folk – and all apparently originals. After a distance similar to the first sloping hallway, the passage opened to the right into an airplane hangar that had a very well-stocked bar with rich woods and mirrors.

"What'll you have?" called the affable man behind the mahogany counter.

"Irish," responded Wilson. "Rocks."

"Bushmill or Jameson?"

"Jameson, please"

"You got it."

The room was deserted. Wilson pulled out a chair from the half dozen round wooden tables in the bar area, sat down, and directed his attention toward the World War Two vintage two engine plane with its large propellers.

"The last flight out is in thirty minutes," said the bartender as he set Wilson's whiskey on a cocktail napkin. Wilson reached for his wallet and the bartender said, "Forget it. You're with the party, aren't you?"

"Right. Thanks," said Wilson. "Where is it going?"

"The flight?"

"Yeah?"

"Won't know 'til it gets there. Depends on 'landing conditions'."

Suddenly a bell started ringing persistently.

"Uh-oh, *there's* trouble!" said the bartender. "I don't smell smoke yet though."

The bell jangled relentlessly, stopping and starting.

Wilson's eyes opened wide, suddenly, dramatically. He had been dreaming a damn stupid dream. Meanwhile the telephone was insisting on an answer. Wilson groped for the phone.

"Hello?" he said slowly, blearily, softly. He wanted to make it clear with that one word that he had been asleep and that their emergency was a sacrifice on his part.

"Sorry to call at this hour, doc," said Ron Weber, but "June has just had a heart attack or something. It was really bad. She says her heart fluttered and stopped. I thought she was dying but she seems better now except she can't get her breath."

"Did she lose consciousness?"

"I'm not sure. Almost. Maybe."

"Can you check her vital signs?"

"I don't even know what that means. Can you come over here now?"

"Of course. I'm on my way." And with that Doctor Michael Wilson pulled on shorts, buttoned up a tropical shirt, slipped on his Birkies, grabbed his leather doctor bag, and headed out the door to the Jeep.

Wilson loved his Rubicon. It was ten years old but garage-kept. The red was not oxidized at all. In a world of smart cars he enjoyed sitting up high in his ragtop. Even the satellite radio still worked. He justified it because one never knew when accessing a medical emergency would require four-wheel drive; and to be fair, getting stuck in the sand was a common enough occurrence that he did not need to risk. And the island bought the gas for this behemoth. Enough said.

Doctor Wilson pulled up to the front door of the Webers. The brick circular drive was surrounded by the lush tropical landscaping for which the island was well known. Located near the western end of West Gulf Drive, the house was impressive even by Sanibel standards. Ron Weber came to the door seconds after the headlights swept the front façade. He anxiously waited while

Wilson gathered his bag and climbed down from the Jeep.

"This way," said Weber.

"Tell me what happened," commanded Wilson gently.

"She nearly passed out on me," replied Ron Weber. "She said her heart fluttered to a stop, if that makes any sense. Since then she has been hysterical; she can't get her breath. I've never seen her like this before, and I've seen her plenty of ways."

They climbed the stairs to the bedrooms. "Had she been drinking?" asked Wilson.

"When has she not been?" affirmed Weber. "She was mostly doing coke though, and some meth."

"Methamphetamine or methadone?" sought Wilson for clarification.

"Sorry, methadone. She uses it to mellow out between her coke highs."

"Not a smart combination," warned Wilson. They entered the bedroom.

June Weber was on the bed, sitting propped against the headboard with decorative pillows supporting her. She was breathing rapidly but had clearly calmed down some from the worst of it.

"I took a few Xanax for the panic attack," June began. "I hope that was OK. I had to do something."

"You did fine, June," reassured Wilson. "Ron tells me you have had a rough night."

"Actually it was a great night until this happened. We had people over and it was a swell party, until this happened. Thank God they had all gone home. They would have freaked!"

With the invitation to retell her story of the night's events, June reiterated the details of the event, the spell, and it was similar to the story as relayed by Ron. Nothing new or surprising was forthcoming.

Wilson said, "I am going to need to examine you now. Is that OK?"

"Sure," said June. "How and where do you want me?"

"Here is fine. Can you sit on the side of the bed?" asked Weber. "Ron, are you OK standing there?"

"Fine, Michael. Can I get you anything?"

"You can boil some water," Wilson quipped. "No, I have all that I need. Thanks."

Doctor Wilson opened his bag and took out some equipment – stethoscope, blood pressure cuff, some items for the neurologic exam – then he took June's blood pressure. He palpated the tissues of her scalp for signs of injury related to the fall. He shined his little flashlight into June's eyes, one then the other, watching for sluggish reactions of the pupils that might indicate a stroke or other neurologic condition. He checked the tongue to determine that it was still midline and had not been bitten by June either during a fall or a seizure. He checked to see if the trachea was midline and the thyroid was normal in size and consistency and non-tender. He looked for enlarged lymph nodes and checked the conjunctivae for paleness that could indicate anemia.

"Can you unbutton your blouse and unsnap your bra, June?" asked Wilson.

"Do you want me to take them off?"

"Either way."

She removed both and Ron stepped into the bathroom to get her robe, more for Dr. Wilson's modesty than for June's. June slipped into the light robe and sat back down on the bed.

"Lie back, if you don't mind." Wilson requested. June did so and Dr. Wilson untied the belt on the robe and separated the opening in front to expose her midchest and inner breasts, but not her nipples.

Wilson listened to her heart for a long time, first with the diaphragm then with the bell to discern the lower frequency tones. He listened at the lower left sternal border, then the right, then at the base, a little above the first locations. "Take a deep breath," he said when it appeared that June was needing to breathe. While she inhaled deeply, Dr. Wilson moved the stethoscope to her upper chest, left then right, then to her lateral rib cage, listening for the first time through the fabric of the robe. Strong breath sounds lowered his index of suspicion for abnormalities in this region. When June appeared caught up with her need to breathe, Wilson again said, "OK, now stop."

He went back to listening to her heart, this time lifting her left breast with the back of his right hand, and with a rolling of the right wrist, positioned the diaphragm of the stethoscope against the rib cage that covered the apex of the heart. June's breast was pendulous and heavy. It warmed Wilson's right hand but did not interfere with a clear auscultation. It was merely a nuisance, not exactly a hindrance.

Next Wilson palpated and auscultated the abdomen, felt for inguinal lymph nodes. He examined the extremities carefully for signs of injury, then as part of the neurologic exam for signs of weakness. A thorough neurologic exam required several little tools, a reflex hammer and a wheel and a tuning fork; and a mental status exam rounded out this relatively complete physical.

"I am going to do an EKG now. Is that OK?" Wilson asked of June.

"Can you do that here?" Ron asked.

"Sure."

"Good, then," said Ron. June nodded.

Dr. Wilson pulled a small lap top computer out of his bag. It was thin and measured six inches by nine. He plugged it into the wall socket, but it could function just as well on battery power. *Why waste batteries?* thought Wilson. He opened the computer and pressed power. The screen responded instantly. "I wouldn't mind having the new holographic model," he said just to make conversation. Along the side were ten jacks into which Wilson plugged ten leads. Two attached to the arms and two more Wilson attached to each of June's ankles. The other six were stuck to her chest over the heart in pattern forming a gentle "S-curve".

"Lie quietly, please," Dr. Wilson instructed.

June did not move.

Moments later the screen presented Wilson with a classic twelve-lead EKG pattern.

"Well, the good news is that you are in a normal sinus rhythm with no residual ectopic beats, meaning your heart rhythm is just fine. The bad news is that your QT-interval is prolonged, meaning that your heart is at increased risk for an arrhythmia called *'torsade de pointes'*. That could be fatal if it happens again. I say 'again' because I am fairly certain that this is what you experienced earlier tonight. Furthermore, I am fairly certain of what caused it and what to do to prevent another episode."

"That's good news, doctor. That's actually rather impressive. Are you really that good? I was expecting more of a shrug of the shoulders," exclaimed Ron.

"Well, don't get too excited yet, you two. The treatment is not as easy as taking a few pills."

"So what was the cause and what do you recommend?"

"You are drug dependent, June. And nobody cares about that and everybody loves you, but it is time to get it under control. It nearly killed you tonight and it might kill you tomorrow. Remember five years ago when the vice president's wife had that seizure and died? Too much cocaine.

Your situation has a little extra nuance to it, though. Methadone is famous for causing *torsade de pointes*. It prolongs the QT-interval and that is what showed up in you. It also inhibits a metabolic pathway, CYP450 2D6, so other drugs build up to toxic levels. That was a bad combination you were playing with tonight.

"So what exactly is it you want me to do?" asked June.

"Take two aspirin and call me in the morning."

"Very funny. You could have told me that over the telephone."

"I know but it wouldn't have had the same effect. Tomorrow, I will take a more thorough history and run some tests, mostly a genomic profile. Then, a little buprenorphine and some pharmacogenomic magic, and you will be fine. Just no more drugs tonight. OK?"

"OK."

At the door Ron was effusive. "Doctor Wilson, I cannot thank you enough. This "intervention" was long overdue. It's just a shame that it took nearly losing June to begin the process of getting her back."

"We will see, Ron," said Wilson warily. "She hasn't shown for that appointment yet. She just might have to 'see a man about a dog'."

"She will be there, doc. She has to."

"We'll see," said Michael Wilson, and he turned and headed for the Rubicon. The sun was just starting to rise and he had a full day at the office scheduled.

As he drove he dictated the entire encounter into the Jeep's onboard computer. When he was finished, he pressed "upload" and the progress note was sent to a satellite that would download to his office computer later in the morning. Voice recognition software had already transcribed the note. It would be on June's chart when she showed for her appointment at the Periwinkle office. "We'll see," said Wilson to no one there.

． ． ． ． ．

A piercing trill of a flute told Sheriff Cochran that he was wanted. Even the most musical cell phone ring tone can be annoying the twentieth time that it goes off.

"Sheriff Cochran," he answered.

"John, it's Liz Forbes."

Cochran recognized his friend's voice immediately. "What's wrong, Liz? Are you OK?" Cochran had recognized the tremor of concern in her voice. He had heard it in too many people recently.

"John. Someone has broken into my studio. They have stolen about a year's worth of my glass fusion art. Why would anyone do such a thing?" She wanted to cry, but held herself back.

"I'll be over as soon as I finish at the Turnbull's, Liz. We seem to have developed a small crime spree on the island. At least I hope it stays small."

"Alright, John. Take your time. I'm alright and I am not going anywhere."

"Good-bye, Liz. Give me about thirty minutes."

"OK." She disconnected from the call and sat down hard, exhausted, and dispirited.

Sheriff John Cochran rang the doorbell and Liz Forbes took a moment to answer. She motioned for her old friend to enter, but she moved slowly, like she was lost.

"Oh, John. I can never replace those pieces. However you become inspired one day, you cannot recapture that the next day, and certainly not a year later. I feel so violated, so vulnerable. Glass fusion has so many happy accidents; you just can't replicate any of it."

"That is what makes your work so great, Liz. It's why you are in such demand by the museums that display your art."

"They took it all. They must have gathered it together quickly because they broke some pieces. They left some broken pieces in the studio."

"Yours is the fifth break-in and robbery this week, Liz. They knew what they were doing, too. It has all been stuff that would sell on the world markets. I can't name names, but someone on the island lost a Rembrandt. I cannot imagine what it is worth. Ten years ago there would have been insurance coverage, but now with those companies all gone, it's all just a total loss."

"I had not heard about any robberies."

"We were trying to keep it quiet to avoid tipping off whomever is responsible, but it seems to be getting worse and I think it is time we started alerting people to keep a watch out for unusual activity and to start locking their doors."

"Any suspects?"

"None. Have you seen anyone hanging around the neighborhood? Any suspicious activity, as they say?"

"No. Not a thing," assured Liz. "Oh, John, this is paradise. This stuff doesn't happen on Sanibel. I could just cry."

"Go ahead if it makes you feel any better. Meanwhile, keep an eye out, lock your doors, and call me if you get anything."

"Where are you going from here?"

"I will need to investigate the crime scene, and then I think it's time to update Island Security. They are using their satellite to monitor, so I can probably watch a surveillance tape and see when it happened, but it's unlikely I will be able to I.D. anyone."

"Good, but don't go just yet. Stay with me a few minutes. I'll fix us some coffee."

"Sure. That sounds good. I could use a cup. Thanks."

Liz headed for the kitchen to brew coffee. She was grateful for the company just now.

Chapter Six

"What are you doing sleeping there?" asked Beverly.

If Jesse was startled, he didn't show it. "I'm not asleep." After a pause Jesse added, "I'm watching for meteors."

Jesse still had not moved, didn't turn his head to look at Beverly. He was lying on his back on the foredeck of *Serenity*, his head near the mast, his feet toward the bow. *Serenity's* curves formed a delicate arch for his back and the clean white fiberglass was sturdy and comfortable.

"See any?" asked Beverly as she took hold of the rigging and swung her long limbs over the railing. She negotiated her way along the side of *Serenity*, around the mast to where Jesse still had not moved and laid down beside him. Jesse moved to his left to balance *Serenity*. When the listing resolved and *Serenity* was again still, he said, "A few. Watch toward the east."

After they lay still and quiet for awhile, Beverly asked, "Hungry? I brought some chicken." She had seen no meteors, but did not doubt that he had.

"Great," said Jesse. "I am a bit weary of fish, but, you know, it's all good."

They climbed down into the cabin. Jesse lit a burner on the alcohol stove and said, "Let me see what I can find to go with it." From the small stock of provisions beneath the stove, he extracted some olive oil, a garlic clove, and a bottle of artichoke hearts. From another cabinet he rummaged around until he produced a bottle of capers.

"What, no wine?" teased Beverly, impressed with the range of small items that he kept on board.

"Maybe..." Jesse teased back at her. He turned to face her in the close quarters of the cabin. She was standing with her back to the steps that led down from the cockpit. Jesse leaned into her and she yielded, pressing her buttocks, then her shoulders against the steps. Jesse's weight against her and the gentle rocking of *Serenity* caused her to flush and the glow felt good. She slowly encircled his waist with her arms and loosely held one wrist with the other hand. She pulled him toward her and Jesse responded by moving his chest and shoulders toward her as well.

Jesse took her lower lip gently in his teeth and let loose only after his lips had taken over that hold. He pulled on her lip with his mouth as it slowly stretched then slipped from his grasp. Then both mouths formed a quiet smile and the couple's eyes engaged one another. They kissed softly, warmly. The night was young.

Gazing at Beverly's face, but keeping still, Jesse lingered over the moment and finally said, "I have a zin, and maybe a shiraz."

Smiling back at Jesse, Beverly whispered in an uncharacteristically throaty voice. "Tough decision. We may need both."

"Hmm," said he. "We may indeed."

They regained an upright position. Jesse had to be careful of his head, but as long as he didn't dash around, he wouldn't hit it. Beverly had more than ample headroom.

Jesse added some oil to a pan and placed it on the stove. He sliced and diced the garlic clove and added that, then the chicken.

"Look over there for a tomato," he said to Beverly, pointing at yet another storage unit. She found one next to two bananas in a small hand-crafted cabinet with tricky sliding doors that could swing down to form a small table between the cushioned seating.

"Found one," she said.

"Cut that up for us, would you? There's a knife in that same cabinet."

"Yes, I saw it." She slid the kitchen knife from its built-in wooden holder and swung the cabinet door ninety degrees in a vertical arch. A table leg fell into place and she had a cutting surface. Beverly diced the tomato and Jesse put it, along with the artichoke hearts and capers, into the pan with the chicken mixture.

"Five minutes," he announced.

"Not enough time," Beverly said with a broad smile, teasing.

"Not *nearly* enough," he promised, and took her in his arms.

"Not ever enough," she said, and they kissed.

"Never enough," he replied, and they kissed again.

"The wine went well with the chicken dish," said Beverly after a long silence. They had gone outside of the cabin and were sitting in *Serenity's* cockpit.

Jesse uncorked the second bottle and Beverly presented her glass in an outstretched hand.

"It could have used a side dish, at least some rice."

"It was great," she reassured him. Beverly inhaled the aroma of the wine as she took the first sip. She held it in her mouth while the world paused.

"Wow," she said. "This is *good*. What is it?"

"It's an *Eileen Hardy* Shiraz. The Aussies are still getting it done aren't they?"

"I'll say! This is good stuff."

"It's all good," he added the catch phrase that says nothing and everything. A head nod would have served as well, but either one was fine. It was both dismissal and reassurance, thoughtlessly co-mingling.

They sat sipping wine, silently for a few minutes, then Beverly moved to where Jesse was sitting and put her head on his shoulder. He put his arm around her shoulder to ward off the growing chill of the night. *Serenity* listed from their unbalanced weight and they slid into the deeper mid-section of the cockpit to balance her. They kissed long and deep, and their breathing deepened. Jesse cradled Beverly's head and neck in his free hand and held that firm embrace through a series of kisses, deep and tender.

Beverly moaned and Jesse's nostrils flared. Beverly was going all moist when Jesse said, "Let's go inside."

"Yes," she replied. "Let's."

.   .   .   .   .

The next morning they made love twice more; five times total counting the one time during the night when he cradled her breast until her nipples hardened and she awoke rather passionately. Turning over to greet his erection, she had abandoned the earlier gymnastics for a deep satisfying stillness. He filled her, completed her, so tremendously that she wanted to cry. Just when she could press him into her no harder, Jesse broke the stillness with a cry of his own. "Aaahhh, God!" he said as he released his arch and buried his head in her neck and hair, and pulsing and spasming down there, mixing the fluids of life one time more.

It's all good, thought Beverly, smiling to herself at Jesse's little saying.

They showered in the marina's facilities. Jesse made coffee on the alcohol stove and they sat out on the marina's deck, watching pelicans dive for fish and osprey soaring, and great blue heron wading, and ibis and egrets. This day was happening the same as if the Earth had not moved, had not shaken, not once but five times during the night. These birds were oblivious to the excitement of mankind's adventures whether on a sail boat or in this crazy world.

"What are your plans?" asked Beverly.

Not contemplating the larger picture at just this time, Jesse replied, "It's funny that you ask, but I seem to have a larger than usual appetite this morning."

"I'll say," Beverly twinkled.

"Well, yes. That, too. But you asked, and right now my plans definitely include breakfast."

"Timbers isn't open for breakfast, is it?"

"No, but we can get some croissants and eggs at the market just a block from here, and I can whip up something in no time."

"You da man!"

"An' you da woman."

"Wouldn't have it any other way."

"Amen."

Before walking over to the market, they kissed again, out on the decking with nobody around to see them, but with the pelicans diving for fish and the osprey soaring, and the great blue herons wading, and the ibis and the egrets silently calling for more. They walked slowly to the corner market with no plans beyond breakfast and with no expectations for a permanent relationship expressed by either. The world was too crazy, and too uncertain. Later in the day they went for a sail.

Book Two

Chapter Seven

Brady Chapman was admiring his tomatoes. He was sacrificing quantity for quality and size by "deadheading" the plants, removing selected blooms based on their appearance and location on the plant. He had dozens of plants, all of his favorite varieties, so he would always have fresh tomatoes. He chose a prize to pick for his *caprese* salad – firm, bright reddish orange, and perfectly vine-ripened. He placed the fruit in a medium-sized shallow wooden bowl next to some basil leaves. With some Spanish olive oil and fresh buffalo mozzarella, his lunch salad would be complete. He carried the bowl to the kitchen and set it on the black quartz countertop. He opened the stainless steel door to the wine cooler, stared at the Caymus Conundrum, and chose a Pouilly-Fuissé. He had a proper wine cellar, of course, but that was for his reds, several thousand bottles of them.

Chapman poured the wine into an antique crystal glass and re-corked the bottle for use later, perhaps as a patio aperitif later this afternoon. He held the glass in the late morning sunlight, not to admire the wine's pale straw color, but just to play with the reflections the crystal generated. He took a sip of the dry oaky wine and set the glass on the counter. *Les vins extraordinaire dans votre vere.*

He was beginning to slice the tomato when his cell phone rang. Chapman set the tomato knife to the right of the bowl, the blade edge facing to the left toward the bowl, and picked up his phone.

"Hello?" he said.

"Hello, sir," replied a voice. "At Rothschild and Rosenblum, we can guarantee superior asset management for your portfolio. May I ask if you are satisfied with your current..."

Chapman disconnected the call without replying. He recognized the significance of the coded message and went directly to a secure room, and sealed himself into the sound proof chamber. He brought the direct satellite connection online and activated the touch screen hologram. Over an encrypted Internet he requested the site www.rothschildrosenblum.net. He knew the one-time use site would be active for less than thirty minutes. The site was simple with no graphics. Chapman entered his twenty symbol password and was immediately provided a coded set of directives. He transferred the coded directives via crystalchip to a separate tablet computer that was not and had never been connected to the Internet. A dedicated proprietary program translated the set of directives, indicated that a seventy million dollar transfer had already been made to his Cayman account as a retainer fee, and indicated that a balance of one hundred thirty million would be paid on successful completion of the assassination.

Chapman returned to the hologram and touched the "accept" panel. With a delay related to the speed of light and the distance to space orbit and then to Europe, additional information and photographs were downloaded. A minute later the website disconnected. Chapman erased the crystalchip and powered down the equipment in his safe room.

He would study the details of the mission later. First he had a salad to make. Later he would need to pack warmer clothes for Ireland.

· · · · ·

"Ping," announced Jesse's cell phone.

Jesse laid down the cloth he was using to apply teak oil to the door panels that led to the cabin. He picked up the phone and pressed the green icon on the touch screen. He listened.

"Hello?" came a voice Jesse did not recognize.

Jesse listened and waited.

"Hello? I'm looking for a Mr. O'Connell?" said the voice.

"This is Jesse O'Connell."

"Mr. O'Connell, this is Bert Krepazhski. I'm with Island Water?"

"What can I do for you, Mr. Krepazhski?"

"Sheriff Cochran gave me your name, sir."

"I'll bet he did!"

"We are having some problems with the reverse osmosis plant. At least three of the wells are in need of restoration, the computer control center has shut down twice this week, and well, frankly, there isn't anyone left with what you might call an institutional memory. All of the technicians are recent hires. Sheriff Cochran tells me you used to work at the plant."

"Yes. As a summer job when I was in college."

"Oh," Krepazhski paused, thinking. "Still it's more that we have now. Could you take a look at our operations? We would really appreciate it.

The island water is going to get brackish fast if we don't do *something.*"

Jesse sighed, "OK. I'll be there after a bit."

"Thanks. We really appreciate it."

"No problem," assured Jesse. He put the top on the bottle of teak polish and slipped down the cabin stairs to find a fresh T-shirt. At the marina bike rack Jesse chose a clean magnesium alloy bicycle for the short ride down Sanibel-Captiva Road to the Island Water Plant. On an island with twice as many bicycles as people, it served everyone well to consider them as community property. Favorite selections were closely guarded by a few particular residents, but they represented a small minority. Jesse was not one of them. He would ride this bike or another. This bike was actually rather nice, Jesse noticed as he pedaled faster. It was a Special Edition Litespeed Siena featuring a 3/2.5 titanium frame, Easton EC90 fork, Shimano Ultegra SL components and Fulcrum Racing wheels. It was all good.

At the plant Jesse reviewed ongoing operations with the new technicians and Mr. Krepazhski, the plant manager. "As long as you are going to do a maintenance overhaul," Jesse told them, "you are going to want to do well restoration. It is better to have all twenty-four wells on line. Only about half of these are providing water to the plant, but you need the others for monitoring water levels and quality and you need a few to standby as reserves. First things being first, you want to start with clean wells. They get choked with calcium carbonate deposits and you need to flush them."

"OK, but how?"

"Easy enough, pilgrim. Take some of the fresh water from the good wells and divert it to the problem wells. Pump in some carbonated water and the carbonic acid will react with the built-up calcium carbonate deposits that are responsible for dropping the production rates of the wells. Flush the free calcium and bicarb that gets formed and – *voila* – a fresh well, ready for service."

"*Voila*" says Krepazhski, enjoying the lesson. "Are you an engineer?" Krepazhski asked.

"More of a Jack-of-all-trades," said Jesse, smiling at the recognition.

"But why do we keep going off line at the computer control center?" asked one of the technicians.

"Could be any number of things," said Jesse. "Probably low flow from the wells if well restoration hasn't been done for awhile, and I'll bet that is the case. The system monitors for pH, pressure, conductivity and several other conditions, and it will shut down to prevent damage to the system or if water is off-specification. Check your variables and control signals and that might point to the problem. I will do a walk-through with you before I go."

"You don't know how much we appreciate this, sir."

Jesse felt strange being called "Sir" by someone older than him. "Not a problem," Jesse reassured Krepazhski. "I drink the water, too, you know."

Jesse told them what he knew as they toured the plant. "There are two deep artesian aquifers beneath Sanibel, the Hawthorne and the deeper Suwanee, about 800 feet deep. It's not terribly brackish, nowhere near what you would get out of the Gulf, and it is stratified with the salinity increasing as you go deeper. Anyway, you pre-treat and filter this. It is standard reverse osmosis technology after that but the semipermeable membranes are really high-tech – complex organic materials only several thousandths of an inch thick. The high pressure pumps seem to be working alright," Jesse observed, glancing at the pressure gauges. "They can easily generate twice the pressure they need to provide. Six of them are reading between 200 and 250 p.s.i." he said reassuringly. "That seventh one is for back-up. The plant is in good shape. I think that all you need to do is restore a few wells. Call me if you run into any problems."

"You are so kind, sir," said Krepazhski. "Is there anything we can do for you in return?"

"Sure is," said Jesse. "Quit calling me 'Sir'."

.   .   .   .   .

The Mayor's office was unusually busy. As the Island administrator, Mayor Farber functioned more as a benign despot ruling a kingdom than as a mayor in the older traditional sense. Henry had no need to please the body politic; he served at the pleasure of the Council. That group of the Island's wealthiest and most privileged men and women felt lucky to have Henry watching over their interests, and rightly so. It could not be easy maintaining supply chains in an uncertain world, assuring a defensive stature that was secure yet appeared unobtrusive, and assuaging powerful egos. On the surface Farber made it appear easy, but scratch that surface and the complexities of the office peeled like an onion to reveal systems within systems. Today was heavily scheduled.

The group seated at the long mahogany table essentially ran the Island. They were there because they *had* to be leaders. It was who they were in an existential sense – a part of their DNA perhaps. In another context they were surviving, not just thriving. In that regard their collective hypothalamus was in the cockpit, issuing orders to the neocortex. If they had known what was driving their behavior, they would have smiled anyway. They enjoyed the game, solving the puzzles, putting out the fires, designing the system, winding it up and watching it run around. They were *eu*stressing.

Jeffrey Rogers was still every bit as cynical as he had been as an NSA intelligence analyst. "We give Island Security too much latitude, Ron," he said, ignoring the Island Security commander seated two chairs to his right. "We do not need to be sending forces off island."

"I agree," interjects Farber. "Projecting power to the periphery is how empires fall, whether you're talking about Rome, England, America, or Sanibel. The center cannot hold. We need to manage our resources. They are plentiful, but not unlimited."

"I am not following this," said Ron Weber, who had come into the board room mid-conversation. "I was on the phone with June."

"General Presswood was sharing with us that he thinks the bulk of this Island crime spree, mostly break-ins and jewelry theft, originates off island. He wants to beef up patrols, which we all agree with, but he wants clearance to follow some of the perpetrators back to the mainland and take out the source," Farber reported. "Is that about it, General?"

Oliver Presswood, commander of the paramilitary mercenaries, Island Security, was typically taciturn at meetings, speaking only when somebody else couldn't get it said. "That's it. Take out their headquarters, otherwise this problem will not go away. Strategy sessions with my officers keep reaching the same conclusion: send the mainlanders a message, or they will continue to test the limits of our patience and the depth of our resolve."

"I don't know about this, people," Cochran spoke up. "I would rather continue to gather evidence before we escalate strategically. We know that some petty thefts are being pulled off by the day laborers that we bring over to the island. We simply do not have enough information about how many robberies are raids from off-island and how many are by day laborers. For all we know it could be a coordinated effort. Day laborers could do the stealing and stash the property in a cache hidden somewhere for a mainlander boat to pick up later. You know the laborers are searched upon arrival and prior to leaving, and Island Security scans our waters with infrared wavelengths. Why are these measures not sufficient? Shouldn't those geosynchronous satellite images alert us to any unauthorized beach landings, General? Isn't that what we pay the big bucks for?"

Eyes turned back to General Presswood. He straightened his spine and considered his response. After a pregnant silence he said, "You are correct, of course. We will do a full scale review, conduct some surreptitious landings ourselves and see if we have holes in our technology or our human resources. We do not tolerate distraction among our monitoring personnel. Thank you, gentlemen." With that conclusion, the general rose to leave. He paused and seemed disappointed that the gathering did not stand as well. He was accustomed to the display of respect from his officers, but realized that he should not expect it from his civilian employers.

As Presswood left, the others turned their attention to a short list of additional agenda items. Farber addressed the next issue, "Where are we with the desalinization plant upgrade?"

Cochran spoke up, "I gave the staff Jesse's name and number."

"Oh, he'll love that!" interjected Rogers.

"He'll be fine with the imposition. It will give him something to do besides sailing. He has the institutional memory for the plant and he can give the crew the pointers they need to keep the facility running. He's a good citizen – second or third generation islander, civic responsibility, has to drink the water, too, and all of that. He'll be happy to help us out." Cochran was wasting words and he knew it. Everyone knew all of this about Jesse. He was their go-to guy and was always cheerful about pitching in, no matter how obtuse the project. Cochran was talking to hear himself talk apparently; must be the politician in him. It was too bad that sheriff was not an elected office: he might find a receptive audience upon which to focus those tendencies and energies.

"Sounds good, John," assured Farber, silencing the sheriff's meandering diatribe. "Who has the report on exotic supply?"

"Here!" barked Ron Weber. As Island treasurer and a former C.F.O. of a credit default swaps brokerage house (and derivatives trader prior to that), Weber was among the wealthiest of Island immigrants. His ways and means skills were unsurpassed when it came to obtaining non-staple items, the luxury goods that truly made Sanibel special. Weber excelled through his contacts and distribution systems awareness. He clearly enjoyed this part of what it took to keep Sanibel humming, and he wriggled in his seat to obtain a posture suitable for his presentation. The others ignored or tolerated this subtle nuance.

Grinning, Weber announced with a certain pleasure, "I am quite happy to say that we are assured at least five cases of the 2017 Bordeaux from Poulliac, different estates, and another three from estates in Saint-Estèphe – private shipping and future allocations guaranteed."

"Strong work, sailor!" said Dr. Wilson, reminding everyone that he was at the table. "I will work for wine, you know." Actually, everyone *did* know.

"And civilization perseveres… God bless the French," smiled Cochran.

"Wait, there's more." Weber was just getting started: cheeses from Belgium; software upgrades from California – now a sovereign nation after surviving an incursion from Mexican nationals; women's shoes from Brazil and dresses from Sicily – an island that had survived relatively unscathed; gems from India and gold ore from Mali.

"Who requested gold ore?" asked Farber. "That's not the best currency for transactions."

"Alison Swanson," replied Weber. "She says she is going to put on a jewelry designing workshop. June has signed up. Hell, I think Mabel has, too. Doesn't your wife ever tell you anything?" teased Weber.

"I guess not," said Farber sheepishly.

"What does she plan to do to keep the stuff safe?" asked Cochran in his role as sheriff.

"Keep the project quiet, I suppose," answered Weber. "It's not that big of an order anyway – $20,000, maybe thirty. It will be a good change of pace activity for the ladies. You can throw only so many garden parties, you know."

"Still," said Cochran, "I am glad for the heads up. Gold is a risky asset when it's not in a vault – very much portable and in demand and untraceable."

"I think we can agree that Alison can manage her assets," said Farber. As the only woman on the Council, Alison Swanson had engendered more than a little respect. Her fortune had not derived from her career as an actress or even following her father's footstep as a major Hollywood producer, both of which had been highly successful and lucrative careers, by the way. Her real fortune came from a determined foray with a few million that she determined she could afford to lose. She bought highly leveraged silver puts over a decade ago, and as the economy turned down so did industrial demand for an inflationary hedge that became just another victim of the great deflation as bankruptcies snowballed. Puts protected her from the price gyrations in a way that futures would not have, and as she profited she pyramided – soon she was worth billions. No; no one doubted that Alison could manage a little gold ore as a plaything.

"Next!" beseeched Wilson. The good doctor was growing bored and restless.

"Time!" declared Farber. "Sorry for letting it run late." Actually the meeting *had* run long. The gathering rose gratefully, lost in thoughts of where they needed to be next. For some it was a late lunch; for others it was golf; for John Cochran it was a chance to check messages and resume the quest for a secure civilization.

Michael Wilson approached Ron Weber. "I haven't seen June, Ron. Is she doing OK?"

"She is, Michael. Thanks for everything you did the other night. She says she is doing fine and uses that as her excuse not to come to see you or deal with the underlying issue. But I suspect you knew that."

"It's a risky way she has chosen to go, Ron. Work on her for us when you can. Tough love and all of that."

"I'll say that I will, but she just spins me around when I go there," confessed Ron.

"You are no different than every other man. I guess it at least helps a little to realize to what extent they jerk us around."

"I don't know. It might be easier not to know that women rule, to just go along with the common delusion that men are in charge – cave man days."

"Yeah, you probably just need a bigger club."

"No. If I came home with that, I would just get bigger lumps on my head."

"I hear that. Alright, then, but do what you can. She's not ready to quit yet. That's clear. But she needs to; it's a bad disease."

"Alright, Michael. Thanks," said Ron as he headed for his golf foursome.

"*De nada*," replied Wilson as he headed for his office practice.

Chapter Eight

General David Douglas was the undisputed regional warlord for southwest Florida. He rarely thought of himself in such terms, but to be sure, others did. Others may have seen him as ruthless, a brilliant tactician, and all business, but Douglas personally declined to engage in the frivolity of self examination. He might describe himself as *focused*, but the finer narratives on his talents or shortcomings, he would leave to others. His heart still beat with its muffled tattoo. He was still counted among the living. That was the definitive accolade. That was enough for Douglas, and it spoke volumes.

Headquarters for Douglas and his officers was a former hotel and restaurant constructed about ten years ago from recycled cypress. It exuded old world charm with a wrap-around porch peppered with rocking chairs, and an ornate bar with dark woods, and large doors that opened out to the veranda. It was at this location, in oversized wicker chairs outside the bar, on the battleship grey planking of the wide porch, that Douglas and his officers congregated with whiskey and cigars to discuss their warlord affairs.

The scene was eerily void of conversation. *This is spooky*, thought one of the junior officers, a Captain Thomas, a local recruit with no formal military training. "How can we plan missions if no one speaks?" he whispered.

"Hush!" snapped a nearby veteran; and chastened, Thomas fell silent, watching the seasoned officers take draws on their cigars and sips from their tumblers.

The challenges presented to leadership were understood, and laughably mundane. It was a recurring dilemma for a marauding paramilitary force: how to pay and feed warriors after years of plunder had stripped the region of its low-hanging fruit. Expeditions were branching further out and soon the risk would be that of violating treaties and territories of allies.

Douglas knew that it was only a matter of time until he would bring his forces to bear against the defenses of Sanibel's famed Island Security. What they lacked in numbers, only two or three hundred by reports from his men who doubled as day laborers, they made up for in sophisticated surveillance and weaponry. Still the island was such a great temptation that Douglas bordered on obsessing about an invasion. He had even moved his headquarters to this lovely hotel retreat on Pine Island, where with binoculars he could monitor first hand some of the activities of the forbidden fruit.

"Let's look at the maps again," Douglas barked, and the men followed him into the bar. Major Brody and Colonel LaFerla went behind the bar, set the box of maps on the bar and began spreading them over the dark wood. They turned up the lights to their brightest level and all gathered around.

"There is too much that we do not know," said Colonel LeFerla.

"Let's begin with what we do know," said Douglas. "Shore patrols!"

"It seems sparse by our standards," began Captain Gribble. "Too few and far between unless they have some kind of electronic surveillance... so you know they must have."

"No reports of cameras on poles, or any other devices," said Brody. "Hell, there're not even any poles. It's like the rich bastards can't have their scenery disrupted."

"Waters!" barked Douglas.

"Mines!" LeFerla barked back. "We calculate two or three hundred, maybe more. They are moored just under the surface and can be turned on and off at will from their headquarters. We suspect they can be detonated by Island Security just as easily as they can be activated, in case someone just gets too close. We've sent teams to look at them at night. They are big mothers. We have to use scuba gear and stay low in the water. The men have to acclimate to the temperature, too. Body heats gets them detected. We lost three squads learning that one. Must have infrared cameras some damn where."

"Troop count!" Douglas was moving on with the inventory.

"250. But it varies. They get 'shore leave'. Some of them use it to travel; some do some recruiting. They get finder's fees for new qualified grunts." LaFerla wasn't requesting benefits for the troops under Douglas. He was just sharing intel. No one took it otherwise.

"Munitions! Vehicles!"

"More than they know what to do with. I don't have photos, but our men get stationed near their Sundial facility whenever they can, and that is one well-equipped barracks, I'm here to tell you," said LaFerla. "They have helicopters, assault vehicles, some of those new urban tanks, and the latest in lightweight body armor. They will be tough to kill and tougher to get to. If they can see a boat, they can take it out. You've seen their war games just watching here from Pine Island. They shoot at a boat, they don't miss. I mean, I'm not afraid to die, but it might be nice if we had an assault helicopter or two. Right now they could mow us down, rake us into little neat piles, and not be late for lunch at the club."

Douglas had no more barks at this time. The general eased his way back out to the porch and sat quietly in the cushioned white wicker chair. After a time he said, "Mission's still on for tomorrow night."

.   .   .   .   .

General Douglas' counterpart, General Oliver Presswood, stood with his officers around a table as well. Electronic holograms of real time images of Sanibel and its surrounding environs stood in contradistinction to the worn paper maps of Douglas' army.

"Gentlemen, I want two exercises to be carried out in tandem," said the general standing ramrod straight. "The first is a war game. We know that there is a contingent of mainlanders, armed and organized, on Pine Island. We watched them arrive on our infrared satellite monitoring setup two weeks ago. It was dark, but they came in as a unit, almost in formation – 330 bodies by our count, 40 trucks, nothing special in the way of equipment. They clearly do not know we have satellite. We think they joined forces with about 40 or 50 others who have been acting as an advance guard, probably acting as some of our day labor. *Walters!*" Corporal Walters stiffened at the attention. "Get me a list of new hires! Last three months."

"Sir!" acknowledged the corporal.

"Now to the war game," Presswood resumed. "Tomorrow at 0800 we launch a surprise attack from Pine Island. Corporal Walters is putting together a list of our sixty most recent recruits. Set them up with ten rafts and position them midway between Sanibel and ten plausible launch points – Panther Key, Demere Key, James City, the mouth of the Caloosahatchee River, Bokeelia, and the other sites on this printout. Landings on Sanibel are projected at diverse locations, north and south, Buck Key to the causeway remnant. It's on your handouts. We will send two groups through the mangroves. The satellite will track them but it's up to your troops to find them and paint them. Pass out the paint ball weaponry tonight. That's all the preliminary intel anyone should need. Walters!"

"Sir!"

"Walters, you are excused from tomorrow's exercise. You are being given an assignment separate from the war games – real issues. Got it?"

"Yes, sir!"

"Walters, you will launch a missile at the individual with binoculars on the porch of that hotel on Pine Island – the individual who watches us on a daily basis. Got it?"

"Yes, sir. With pleasure, sir!"

"Good man," Presswood said turning his attention back to his officers. "Gentlemen, are we clear with regard to the exercise? Standard procedure and protocol should suffice."

"Clear, sir," said one.

"Crystal," said another.

"Good," snapped Presswood. "Now...*If!* – and I say 'if' because it damn well better not – but *if* somehow Sanibel's council or the civilian leadership gets wind of a missile launch on mainland forces, then this was just a stray bird during our war games. Got it?"

There was widespread agreement. This was a loyalty issue.

"Next I want to turn our attention to the very real possibility that these mainlanders are conducting incursions into civilian neighborhoods.

Sheriff Cochran has investigated numerous incidences of break-ins and thefts that appear to be originating off shore. Our satellite should be catching these but only if we know what to look for. This next exercise is no game. Tomorrow night when our troops are tired from this war game diversion we are throwing at them, tomorrow night will be the true test."

"Tomorrow, bring me the first ten soldiers hit by paint balls. I will read them the riot act for their incompetence. They will be given one and only one chance to stay in good standing with our security forces. They will be charged with invading the island by raft from off shore, capturing some specified trinket at a location to be disclosed later, and getting away undetected back out to sea. There will be no forewarning to our surveillance squads. Let me make this last point abundantly clear: there will be no forewarning to our surveillance squads. Am I clear on this point?"

The cacophonous reply indicated in the affirmative.

"The real purpose for these two exercises is to probe our own fallibilities. How have we missed landings from off island? What nuances must we be attentive toward? Is it personnel error, or is it a pattern that we need to learn to identify? Regardless, we have improvements to make in our defenses. We start now. Am I clear on this point?"

"Sir. Yes, sir," came the cacophonous reply.
"*Very* good. Questions?"
Silence.
"All right then. Dismissed."

.   .   .   .   .

General Douglas was up early as usual, taking coffee on the veranda of the cypress hotel, appreciating the cool and quiet of a day that promised anything but cool and quiet later on. As he stood watching the activity in Pine Island Sound, he recognized the beginning of activities consistent with war games. Troops were playing soldier, only with better toys than they had when they were children. He turned to his second in command, "It looks like they are in for some amusement today, LaFerla."

"That's a good thing for us, isn't it?" LaFerla was validating his own impression of the situation.

"Yeah. It should be. The boys will be worn out this evening – probably boisterous and drunk on the side that wins and dejected if not asleep on the side that loses. It couldn't get any better for our landing tonight. We'll let the others finish their breakfasts and go over the details. Good with that?"

"All over it, David," replied his friend.

. . . . .

At 0800 ten rafts surrounded Sanibel Island; six men from Island Security surrounded each raft, each red team soldier floating with his head and one arm above water, paint ball weaponry in the raft, minimizing their infrared signature, slowly maneuvering their raft toward an assigned target, hoping to grab the porcelain prize and make their way back to sea without being spotted by their island counterparts, the blue team.

The first team to go down was J Raft. Assigned to a landing at the lighthouse, they didn't stand a chance. Two were dragging the raft toward the nearest cover of sea grapes and the other four were flat out running for the same cover when blue teamsters popped up on signal to take out the red teamsters with one coordinated volley.

"You're dead!" declared the blue team leader. "Get your sorry asses back to headquarters. There is a truck in the parking lot."

The red teamsters looked pathetic as they were escorted by blue teamsters in their death march along the path to the parking lot. They even had to endure the indignity of an armed escort for the truck ride, an added assurance that they were out of today's game for good. It was a quiet ride.

Back at headquarters another unwelcome surprise awaited them. Rather than being given the run of the Sundial facility, the young troops were taken to a holding cell. They were not only dead; they were prisoners of war.

"What the hell!" one of them complained.

"Shut up, dead man!" came the reply as the steel door slammed shut. They looked around their small holding cell. It didn't seem to be designed for six. Some of them had to stand.

.   .   .   .   .

Douglas and LaFerla greeted the other officers as they convened in the bar room, now harshly lit by the four floor-to-ceiling double doors that opened to the veranda – the bright morning light streaming in. A coffee urn served up a rich dark roast and was in justifiable demand.

"Listen up, ladies!" What sounded like an insult from their general was taken for the good-natured sign of respect that every soldier recognized. "LaFerla, tell them the news."

LaFerla stood and looked around. He had their instant attention, another sign of respect. These men had been through a lot together. "First, as I hope you noticed, Island Security is playing war games. They look like they are training to encounter an island invasion from troops much like ourselves. They clearly do not mind broadcasting the exercise and it may be as much for our benefit as for theirs. Maybe we are supposed to be scared off by their show of force, but so far it looks pretty damn weak. We're not really sure what they are up to, but keep heads up. I doubt they will show us anything we don't already know, but keep a few surveillance details at various points around our side of the bay and maybe we will learn something. I'm guessing their mines are turned off, so we will get no new areas added to our mine maps. Can't tell if they are using live ammo but I gotta doubt that, too. They are hanging low in the water, so that fits with our thoughts about them having some kind of infrared imaging. We'll just watch for what we can see and analyze the findings later."

"Next thing is the landing tonight. It's part mission and part exercise. There is a cache of items for us at a drop point – location is need-to-know. This will be our biggest landing yet. Two rafts, invisible to radar and damned hard to see on infrared, at two different locations: here, and here."

LaFerla was tapping his finger at a map. One location was the western mangroves along the former J. N. "Ding" Darling National Wildlife Refuge; the other was a populated bay front area with a sea wall, near the causeway remnant. They had abandoned plans for a third landing south of Knapps Point. The sea wall area landing would be the trickier of the two. A probing break-in of a single dwelling plus the retrieval of a nearby bundle were the dual objectives of the causeway mission. Hopefully Island Security would put in a full day's activity and readiness would be degraded. Four officers would lead the two teams. Team members would be hand selected by each team's two officers with additional input from the first men chosen. It came down to whom do you trust with your life *tonight*. Who is off the sauce, not drugged and not craving. Who is sharp; who wants it more. Whose morale is high; whose star is shining bright. Who's your buddy?

. . . . .

C Raft team was slogging through mangrove. They had taken their raft as far as they could and were making their way through waist deep waters to the marina. A porcelain prize awaited them at the marina in the soft drink cooler – an old Coca Cola chest style cooler. They were getting close. They had been totally immersed in natural surroundings. When you are alone and quiet in nature, manmade intrusions are fairly blatant. They could sense, then hear, then smell the marina long before they could see it. As they drew closer, they could begin to make out voices.

"So, do you think the games are over? I heard that they made a run on the lighthouse. It wasn't even close," said one blue trooper.

"I don't know. They haven't shared intel with anyone that I know of. What do you think, Grump-butt?" asked Evans.

The soldier he referred to as "Grump-butt" just looked at him sourly and turned back to scanning the mangroves for intruders. "Stay alert," he replied. "And keep quiet, for Christ's sake."

Evans smiled at "Grump-butt" and looked out over the waters of the marina. A pelican splashed down, then it was quiet again. Too quiet.

"Shit!" exclaimed "Grump-butt". The others turned to hush him and noticed the bright red spot on his uniform.

Then in unison the others were splattered in red paint followed by their own epithets. "Gentlemen, we've been had," declared Evans. "It's been an honor sharing the field of battle with you."

"Grump-butt" wasn't having any of this good humor. He scowled and went inside. Evans turned to the two teammates remaining on the deck and said, "As me sainted grandmother always used to say, 'fuck him if he can't take a joke'."

"She didn't say that," protested a teammate.

"She might have," Evans postulated. "Anyway, I'm dead. Might as well light up a cigar." And with that he proceeded to produce a short cigar from his breast pocket, clip the tip and light it with a wooden match. "Got to come prepared, gentlemen." Clearly he had none to offer around.

Evans was halfway through the cigar when the first of the red troops came ashore. "You've been swimming, trooper," said Evans. He recognized Private Raurk from training camp.

"I see you didn't waste any time celebrating our magnificent victory over your pathetic little band of boy scouts," said Raurk, grinning back.

"How do you know you've won?" teased Evans. "We could have a division of sharpshooters in the woods over there."

Raurk scanned the tree line nervously, then relaxed. "Well, first, that would violate the spirit of the games. War game conditions need to mimic real life conditions, and that includes troop strength patterns. Second, if you had people in the woods, you wouldn't say anything about it. Third, if someone's out there, at least they won't open fire until the rest of my guys show up. That gives me time to wet my whistle."

Raurk went to the cold drink box, opened the heavy steel top, and reached inside. "Well, well. What have we here?" Raurk pulled out a porcelain rabbit and turned to Evans. "I don't suppose they let you carry the radio, do they?"

Evans took the radio off of his utility belt and handed it to Raurk, who turned the frequency to channel 34.

"Red Command, this is Red Raft C! The day is ours! Come back."

"Red Raft C, this is Red Command. Strong work, son."

"Red Command, our raft is in the mangrove about two klicks west. My team is in position. I am the only one exposed. We have the object and are ready to return to point of origin."

"Negative, son. Hold course until transport arrives, then report for debriefing. No use putting you back out there just to let some blue sniper get lucky."

"Roger that. I'm pulling troops out of the water if you say we are done, sir."

"Go ahead with that, private. Your work day is done. Tell those dead blue troopers not to make plans, and place them under house arrest. Transport will be there in five."

"Yes, sir. Thank you, sir. Red Raft C, out!"

At the end of that rather earnest and startling exchange, Raurk unholstered his sidearm and leveled it at Evans and the other. Next he removed a flare pistol and shot a round in an arc over the waters of the marina. Raurk motioned the others inside and held the four at gunpoint while he collected their weapons. "You heard the major, gentlemen, house arrest."

"We're already dead, Raurk. What more can you do to us?" Evans asked with a wry smile.

"Run out the door or lunge for my gun. Either way we'll find out." Raurk's thumb slid over the side of the gun, instinctively feeling for the safety, but the Glock didn't have one. The Glock's safety was in the trigger itself. What was the point of even having one? *Old habits die hard,* thought Raurk, running his thumb along the smooth side of his handgun a bit more self-consciously. His personal weapon was a 9mm Ruger. He preferred the Ruger; it was his first love. It had a proper safety.

"Wait a minute. Your gun has been under water for an hour, maybe two. You pull the trigger, it will explode in your face," Evans bluffed.

"Ooh, let's test that theory," smiled Raurk. He knew the torture test results associated with Glock abuse.

The banter was still in progress when the remainder of Raurk's team came dripping in. The other five looked at the live weapon in Raurk's hand and then at each other. "Report, Private Raurk," said Sullivan, C team's leader.

"Red Command told me to hold 'em for real, Sully. Called it 'house arrest'; said Transport was on the way."

"He got that last part right. Two trucks coming up the road," said a red trooper. "I hope there are no more surprises."

"Roger that."

Four staff sergeants entered the marina gift shop with stiff military bearing. "Blue troops, ten-hut!"

The blue team came to attention and stared, straight-faced, straight ahead.

"Red troops, at ease," said the sergeant. "You men go with Sergeant Adams there," motioning. "I'll need their side arms, please, Private."

Raurk stepped sharply and handed the sergeant the handguns. He and the others in the C Raft unit followed Sergeant Adams to a troop transport vehicle modeled after a Chevy Yukon. It was as nice as Island Security had – the equivalent of a ticker-tape parade.

Evans and his blue teammates were roughly thrown into the back of the military equivalent of a paddy wagon. When the back door was closed and locked, "Grump-butt" stared at Evan's "WTF" expression with a look that combined disgust with vindication. He didn't have to say, "I told you so." It was understood.

At the Sundial headquarters, the men of the blue marina guard were left waiting in the hot truck enclosure a full thirty minutes before being let out and again roughly handled. They exited the truck under full guard in an otherwise empty courtyard. If command was trying to make a point, it could not be made more clearly. Under escort they were taken to the crowded holding room occupied by the six red troopers, still splattered with blue paint marks. The day no longer felt like fun and games. Not even to Evans.

One of the J Raft team members spoke first as the steel door slammed shut and was locked. "I guess you guys died, too."

.   .   .   .   .

Douglas had seen enough to realize that the groups in rafts were hitting shore at all of the best locations. He wondered what their success rate had been at the various landing spots, but he knew the island teams had the advantage: daylight, anticipation, and defensive cover and posture. Still it was disturbing to see all of your best moves, locations, and tactics anticipated so precisely. "Presswood's no fool," Douglas said to LaFerla grudgingly.

"You an admirer now?" asked LaFerla.

"Hardly," came back Douglas. "He's not doing anything out of the ordinary. I guess I just hate to see the reality of how difficult it would be to actually carry out some kind of mission on

Sanibel. These troops are professional and funded. That's a tough combination to be going after."

"Ten-four."

Douglas looked at LaFerla in a funny way for using trucker's slang after he had just talked about professionalism. "Tell you what, Jacques," said Douglas. "You keep an eye on their operations. I need to go up north near the old submarine pile and see if I can get a better look at their defenses near the old causeway ruins. I'll be back before dark."

.   .   .   .   .

General Oliver Presswood strode briskly into command and control. The officers straightened imperceptively and high alert notched a click higher. "Report!" requested the general. "How goes the operations?"

"Mixed bag, sir," said Captain Rodriguez. He brought up a hologram of the island. "The lighthouse capture was too easy. No cover for the landing party. It was a waste of our time. They could have been given a more likely landing site for us to test our detection skills."

"Are you saying I chose poorly, Captain?"

"Yes, sir. If you were the one who chose the site, that is. We could have benefitted more from a greater challenge is all. But maybe you had other reasons, sir."

"No not really, but I do appreciate this 'truth to power' schtick of yours. I suppose I could postpone your court-marshal."

"Thank you, sir," said Captain Rodriguez, smiling a little at the general's humor. "We learned a little at the marina, however, such details as standing around talking on the deck will get you the wrong end of a sniper's round."

"Red team took the marina?" asked Presswood, eyebrow raised.

"In a heartbeat," Captain Rodriguez confirmed.

"I hope those blue slackers are part of tonight's exploits."

"They are indeed, sir – numbers seven through ten."

. . . . .

Corporal Walters was in position on a finger of land to the west of Tarpon Bay when his ear piece clicked on with a faint white noise.

"It's 1600 hours, Corporal. How's your position?" asked General Presswood.

The general himself, thought Walters. "Ready and able, sir."

"Good man. Launch at will."

"Yes, sir!" Walters sighted on the hotel about two kilometers away across the eastern waters of Pine Island Sound. He briefly pressed the laser sighting button on the side of the missile launch tube. The action sent computerized instructions to the missile's navigation system. Nothing was left to chance.

So easy a corporal can do it, mused Walters, and not for the first time.

Across the short expanse of water, LaFerla stood sentry for Douglas. Scanning the northern edge of the east half of Sanibel was made more difficult by the lack of visual targets. Truth was, since the war games died down, it was boring, like looking for something that you know isn't there. Then his attention was drawn to a red dot, like a laser spotting scope. LaFerla focused on the area just in time to see a flash. If he had not been focused on the area of the flash with Douglas's powerful binoculars, he might have seen the vapor trail rising in a gentle arc, then less than a kilometer away changing angle downward to stream directly toward the hotel, directly at LaFerla. LaFerla eased the binoculars from his eyes in time to see, as well as faintly hear, the approaching projectile. He had no time for last thoughts.

From the north, Douglas heard the explosion then saw the smoke and flames billowing from the site of his most recent headquarters.

LaFerla!

Douglas grieved for his old friend as he ran toward his former base of operations. *It was meant for me,* Douglas thought. He realized that Island Security was taking notice of them. *They think we're getting too close,* he thought. *Maybe they think we are a threat. Well, who am I to disappoint them?*

.   .   .   .   .

Blam!

Somebody hit the steel door with his baton just to get the small room's attention before they opened the door.

Jerk, thought Jeremy "Grump-butt" Andersen.

When the door did open, the ten "dead" individuals were brought from the crowded room into a spacious hallway. A military detail escorted them to another building in the Sundial complex. The ten had never been to the command and control center before; they had never seen General Presswood; and particularly, they nor anyone else had ever seen him this livid. These ten recruits needed no additional intimidation after their hours of internment in the small and poorly ventilated holding room. The entire group was striving for bladder control.

"You gentlemen stink!" began Presswood. He was standing at a holographic map of the island and nearby mainland. The map showed strategic troop movements, locations of today's incursions, and indications of conflicts and outcomes. None of the ten noticed the map. The general was in the room; he was all that was in the room; and he was standing erect and proud with his back to the group.

"Gentlemen, we have no place in this organization for incompetence. We recruited you from thousands of applicants with the expectation of higher performance levels. We have no room for slackers and slugs. The decision for me today is whether to have you shot or send you back to the mainland."

The room got extremely tense. The ten recruits had no idea the games were so serious to high command. Some like Evans had thought today would be fun, even if they got "shot" and had to quit early. Now he might get shot for real!

General Presswood turned and faced his men. "I cannot send you to the mainland," he reasoned. "Not with incursions from a mainland war lord military force happening. For all I know you would provide aide and succor to the enemy – troop strength, deployment patterns, tactics. No, I cannot send you to the mainland. But, by God, I can have your sorry asses hauled in front of a firing squad and replace you with some troops that know what they are doing. I will not have my men placed at risk. My soldiers will have support troops they can depend on in a pinch, and you men would not appear to be up to the task."

The general became silent. The room was pin-drop silent.

"Sir," requested Evans after the pause.

Presswood looked him in the eye, deciding whether to acknowledge him. Finally he said, "Permission to speak, Private."

"Sir, I just wanted to say that we are sorry we let you down."

Presswood fixed his gaze again. He was surprised the private made no plea for his life. *Good move, soldier.* Ready to take it like a man; fall on that sword.

"OK. Here's the deal," Presswood began. "I am giving you one chance and one chance only to redeem yourselves."

A collective sigh was not so much heard as felt.

"You will go on a new mission tonight: two five man teams, a mix of today's teams, red and blue in each. You will be taken out to sea and set adrift with rafts. Each team will be given two addresses of civilians on the island. They will know you are coming and they will not interfere, but their houses will be locked. Your target is their cutlery – one spoon, knife, and fork from each dwelling. It must match the known pattern from the specified household, so don't think you can run by Bailey's and buy your way out of this."

"Gentlemen, this is a serious exercise. You might get shot by our security forces. I will not be informing anyone of your mission, other than your patrol boat crew that will take you out and, hopefully, bring you back; but I will issue new orders, effective immediately, to capture and detain any suspected insurgents for interrogation purposes. I am very interested in how well Island Security will perform after a busy day of war games, especially since no one will be suspecting you. I will allow each of your teams to choose your landing sites, and you need not tell even me, but you will probably want to choose a site with some proximity to your hard targets. Get your rafts back out to sea with your two sets of cutlery and activate your GPS locators. We will pick you up with a dedicated patrol boat. Questions?"

Silence.

"Alright. Squad leaders from today, pick your men; alternate picks between the two of you; alternate colors, blue one time, red the next. Maps with targets marked are on the table. You have two hours to work on strategy, then take a shower with unscented soap. You really do stink, and you don't want to die because they smelled you coming."

Chapter Nine

It had been an outstandingly beautiful day on Sanibel – deep blue sky, fresh gulf breeze, mid-80s. Beverly always thought it to be a privilege to be the one to tend Chapman's gardens. These particular gardens were so much more than pretty plantings. Brady Chapman, for all of his athleticism and world-wise philosophy, had a unique artistic side to him, too. Chapman's gardens flowed with dynamic curved borders that swept the eye to more exotic plantings with color and texture that complemented the whole. The yard was like an inspired painting. It was not some rigid Japanese style with rules; it was not some western attempt at *feng shui* either; and it was certainly no Jackson Pollack canvas abstraction. It was a masterpiece of original beauty: not classical, not modern, but highly original. There was peace here. There were spaces for reflection and others for meditation. There were areas that worked best, it seemed, for letting the mind wander and other spaces that helped you focus; problem solve. There was a court yard for dining and another for reading. There was a walk path to the canal and another amongst water features. All of this was neatly packed onto less than one and one-half acres, and one of the garden's miracles was that a visitor never felt crowded by the vegetation or overwhelmed by its scope. It managed to flow that smoothly. One planting would draw your attention, by color gradation, textures, and height, to another area, then another. The graceful curves of the borders and walkways gave hint to what lay beyond but, like a well-mannered woman, the hint never revealed too much too soon.

There was always plenty for Beverly to work on, and her gentle coaxing of the vegetation kept the areas lush. Chapman hired a pool service that also maintained the water features and koi ponds. Beverly had said numerous times that she would be happy to do that work, too, but Chapman valued her too much for her horticultural artistry to allow her to divide her time with the more mundane chores. He also seemed to value their "patio time", after the work was done, when they could share conversation and a glass of tea or a cool white wine.

Beverly had been working a tall bed of elephant ears, made taller by an artificial uphill slope that led to a raised bed planting of salvia, gaillardia, Lily of the Nile, and Ageratum. She had finished adjusting and replacing the stakes that supported the elephant ears and was cleaning her gardening tools when Chapman appeared.

"When you finish cleaning, can you join me on the main patio?" he asked politely. He was never one to assume.

"With distinct pleasure." Beverly enjoyed their talks as much or more than Chapman did. She especially liked it when he told of personal experiences abroad. No one else she knew traveled as much or as often as Chapman. Travel used to be more commonplace, but now even those who could afford it chose not to risk the kidnapping for ransom that was still prevalent. She sometimes mused as she divided bulbs or fertilized the azaleas about how Chapman appeared to disappear without warning, as if he had *not* been planning the trip but chose to leave on the spur of the moment. Often at these times he would seem more focused than usual, not at all spontaneous. He might be gone for days or weeks, but never months. They did not broach the subject, but upon his return, he was always grateful that his absence had not interrupted Beverly's work on the gardens. He was grateful and generous, offering her valuable and exotic items, which she accepted without hesitation; but for her actual labor, he paid her in gold.

Beverly found Chapman on the dining patio, at a table with six chairs, on a flagstone expanse near the largest of several koi ponds. He smiled as she approached and seemed eager to announce the details of a wine that he had waiting, chilling in its cylinder.

"The gardens have never looked lovelier," he said, starting the conversation with the compliment she had heard many times.

"Why 'thank you', kind sir", she responded with a modest curtsey. "What have we here?" she added moving her eyes from Chapman to the wine.

"This little beauty is not our average unassuming patio wine," Chapman announced in an attempt to build anticipation. "This is a varietal that I brought back with me from a trip to Napa. It's a Forman chardonnay. Not a very impressive sounding wine, I know, but it really is a magnificent example of the winemaker's art.

"I'm sold, not that you would need to convince me ahead of the tasting. The worst you have ever presented was wonderful."

"Yes, well, that is the point. We strive for something a bit better than 'wonderful' here at Chez Chapman." Chapman twisted the pronunciation of his name to a distorted and comical French parody: *Chez Shapp-moan´*.

"*Tres bien, monsieur. Merci,*" she mimicked his French accent as she extended her glass.

As he poured the wine – her glass first then his, as always – he inquired, "Do you realize that you never speak my name?"

"No, I had not realized that," she said softly as she looked up at him with her eyes while keeping her nose deep in the glass to appreciate the burgeoning bouquet. "You know I feel very comfortable and relaxed when I am with you, but I had not realized until just now that I really do not know what to call you. It's a funny thing when your employer is also your friend. So, how would you like me to call you?"

"*Je m'appel* 'Brady Chapman' (again with the *Shapp-moan´*)," he said playfully. He added seriously, demurely, "but I would like it if you would call me 'Brad'. It's a nickname that a few friends use. I would like to count you among them."

"I would be honored to be counted among your 'few friends'," Beverly smiled and clicked her glass to his. "¡*Salud*! Brad."

"¡*Salud*! Beverly," Chapman replied.

They sipped the wine carefully, appreciating its nuances. Neither spoke for a while, but Chapman noticed Beverly following the koi as they moved from one area of the pond to another. "Enjoying the koi?" he asked.

"Yes," she replied, "but more specifically, the *nishikigoi*."

Referencing the Japanese carp so precisely caused Chapman to raise an eyebrow. "You never fail to surprise me," he said. "Where did you attend college?"

"No place you would know," Beverly said. "A small school in the Kentucky hills – Centre."

"I do know Centre. It's a major bastion for the liberal arts. What did you major in? Let me guess – philosophy? Japanese? Russian? Creative writing?"

"No. You just think you know me," she laughed. "Biology. I was a biology major. I was lucky to graduate. The school hung together just long enough to graduate my class when the country fell apart. Of course there were no jobs in that field or any other. How about you? Where did you go?"

"Harvard," he said; and she believed him. Why not? But he said no more about himself. In fact he turned the subject back to the topic of Beverly.

"Biology major," he mused. "Well that explains your vocabulary: referring to the koi as *nishikigoi*."

"And the hibiscus as *Hibiscus rosa-sinensis*?" she joined in the game.

"Which is what I take as a tea to lower my blood pressure, by the way," Chapman added.

"Does it work?" She continued to follow his lead.

"Quite well," he said. "Really. My hibiscus tea has lowered my top number about ten points."

"So, what was *your* major?" she pressed. "Pre-med?"

"Political science," he said. "I had ambitions," he added after taking a longer sip than usual, "before things... you know. And afterwards I spent some time in Iran."

"Special forces?"

He looked at her for a moment, deciding. "Yes," he admitted. "Does it show?"

"Maybe it's just me, but yes. You have a way about you." She added, "Yet you also have this gentler side to your bearing. I think it's a remarkable balance, actually."

He smiled at her observations. "Do you examine everyone so closely?"

"Maybe not," she was required to examine herself now; and like everyone, she was reluctant to plumb those depths. She was also starting to realize that he had skillfully turned her – like a social jujitsu artist. "Hmmm!" she mused, fixing his eyes with her gaze and smiling broadly and knowingly. She had caught him deflecting the attention back to her and she appreciated the clever talent he had revealed.

"What!?" he protested.

"Nice wine," she deflected back.

He knew she knew; and she knew he knew she knew; and it was a quick silly exchange about a relative nonevent. Yet they were both amused by it, and they paused the conversation long enough to enjoy the moment, and the wine, and the nonthreatening company. After awhile, Beverly broke the still evening air, quiet except for the occasional *caw*, or the brief *pssst* of insect repellant being released by the timers in an installed system.

"Brad," she said.

They both realized the weight of the name on this occasion of the first time it was evoked. There was a mild tension in the anticipation.

Chapman looked at her with soft permission to proceed.

"Brad," she said again, this time to soften the impact of his name by using repetition to make it more familiar, less intimate. "When you go away, off island I mean, I am curious about where you go, and I suppose I am curious about why you go, too. Can you tell me?"

"No; not really." Chapman was speaking matter-of-factly and softly – a straight answer to a straight forward question. "I can't discuss where or why; but that does remind me to bring up the when. I need to be away again soon. I can give you more details later, but I don't want to discuss planning and schedules just now."

"OK; sure."

Chapman broke the next silence. "I do really like you, Beverly. I value your friendship and our quiet times together as much or more than the efforts you put into this island sanctuary. I hate to put it so analytically, but you are an important measure of the quality of life that I am afforded, for however little time that we are granted."

"Oh, damn," said Beverly. "That is so... *je ne sais quoi...* so friggin' real, or sweet, or deep, or something. I like you and our times, too, Brad. But you know, a lot of people feel close to one another and never get around to expressing the appreciation; so here's back at you!" She stretched to put her glass in his space and he stretched to clink hers with his – a silent toast otherwise: eye contact, a warm look, and mouths tightening shut into knowing smiles.

Beverly broke the next silence. "I'm meeting Marti Leinhart for drinks and probably dinner. Want to join us?"

"No, but thanks. I have things I must attend to this evening. I have that trip to plan and some details demand my attention."

Beverly drained her glass of chardonnay and rose to leave. "Well, I better be on my way. Thanks for a great evening, but," she hesitated.

"What?" he asked.

"I would like to hug you, Brad. If that is OK."

"Indeed." Brad stood and they embraced. Neither felt sexually stimulated so much as simply appreciated.

"That was nice," said Beverly.

"Yes," agreed Chapman. "It was."

.　　.　　.　　.　　.

"What's up, Buttercup?" asked Marti as she came up behind Beverly on her walk home.

"Hey, Marti," Beverly replied, shaking off the daydreams that come when one walks alone for a stretch. "What's up with your own bad self?"

"Well, actually…there is this… dilemma," Marti began.

"Uh-oh, now what have you done?"

"Nothing noteworthy," said Marti, "but I do need to run things by you. It's crunch time."

"Uh-huh. OK. Let's go for a glass of wine and if that doesn't set things straight, we may have to take a bottle with us for a walk on the beach," suggested Beverly.

"OK," replied Marti, "but I'm picturing the little bottle growing legs so it can keep up with us."

"Sorry, what?"

"Never mind. I'm just having loose thoughts."

"So, my place or yours?" Beverly asked in an attempt to move things along.

"I have several reds to choose from, and I need the time walking and talking just now. So how about we go over to my place?" offered Marti.

"OK, good. Let's walk along the beach if it's OK with you," suggested Beverly. "It will take longer but it sounds like you're in no hurry to get anywhere and I would like to let my head get clear while we catch up on things."

The two friends walked along the moist cool sand at the water's edge, sandals in hand, and surprisingly quiet. They were enjoying each other's company in a wordless saunter, rotating their bodies unconsciously in a yaw motion as if to deliberately slow their pace so they could play barefoot in the shallow surf. Marti was wearing shorts and a sleeveless blouse, tails tied at her midriff. Beverly was wearing a light cotton print dress, her usual attire.

"So, is this about a man?" Beverly said to break the reverie.

"What else?" replied Marti with a wry laugh. "Actually more than one."

"Uh-oh," Beverly teased. "So spill it."

"OK, so there's Greg, who's very sweet, and there is Clyde, who makes me laugh, and I don't want to rule out Jeffrey, who is more about maybe someday."

"Well let's deal with the here and now. Two birds in the hand are worth more than whatever is out there in the bushes, or something."

"Alright, granted. So here's the deal. Greg and I have been on again off again, but mostly on, for a few years. You know that. But now he's making noises about going away together."

"Going away!" exclaims Beverly. "Where on Earth? And why? Where else is there?"

He keeps talking about this place in Tennessee; calls it *the Farm*; says it's an old hippie commune. It would be more... what's the word?... *rustic* than here on Sanibel."

"Ya think?!" cried Beverly. She was not prepared for her friend to be moving away. "Oh, I don't know, honey. This doesn't sound like you, and it's not like it is your idea." She left it at that.

"The big deal for me is not only would I be leaving you and my other friends, I would be committing to one man, and I'm not sure I am ready for commitment," Marti spoke as if she had rehearsed the issue. She had probably gone over it in her head many times.

"I hadn't even thought of it that way," said Beverly. "That seals it for me. Let me validate your parking ticket, girlfriend. You are definitely not ready for monogamy. And I am not interested in you going to some farm a million miles away. So, is he definitely going?"

"No, not for sure. He talks about it enough, though."

"What's his issue with Sanibel?"

"Multiple issues," replied Marti. "He is a workman among the rich elite, and looked down upon that way. He's a competent hands-on guy and he is sweet – nice, gentle, you know. He doesn't deserve to be so... I don't know... second class. He doesn't like being in a place that has to be defended so aggressively either. He feels like we are in a police state, and the benevolence is at someone else's whim. His words, not mine, but I see his point. And I think he's just restless. He says he's been here two years and that's the longest he has stayed anywhere."

"OK. I can see it from his angle," Beverly said, trying to be supportive, "but why does that mean you have to go with him." Beverly stooped and came up with a whelk. She inspected it and said, "Nice one," before tossing it into the gentle surf.

"Well, you know. I do like him," Marti continued. "He has never been anything but a gentleman. He's kind and he's a good person. He loves me and would always be there for me – my protector and provider. A girl could do worse. And, you know the other thing. I've told you time and again; the sex ain't bad." She smiled big at the thought. Beverly thought she caught Marti in a quick shudder. "I don't want to give that up, and I think I really don't want to lose Greg. It's almost that simple."

"Nothing is simple," Beverly said, grounding the conversation.

"Spoiler alert!"

"True though."

They had come upon the boardwalk to Marti's condo.

"We're here," Marti said. "Come on in and we can finish this and talk about Clyde."

"And see what your cellar offers," Beverly continued the flow. The problem solving had them, not at odds, but pitching different viewpoints never-the-less. It was good to get back on the same track.

They entered the spacious second floor apartment and Marti offered, "What's your preference?"

"Let me see what you have," said Beverly, not one to turn down a better varietal if it were offered.

Beverly looked into the EuroCave wine cooler. The whites were kept at a colder setting than the reds. Beverly had a nice white wine earlier and now was thinking, *the whites are what you drink until the reds get here.*

Beverly turned the reds bottle by bottle, inspecting the labels, noting the vintage and pedigree. She pulled out a Vincent Arroyo Petit Syrah, saying, "Nothing 'petit' about this one!"

"Oh, wow!" said Marti. "I was saving that one. Good choice."

Beverly looked at her friend to make sure she had permission.

"Oh, hell yeah," exclaimed Marti. "I'm saying I was saving it for you and me; right here, right now."

Beverly grinned and looked around for an opener before Marti changed her mind. "Where do you get such good stuff?" she asked.

"Clyde works at that jazz bar restaurant, Ellington's. Part of his pay is worked out in wine. Doctor Wilson has a surprisingly good selection, too. Why do you think he still makes house calls? That's his little tradition – to get a nice wine as a gratuity, so to speak. He gives me one now and then. And several of my hair customers really

145

appreciate what I can do for them. The stuff just seems to come out of the wood work sometimes. Why do you think I put in the 150 bottle cooler?"

"Tough life," Beverly conceded.

"Yeah," Marti agreed. "I don't think I could move away from it just yet."

"Or ever?" asks Beverly.

"Can't say anything stays right forever, you know?"

"One can hope," Beverly mused aloud as she poured the petit syrah into appropriate glasses. "You even have the crystal stemware. I *am* jealous now."

They swirled the wine and inhaled the aroma, and swirled again. Then with a mutual glance they tasted.

"Damn, girl," Beverly said in wonder after holding the wine in her mouth for as long as she could delay its passage through less appreciative areas of her system.

"Damn right," echoed Marti.

Moments passed. Beverly asked, "Got any cheese?"

"No, fresh out, but you are right: it needs something."

"Yeah, it's too big for just sipping."

Marti checked the refrigerator and came back with a chocolate bar. She looked at Beverly, enquiring silently if this would do.

146

"Oh, yeah," said Beverly. "Life is short. Eat dessert first."

The chocolate changed the character of the wine; made it even richer somehow. They corked the bottle for later.

"So," Beverly again broke the reverie. "What *about* Clyde?"

"Clyde's *Clyde*; he makes me laugh." Marti repeated her earlier observation. "He's playing tonight. Want to go?"

"Actually, yes. That would be great. It's been awhile since we hung out at Ellington's," Beverly said. "What is your relationship with Clyde? Would I be intruding?"

"Not at all," Marti assures her. "Clyde loves a movable feast, and he thrives on an entourage. That's the thing! Clyde is fun to hang with; he is funny and talented, and he is a great lover. He drinks but he doesn't do coke. I will tell you something else. He knows more than he lets on about how this island really works – what goes on and all. But he gets so full of himself sometimes, you know? He has this ego the size of Kansas, and he gets into these mind games. He gets so – I don't know – irrepressible; like he has to 'hold court'. I just don't see settling down with him; he's not commitment oriented."

"Well, let's go hear some jazz and eat some seafood and not worry about it," suggested Beverly.

"Now you are talking. What would I do without you?" gushed Marti.

"Don't even think about it," reassured Beverly.

.　　　.　　　.　　　.　　　.

Fernando Lopez was an island staple, a Hispanic handyman, a jack-of-all-trades, and very much in demand. He and Greg Johnston, his coworker, were watching as the last of their day labor crew boarded the small armada of pontoon boats destined for the main land. It was growing darker and Island Security had been delayed by some other activities from earlier in the day – some war games, they had heard. *Must be nice*, they thought of the 'soldiers', *to get paid so well to 'play games'*.

Island Security always escorted the laborers to the mainland where they would conduct cavity searches. Anyone caught hiding an emerald or whatever would be shot. It was as simple as that. Of course they could not risk a Sanibel resident witnessing their methods: the island needed to maintain its air of gentility. Everyone knew the policy, the consequences; but no one wanted to be reminded as to the extent of their deterrence practices. The laborers – those who culled the dead fronds from the palm trees and manicured the lush lawns and landscapes – they needed reminding, however, on the trip over and again on the trip back. No one wanted to lose good help – retraining was expensive – but no one wanted to lose good jewelry either. Deterrence had proven to be an effective policy. The Sanibel residents paid well – a fair wage – but times were tough and was a salary ever enough?

"I'm just sayin'," said Greg, "I wish it didn't have to be this way. Look at Roberto. He's a good man, a hard worker. Why do they have to herd him around like he was a steer?"

"I hear you," agreed Fernando. He was feeling a special sympathy for his Hispanic 'brother'.

"This place ain't right, if you ask me," Johnston continued. "Too much money in a tight little space. Wealth concentration like that goes against the laws of the universe."

"What do you know about astrophysics and stuff?" Fernando Lopez was egging him on.

"I'm just sayin'," said Greg, "I wish it didn't have to be this way. These Island Security troops could turn on you and me and we would never know why. It's a dangerous thing being a peon in the midst of so much power. One day we will get caught in the middle of somebody's pissing contest and it won't be pretty. They need us now for carpentry and renovation and whatnot, but we are expendable. There's hundreds more like us a satellite phone call away."

"You're right, buddy."

"I'm just sayin'."

"So, what about it? You got some other thing happening?"

"Maybe."

"Or are you just blowing smoke rings?"

Greg looked at his friend. "Maybe," he said.

"Maybe you're full of shit. That's what I think. If you didn't want to be here, you know the way off the island. And good luck over there," Fernando gestured toward the mainland. "I hear it can still be rough, although I hear it's starting to get a little better, too."

"It would have to sooner or later, wouldn't it?" asked Greg, reminding them both of lost lovers and family.

"*Si, amigo.* It would have to get a damn sight better."

"I'm just saying, *amigo.* I can't run with this godless crowd no more."

Fernando looked at his friend and nodded. He understood.

They climbed into Fernando's truck after the last of the day's laborers were loaded onto the boats and headed for Periwinkle, away from the "Port of Sanibel" – the causeway remnant. They each had small condos near the northern tip of that area of Sanibel, close enough to walk if they hadn't needed the truck for men and materials. They parked the truck a short distance from Periwinkle, midway between their condos.

Sometimes they would take their fishing poles out on the causeway remnant and try their luck, which was usually good. Tonight was as good as any, they decided, and they arranged to rendezvous after dinner. It was too close to drive from their condos, and besides, the weather was too nice.

"First one to catch a fish buys me a bus ticket to the *Farm*," declared Greg.

"In your dreams, farm boy," said Fernando. "I started to say that you couldn't lose no matter who got the first catch; then I remembered that there are no buses any more. But feel free to walk to Tennessee."

"I just might."

"Yeah, and say 'hello' to all those road jackals for me. Sure sounds like easy sailing," warned Fernando.

"Yeah, you're right. I'm aware of all of that, plus – and I am serious about this wrinkle – I don't think I can talk Marti into going with me."

"She's a smart girl, that one."

"I know," said Greg. "I know that all too well."

"See you in a bit," said his friend.

"Not if I see you first," Greg teased.

"You better watch how you talk to me." They were still talking to each other although they had been walking in opposite directions long enough that they had to raise their voices for the other to hear. "I can always find another partner." Fernando was just shy of having to shout.

"Not one as good looking as me," Greg boasted.

"Why would I care about that?" Fernando protested.

"Who else is gonna attract some *nueva pareja* for you? You are too *ugly*." Greg raised his voice for that last jab.

The distance made conversation too much trouble, and they each stepped up their pace towards their condos. It was a credit to them both that they could work together all day and still want to hang out – fish and drink beer – that evening.

Chapter Ten

Jeremy Andersen, the gruff soldier that Evans called "Grump-butt", was serious about carrying out a perfect mission. He turned to Ben Evans and said, "Listen kid, no more clowning around. I don't know the general's game, but he has it out for us or somebody. We're going to come through this smelling like heroes or smelling like death itself. I don't know which, but I'm telling you that there is no in between for us on this go-around."

"We are all corporals and privates here, but you guys gave me command authority when we were reviewing the maps back on land, so as far as

I'm concerned, I'm your lieutenant or something until this mission is behind us," Andersen continued. "Any objections? I'm just saying someone has to take charge, make decisions. Anybody else here rather do that?"

"That's good with us, Corporal," said Evans with a tone of respect. "You lead." The others murmured approval. They were all worried about getting this done and not getting caught.

They were on a patrol boat out to sea but still in sight of Sanibel Island. They would deploy momentarily and no one, not even the general, knew where they would make landfall that night. The team had chosen an unpopulated area, problematic because surveillance would be higher ordinarily in those areas void of eyeballs; and the site was reasonably achievable with existing currents and the tide. The real trick was to become invisible to satellites and infrared technology.

"OK, listen up. First tactic is to go invisible early. If they were expecting us, then we would try going with misdirection – paddling toward where we were not going then hitting the water and changing directions. But they are *not* expecting us – not at all – so we need to be invisible from the get-go. Our boat captain is under orders: he's part of our team. He will drop us off and pick us up when and where we say. We will hang out with him until midnight; plan a two hour swim, more of a float really; then try for a two a.m. landing; a two hour mission; and, if all goes well, a five a.m. rendezvous with our captain. Clear?"

"Clear," said Martinez.

"OK, moving on. Here is a quick physics lesson. Satellite optics cannot see us at night. Infrared can detect us, but only if our surface temperatures exceed our ambient temperatures. That is why we will float next to our raft. Do not let go of the perimeter rope. We will push the raft overboard before long and let it cool down to gulf water temperature. By the time we float to shore, we should be cool enough to stay invisible long enough to reach the interior canals. We will stow the raft and float the canal to our destination. The target is a friendly, so we should be quick in and out. Then we retrace to the raft, launch and rendezvous. Questions?"

"We float? Not swim?"

"Float and *guide*. We will need to stay alert to keep the rafts on course. We calculated the launch coordinates based on currents and tides. Wind should not be a factor."

"Pick-up coordinates were determined the same way?"

"Yeah, pretty much," said Corporal Andersen.

.   .   .   .   .

On Pine Island General David Douglas was taking that evening's mission very seriously. LaFerla was a good friend; and damn well respected by the men. The landing on Sanibel tonight was becoming, in the general's mind anyway, only the opening salvo for a series of missions. For Douglas it had become personal.

Captain Lloyd Birch and Captain J. D. Robinson were focused on a small map of the island when Douglas walked into the kitchen of Birch's Pine Island home.

"Not as detailed as the ones we lost to the missile strike, is it gentlemen?" asked Douglas as he entered.

"No, sir," the men responded with obligatory agreement. "They will get us there, though," Birch assured him.

"And back again," added Robinson optimistically.

"That *better* be the case," commanded Douglas, like a worried old mother. Then he got down to business. "Show me the planned locations for the deployment, timing, defenses, troop strength and the rest."

"Sir," the men responded, and the three of them hunched over the maps, pointing out areas of potential engagement and strategies to avoid detection. Douglas seemed satisfied.

"So much seems to depend on the men's stealth and our hope that Island Security will be sloppy tonight, either tired or celebrating after their war games," said Douglas.

"We are sending good men, sir. We should not have to depend too much on luck," Robinson reassured.

"Nothing is certain, but that's the game we are in, isn't it, sir?" Birch asked rhetorically.

"Nothing is certain," agreed Douglas, "except perhaps your point that 'nothing is certain'."

The captains just looked at him. It was uncharacteristic for him to wax philosophical. Douglas ordinarily stayed focused on the mission. LaFerla must have been a good friend.

.　　.　　.　　.　　.

Captain Rodriguez was two men short for the night shift at the Sundial headquarters. One corporal was a runner and minion with no mission critical functions, just an extra set of eyes to sit at the satellite screen if one of the more experienced men needed a break. The other absentee was Private Markowitz. Despite his low rank, Markowitz had stood out for his pattern recognition skills. He also had logged more hours on the newer system than almost anyone. To make matters worse, Markowitz's excuse was lame – something about his landing party having seized the day as well as the objective in the war games. High command had rewarded the victors and incarcerated the losers. It was a clear cut reward and incentive package, but their champagne and lobster was degrading Rodriguez's roster.

.   .   .   .   .

Floating quietly on the Gulf waters, Corporal Andersen looked at his watch: midnight. He roused the men and muttered some final instruction to the boat captain. With stealth and efficiency Andersen and his men rolled over the edge of the boat and eased into the cool gulf water. It would have been dangerous if it were not for the wet suits, but there was no real concern about hypothermia, especially once they got moving. They floated next to the motor boat, holding on to the raft, for another ten minutes as the boat drifted away from them slowly. Once they had avoided the possibility of one object becoming two on surveillance satellite imaging, they began moving their flippers slowly toward shore. That was the cue for the boat captain to take the boat away in a patrol search pattern. Nothing could look suspicious back at headquarters. No one knew they were coming. That is why shore patrol troops were being instructed to take prisoners; not to fire unless fired upon.

The new strategy for Island Security, starting tonight, was to capture enemy combatants, interrogate them through whatever means necessary, and obtain critical intelligence regarding mainland troop strength and intentions. The raids were increasing in frequency to the extent that they were widely recognized as occurring. Perhaps more important than the loss of property was the chink in the armor of perfect security on Sanibel. Perhaps most important to General Presswood was the idea that until now, Island Security had been window dressing – a trial run of some very high tech toys and well disciplined troops. Now the rubber had hit the road: it was time to shift gears. Now he would test his military power and tactics against a seasoned adversary. Now he was presented with a challenge that carried with it an uncertain outcome.

.   .   .   .   .

The Pine Island expeditionary force was divided into two groups. Captain Birch commanded one squadron; Captain Robinson, the other. They had worked together to choose separate but complementary landing sites. They had information about two wealthy, and therefore worthy, targets on Sanibel. Neither would be a walk in the park.

Captain Birch would make landing just east of the causeway remnant. The journey over water would be relatively short compared with Robinson's assignment. The tradeoff involved Captain Birch's foray into a denser residential area, whereas Captain Robinson and his squad would target a relatively isolated dwelling near the "Ding" Darling sanctuary. In order to reach the sanctuary, Captain Robinson's crew would launch from Pine Island and engage in some island hopping. There were a number of small uninhabitable islands and keys in Pine Island Sound. Captain Robinson would float his troops from Galt Island to the MacKeever Keys to Chino Island. From there they would take the raft under power of an electric motor across Pine Island Sound to the waters of the "Ding" Darling sanctuary. Robinson's men would alternate riding in and steering the raft while the others were pulled through the water holding to its side. The pilot could not stay in the raft long before the breeze would dry his wetsuit and raise his surface temperature, but they could not all stay in the water and expect the little electric motor to know where the group was headed. Each looked forward to his turn at the helm.

Captain Birch took a troop truck loaded with his squadron and the raft off of Pine Island and onto mainland roads. He could not have known that Rodriguez was tracking him from the moment he started the motor and generated heat. By the time Birch's troops rolled out, they were being monitored by two groups back at the Sundial headquarters. By the time Captain Birch crossed the Caloosahatchee River and unloaded men and gear at Punta Rassa, he was feeling pretty good about his progress. He could not sense the eyes following his every move, filtered through the technology of a geosynchronous satellite.

Captain Birch and his squadron eased into the waters of Matanzas Pass and floated their raft along the eastern rim of the causeway remnant. Where road stretched above the water they took advantage of the cover to float beneath the concrete. The electric motor was very quiet and no troops patrolled the mainland portion of the causeway remnant. They were forced to skirt the shallow waters of the small islands that dotted the path of the causeway. Soon they were close enough to Sanibel to scout visually for a potential beachhead. They chose a site with a seawall. They could scale the rocks with no clear line of sight from the neighboring homes. Moments later they were tying their raft to an iron ring, decades old, placed just for such a purpose.

.   .   .   .   .

Douglas's other squadron of troops made its Sanibel landing at a more amphibious location. Once inside the boundary of the sanctuary they stayed with their raft as they negotiated the waters on their way to one of the few adjacent neighborhoods. Glass and rich wood beams dominated the architecture of the homes that increasingly brought a light source to Robinson and his men. The closer they approached, the brighter the woods and waters became. Robinson began to fear detection by the homeowners when he detected a dark dwelling. The home was empty or the owners were asleep. In either case Robinson had his target.

Robinson's men secured the raft to one of the pilings that supported the modern house with its perpetual views of the Sanctuary's wildlife. Three men were dispatched to reconnoiter the home. More than that would have been unnecessary for a target this small, and would have increased the likelihood of detection. They searched the home in silence until they had checked the most likely spaces where the family might be located. Finally from the master bedroom, where the king size bed was clearly untouched, came the call, "All clear!" A series of confirmatory shouts of "Clear!" came from other rooms as closets and sundry areas were checked. Robinson and his last two men climbed the stairs adjacent to the small dock and joined their comrades. The rapid and systematic looting of the family's treasures followed. The dining room table was employed as a staging area to decide what was more valuable, salable, and portable. They had found enough in the form of gold coins that weight would be an issue. Diamonds had top priority, and Robinson produced a jeweler's glass – a triple loupe – to avoid the embarrassment of returning with cubic zirconia or other fakes. These gemstones were the real deal, he concluded, and they were added to the pile to take. After fifteen minutes they were looking around for something else to examine. Finding nothing else, they bundled their take into two backpacks and moved quickly down the stairs to the small dock. Moments later their raft was in the channel that drained "Ding" Darling, headed toward Pine Island Sound and home. The barracks bunks would feel warm, dry, and quite welcome.

.   .   .   .   .

Andersen and his crew were near their destination. They had been floating approximately ninety minutes from the time they separated from the patrol boat and had arrived slightly ahead of schedule. Still his men were frozen. It would feel good to move on land. They reached the northwestern aspect of Sanibel where vegetation met the shoreline. Through the thickets they crept before they hid the raft under a thick swath of sea grapes. Then they proceeded to one of the many inland canals. They made their way in water up to their necks long enough to reach Doctor Wilson's back yard. Wilson lived in a newer development north of Rabbit Road. He would be expecting them. Andersen sent two men to the house. They unlocked the back door and let themselves in. As they passed Wilson, he gave them a half-hearted wave, chest high. They nodded toward him but went straight to the kitchen where they opened drawers until they found the silverware. They removed one knife, one spoon, and one fork. With another nod, but not one word, they went out the way they had come in. Andersen and the other three men had not left the canal. He took the loot, wrapped it in a canvas cloth he had brought for just that purpose, and the team disappeared up the canal.

The next house was Jill Tucker's. The mission went even smoother, if that could have been possible. Jill was sitting in her screened-in cabana smoking a joint. When Evans and Andersen approached her, she held out the cutlery. She did not want the wet and muddy soldiers tracking through her kitchen. So much for negotiating locked doors.

"I want it back, gentlemen," she said. "It was my grandmother's."

Evans smiled at the young lady as he and Andersen made their way back to the canal. He was glad to stretch his legs on solid ground.

"Two sets of cutlery," said Andersen as he placed the set in the canvas roll-up with the doctor's set. "Let's see if we can get off of this island undetected. No talking," he whispered for emphasis.

Thirty minutes later they were retrieving the raft, again grateful to be walking on land. They crept alongside the thicket to the water's edge, launched the raft, and began the swim-float to the patrol boat. They were all amazed that they had encountered no troops. The mission was kept secret as promised. They avoided satellite detection. They had their way in a prominent residential neighborhood. This was good for Andersen's team: they were redeemed. This was not good news for Island Security: Sanibel was vulnerable. No wonder General Presswood was searching for holes in the system. He or somebody needed to plug them before they sprang a serious leak.

.   .   .   .   .

At the Sundial headquarters, Captain Rodriquez had his hands full. He and Corporal Childers had discovered not one but two groups invading Sanibel. The first was from Pine Island by way of Punta Rassa and along the causeway remnant. They were landing now and appeared to be set to enter the home of the Widow McIntyre. Island Security forces were closing on that scene rapidly. The other satellite image that might suggest an incursion was less certain. Faint images that were no more than ripples appeared intermittently. Without a distinct heat source, the infrared technology was nearly blind. Childers had done well to focus in on an imperceptible motion that others might have missed. As it stood now, a group of individuals beachside of West Gulf Drive was working hard to avoid detection. Even more strange was their proximity to Ron Weber's house. No one in their right mind would think of crossing the big dog himself. Island Security forces were closing on that scene also. The troops were again reminded to capture, not kill, if at all possible; but only time would tell *that* tale.

.   .   .   .   .

Captain Birch and his squadron had secured a beachhead and scaled the seawall. They ran low and fast from tree to shrub to exterior wall,

all the while expecting motion detectors to trigger flood lights, exposing them to all the world. They tested the Widow McIntyre's sliding glass door and found it locked, not by the worthless hardware at the handle, but by the tried and true wooden rod filling the length of the aluminum track on the floor. The windows were locked also. The front door was their last source of an easy entry. Birch unscrewed the yellow porch light, but the nearby street light still provided more illumination than they wanted. The door was locked, but it was an older simple doorknob with a central keyhole. It took less than one minute to gain entry.

The team entered and filed through the foyer. In the living room they came face to face with the widow as she came from the bedroom hallway. She was armed.

"I thought I heard a noise," said the Widow McIntyre. She leveled her Walther PPK at the group and said firmly, "You boys need to leave, right now."

"We can't do that, ma'am," said a young slim man in a wetsuit.

The Widow McIntyre shot the young man and would have shot another if several of Birch's team hadn't returned fire. Birch's men had silencers on their handguns but the Widow McIntyre's .380 caliber handgun was loud enough.

"Shit!" was all any of them could think. The sentiment was magnified as wheels could be heard rolling on gravel outside. Island Security was here; they were clearly on their way before shots were fired and they were probably close enough to hear the Widow McIntyre's explosive noise.

Birch's men removed the wooden rod from the sliding glass door track and bolted through the back yard toward the raft. They knew that they had no chance. If they made it to the raft they would be easy targets in the water.

"Halt!" shouted Sergeant Bell as he shot a rapid fire burst over their heads. Birch turned and shot toward the area from where the burst originated. He took cover behind a large palm tree. Bell slumped to the ground as his men ran past, one kneeling to provide assistance. "Medic!" cried the corporal.

Birch's men were surrounded on three sides. From the house and the side yards came a withering hail of automatic firepower. Then the firing stopped abruptly. "Last chance to surrender," called one of the Island Security force.

As before the response was a muffled gunshot. Again came the overpowering response of automatic weaponry. This time Birch's men began to fall. Four were on the ground. They did not move. The two remaining looked at each other and decided to live, if that was an option. They stepped out with their hands high and made a show of tossing their weapons.

"Hold fire!" shouted a Sergeant Russell. Island Security troops moved rapidly to subdue and bind the two, and check the fallen. Two were still alive. "Bring them," shouted Russell. He went over to his fallen comrade.

"Sergeant Bell is dead, Sarge," the corporal said to Russell.

Russell watched as his men gathered the injured Birch to his feet and half drug him toward the house. When they were closer Russell spun around and slammed his heel into Birch's sternum with such force that Birch fell backwards to the ground as the troopers lost their grip on him. One of the troopers was spun around and fell next to Birch. Looking at Birch, Russell said, "That one may not make it. His wounds look pretty bad. Bring him anyway."

Birch lost consciousness.

.   .   .   .   .

From his vantage point on Captain Birch's front porch, General Douglas was watching as automatic gunfire swamped the position where he knew Birch and his men to be. He also knew Birch and his men to be a lost cause at this juncture. He set the replacement binoculars aside. He missed his old pair, but he missed LaFerla more. He would grieve for Birch and his men soon enough. It's not over until it's over.

.   .   .   .   .

The last landing party to join the fray was led by Corporal Harrison, the Island Security recruit who had already botched his first mission during the war games. Green by any standard, he was chosen for his height and his square jaw. He certainly looked the part, and no one in the squad had any more experience. Harrison and his men were chatting with Ron and June Weber when the door was broken in. Fervent troops charged into the room fearing for the safety of the Webers. It is good that they had orders to capture rather than kill, otherwise it could have gotten messy.

"Whoa! Hold it!" cried Weber. "It's a training exercise and we were in on it."

"We are unarmed, Sergeant King," said Corporal Harrison.

King recognized his fellow soldier and cocked his head sideways in surprise and curiosity. "Search them anyway," he ordered his team. Turning back to Harrison, he demanded, "What's going on here, soldier?"

"Like the man said, Sarge, it's a training exercise. I guess we could use a bit more training yet. We thought we had avoided detection," said Harrison.

"You damn near did. Some wrinkle in the satellite image was all that was generated. We didn't know what to expect. You are lucky we didn't blow your pointy little head plum off."

"Well I'm glad you didn't, Sarge."

"We are, too," June Weber chimed in. "Your troops were messy enough as it is." June shifted her gaze from the muddy boots on her oriental carpets to a pale Corporal Harrison. "May I have my silverware back now, please?"

Harrison and his squadron were escorted the short distance back to headquarters. General Presswood was waiting. Only five minutes before, he had received an update on the capture of enemy combatants at the widow's residence. This was followed by word that Andersen's squad was being picked up by their patrol boat.

"I think the general is pleased," someone shared with Harrison as the squadron waited in an anteroom.

"God I hope so," said Harrison, but he did not appear to believe it. He still had visions of a firing squad.

When the general entered the room, it was as if all of the air was sucked out of it. Harrison and his troops stiffened. They could not help themselves.

"At ease, gentlemen," barked General Presswood. "The purpose of the exercise was to find defects in our tracking system that we can fix. A small wave form was generated by your squad even though your surface temperature matched your surroundings and made our infrared technology *nearly* worthless. We are installing new computer algorithms to color code these for our technicians. Your mission was particularly successful, and I thank you for your service."

"Dismissed," Presswood ordered. Harrison and his men barely had time to absorb the message that they were not going to be executed when the general spun around to face them again.

"There is steak and lobster for you in the mess," he added. Then he turned again and disappeared through the double doors that led to his situation room.

.   .   .   .   .

Captain J. D. Robinson was being debriefed when Douglas walked into the kitchen of Birch's home. Both men stared at each other in a silent vow of vengeance. It would be wise, thought the general, to move headquarters from their current vantage point to a new location; maybe they should fall back to the Caloosahatchee River enclave where they were established before Pine Island.

Chapter Eleven

Brady Chapman arrived at Lough Eske Castle like any other well-to-do tourist in Ireland. He had flown into the Shannon airport and taken the train to Donegal. He was now on the Atlantic coast at about the same latitude but directly west and across the island from Belfast on the Irish Sea. There was no point staying in a city where he would carry out his assignment: a city where he would not wish to be recognized later by some bellhop.

Lough Eske Castle was a mere 180 km, or two and one-half hours from Belfast. The accommodations were unparalleled. With its ornamental stone work and the imposing four-story tower, Lough Eske Castle was at the same time discrete and attentive. The degree of relaxed elegance was a luxurious departure from the task at hand. The contemporary renovation preserved much of the original fifteenth century roots, the seventeenth century charm, the Gaelic heritage, and the surrounding natural beauty from the water's edge of Lough Eske to the fabled Blue Stack Mountains. Antiques were juxtaposed with specially commissioned works of art.

Chapman treated himself to the presidential suite with its private access to the castle tower. Chapman was not interested in the surfing or sailing in Donegal Bay, rather it was the mountain hiking amongst the seaside cliffs, waterfalls, ruins, and vistas from numerous peaks. The daylong hikes made him pleasantly tired by evening; Chapman then relaxed and refreshed by swimming laps in the 12-meter pool in the Lough Eske Castle solarium. Dining at Cedars was stunning, surrounded by lawns and woodland views from the terrace and feasting on local ingredients, fish from nearby Killybegs, and superb wines. He certainly slept well enough after the day's activities, nestled in the down of his four poster canopied bed.

As the week progressed, Chapman exercised more and ate less. His trips to the top of the tower increased each morning as did the length and scope of his hikes into the countryside. His meals got lighter, albeit no less masterfully prepared, and he limited himself to one glass of wine per evening, sending back to the kitchen rare bottles of Pomerol or Pouillac Bordeaux for the wait staff to enjoy. He became very popular very fast. He would be remembered for being at Lough Eske Castle if anyone needed to know that he was not in Belfast. Chapman's training camp was ideal.

Nine days into his two-week stay at Lough Eske Castle, Chapman ventured out for his daily hike in the mountains as usual. This time, however, in his backpack was a change of outfits. The traditional hiking clothes were exchanged for the slightly worn suit of a typical Irish commuter, off to work. With cap low over his eyes, Chapman boarded the bus to Derry, a mountainous journey too challenging for rail service. His route took him south initially, then southeast, then north – an unusually lengthy circuitous trace that none would connect to events in Belfast. From Derry (Londonderry to the Northerners) he took the eastbound train to Belfast, as quiet and alone as any other pathetic working man. As far as the hotel staff could know, he was merely out for his day hike.

The Translink train was three cars long and streamlined with large windows and yellow, blue, grey, and white colors. Even if it had been full with 200 people, it could obtain speeds of ninety miles per hour. That was theoretical. Even leaving at just after 10 a.m. local time, with several stops along the way Chapman would not arrive at Belfast (Centre) City Hall Station until 12:36. It was simpler and more anonymous to use his train ticket to board the metro bus system. It was ironic to Chapman that his entire travel itinerary on this of all days was supported by the government of Northern Ireland. It was one of a few functioning public services, but one of which they were duly proud.

At Belfast City Hall Station the hustle and bustle was some high multiple of the usual numbers of commuters, police, lunch seekers, and citizens – especially citizens. McMasters had been voted in as Northern Ireland's Prime Minister two weeks ago against accusation of first, vote rigging, and later, justice tampering, after the judicial system halted vote recounts to declare him the victor. McMasters was sworn in the following day during an officious ceremony at an undisclosed location. The newly elected Prime Minister was scheduled to speak at 2 p.m. and seats with a good vantage point were at a premium. It served one well to arrive early to obtain a better seat.

The journey from Donegal Town to Donegall Square, despite the minor difference in spelling, was a coincidence not lost on Chapman.

The City Hall dominated the city center skyline. The dominant features were the towers at each of the four corners, and the lantern-crowned copper dome in the center. A one and a half acre courtyard enclosed the Baroque Revival Victorian wedding cake, with its Portland stone icing of great columns and massive arched windows, and the distinctive green copper decorations.

The northern portico of City Hall was festive with banners and flowers and one unexpected feature – a giant screen rather than a stage and lectern. In their collective wisdom, the event organizers had moved the stage to the smaller venue of the south-facing back of City Hall. Tradition called for a City Centre ceremony; but security concerns called for a break with tradition. In a city with a history of violence, it served a good purpose to throw the adversaries off their guard. The larger crowd in the courtyard would be quite content with the big screen images. The southern portico of City Hall was festive with banners and flowers also. The streets were crowded with well-wishers – private citizens and minor politicians. There was the requisite lectern with official markings on the upper level with the stone columns; and the omnipresent world news media clogging the streets.

It was from this south-facing spectacle that Chapman headed further to the south down

Linenhall Street, a mere three blocks, past Clarence Street and the Ulster Peoples College, to the adjacent parking garage. Chapman quickly climbed the stairs to the rooftop parking level. There among two rusting vehicles, one with flat tires, was the vintage Mercedes he was expecting. Removing a key from his pocket, Chapman swiftly opened the trunk to find the prize that Kobayashi (Chapman's handler and agent) had promised. Chapman removed the case from the Mercedes, placed the strap across his chest to keep his arms free, and moved his operation to the next level, literally.

From the walled enclosure of the last parking spaces marked on the garage roof, Chapman rapidly climbed the drain pipe to an adjacent roof structure that was providing shade to the three cars on the roof. There was no foot traffic and there would be no one coming to retrieve their automobile: there was no gasoline available to power the vast majority of cars. Most of what was being refined went to military and paramilitary operations, which in turn yielded more gold with which to buy more gas for more military operations. There was limited gas for public transportation, but there had not been any gasoline available to ordinary people for years. Horses were getting popular again in the countryside where there was sufficient forage, but bicycles and public transportation were the conveyance measures for the city. At any rate, the garage was deserted and would remain so.

The roof top geometry sported a slope, a flat surface and another slope that shared a series of windows, and a flat surface at the edge overlooking Linenhall Street. At the northern and southern aspects of this higher flat surface were two parapets. The northern parapet was like the other in design – a rounded concrete structure with a perimeter of a low concrete circular wall with notches like those of a medieval castle – a perfect sniper's nest. Chapman climbed into the circular parapet. Cocooned within his secret space, Chapman began unpacking the case. With the sun over his left shoulder, he was positioned in an ideal vantage point. Sighting north from the highest point along Linenhall Street, Chapman had a clear view of City Hall – the southern portico and stage anyway – and soon enough, Northern Ireland's first elected Prime Minister in nearly a decade.

Chapman unpacked the padded gun case. One piece at a time, Chapman assembled the coveted AS50 fifty caliber sniper rifle – the 15-year-old development of the famous British company Accuracy International Ltd. The inherent accuracy of the rifle was due to the action being bolted with four screws and permanently bonded with epoxy material to an aluminum frame which kept the action from moving away from zero. The accuracy of the rifle was both cause and effect of the military specifications underlying its development, especially for US Special Operations in multiple branches of service. The AS50 was designed to provide combat operators with highly accurate and rapid aimed fire at extended ranges, and it has overachieved in those parameters. To achieve this goal, the designers built the AS50 around a gas operated, semiautomatic action, a two-part receiver machined from high grade steel, a free-floated barrel fitted with an effective muzzle brake, and a detachable buttstock fitted with a recoil-reducing buttpad and a folding rear grip that also served as a rear support leg. A folding quick-detachable bipod with adjustable legs was fitted as a standard. A Picatinny type rail accepted the high powered scope, and within three minutes, Chapman had assembled one of the most accurate and highest powered rifles on the planet. Complete now with a single stack detachable box magazine, the rifle was ready to fire any or all of its five rounds of ammunition After the shots the rifle would be brought down to its basic sub-assemblies within a similar three minute time span for compact storage in its padded case, snugly within the trunk of the nearest convenient Mercedes.

Chapman slipped the polarizing cover over the distal end of the scope. He wanted no flash of reflected light to alert the dense squadrons of military security at the City Hall ceremony. Chapman sat cross-legged behind the north-northwest notch in the parapet. Resting the bipod in the space and leaning his left shoulder against the cool concrete wall, he sighted and focused on the central microphone of the lectern. With skilled and steady hands he could read the brand (Shure) and almost the serial number engraved on the microphone. Prime Minister McMasters had taken the stage and was seated with other officials. Any shot would thread close to nearby buildings, but this would not impede Chapman in any respect. He could take his shot now, with the Prime Minister seated, or after awhile, speaking at the podium.

Why wait for something to go wrong? thought Chapman. Any perceived threat – firecrackers in Donegall Square, anything – could generate a flurry of activity. Duck and cover maneuvers would hide the Prime Minister and cancel the day's activities – opportunity lost! Special Operations officers would spread out in routines honed after decades of the "troubles" and with an expertise unrivaled globally. Why take the chance?

Chapman straightened his spine and balanced the AS50 on the bipod support. He tweaked the focus on the scope and played a game with himself – left eye or right? Left, he decided, and squeezed the trigger. The reports bounced off buildings left and right. The sound could have come from anywhere, witnesses near Linenhall and Clarence would later confirm to authorities. Some would swear the shots rang from one direction; others swore they came from another.

The sounds of the shots were not noticed at the portico stage of City Hall; but McMasters' head exploding, that *was* noticed. It was like stomping an ant hill. *Save the eggs!* Everyone in the densely packed intersection of Linenhall Street and Donegall Square South was moving, running, scanning, directing, cowering, and generally doing so noisily and hysterically.

Chapman calmly packed the AS50 in its case, rolled smartly over the eastern edge of the circular parapet, slid the short distance down the sloping roof to the flat landing, then slid the remainder of the way down the next sloping section. With case in hand he landed on his feet, knees bent and hand completing the tripod landing. He would have rolled if the height had been greater, but the ten feet from the roof edge presented no challenge. Chapman replaced the case in the Mercedes trunk. It would be found eventually and identified as the potential weapon, but without finger prints (Chapman wore gloves) or ballistic evidence (the bullets would not survive the impacts sufficient for scrutiny), the rifle would not achieve legal authority.

Chapman exited the parking garage without enquiring about the confusion. He wanted to remain as inconspicuous as possible, and unmemorable. He made his way to City Hall Station and took the train to Londonderry. Two and one-half hours later he transferred to the bus heading back to the west coast of Ireland, a country suddenly thrust into new levels of political chaos.

In Donegal Town he had stored the backpack in a public locker at the Donegal Station prior to his commute. He retrieved it upon his return to complete the image and the ruse. He locked the door to the men's restroom and changed into his familiar gentleman's hiking clothes. Stuffing the worn suit in the backpack, Chapman let himself out of the restroom and hiked the short distance to Lough Eske Castle.

Upon his arrival, the desk clerk was effusive in the warmth of his greeting. "Good evening, Mr. Johnson!" beamed the clerk to Chapman. "How was your outing today?"

"Marvelous, my good sir! Simply splendid!" smiled Chapman. Without a hiccough, he realized, he had just paid for his time at Lough Eske Castle and two years privilege on Sanibel. Not bad for a day's outing!

"Oh, Mr. Johnson," added the clerk emphatically. "There is a message for you, sir. I trust it is not bad news."

"Thank you," said Chapman, accepting the envelope.

Minutes later, Chapman was in his room, slipping off outer layers of clothing and taking a few moments to lie in bed. He tore the corner flap loose with a finger and opened the envelope along its side, retrieving the paper with the handwritten message. It was coded. Chapman would need secure Internet access.

After a sumptuous dinner at the chef's table – a traditional reward he permitted himself in moments of triumph – Chapman walked into town in search of a computer store. He hailed a bicycle taxi and was taken straight away to the nearest Best Buy in Donegal. As a global retailer, the chain store would have a small computer that he could purchase for the sole purpose of responding to the message he had received earlier. Chapman did not trust the business center at Lough Eske Castle. He was certain that it was discrete and all, but he required that no trace of any contact would remain. A public Internet connection would not do at all.

In the electronics section of the store, he found a satisfactory product: a 32-gigabyte webbook the size of a small paperback novel, complete with satellite service and optional holographic projection. He paid cash, as always, and returned to the waiting bicycle taxi for the short trip back to Lough Eske Castle.

In his room he logged on to a secure website where he was able to decode the missive with its cryptic message promoting an asset management opportunity from the venerable firm, Johnson, Johnston, and Smythe. He knew that he had but thirty minutes from the moment he logged on to the secure decoder website to log on to www.johnsonjohnstonsmythe.net before that site would no longer exist. He did so immediately, entering his unique twenty digit identification.

Kobayashi had a new assignment already. This was unusual – two jobs in such a tight time frame. Chapman's juices were flowing like a vigorous mountain stream. *Bring it on*, he thought. He was going to Paris. He hit "accept".

.   .   .   .   .

The next morning Chapman visited the concierge of the Lough Eske Castle. "I wonder if you could tell me when and where the next Formula One race will be held," began Chapman, although he knew the schedule as well as anyone. "I am a long time fan of Ferrari," he confessed while the concierge turned back to him from his computer screen.

"You are in luck, Mr. Johnson!" cried the concierge with delight. "The next series is this weekend in Belgium – a mere hop, skip, and a jump from here."

"Delightful! Arrange tickets for me, would you?" asked Chapman.

"My pleasure, Mr. Johnson!" replied the concierge. "Does that mean you will be needing an early departure?"

"I am afraid it does. I do love it here, but I haven't seen a Formula One race in person in years. I follow them by satellite, of course, but it is not the same."

"No, indeed not."

"I shall pay the full two weeks, of course, if I do leave early."

"That's very generous, sir."

"Could you also check on flights to Paris?" asked Chapman.

"Of course, Mr. Johnson!" the concierge gushed. "Would there be anything else? Anything at all?"

Look up the word *obsequious* online and you ought to see this man's face, thought Chapman. He smiled, "No. No, thank you."

.   .   .   .   .

Chapman explored Paris long enough to discover that the man targeted by his newest assignment was an art dealer with ties to Russia and the Middle East. His profile, as gleaned from the Internet and news reports, also recounted how he had survived more than one assassination attempt, and now he never went anywhere without his bodyguards.

He has dangerous associations, thought Chapman. *No wonder he has been targeted.*

A visit to the man's gallery in Paris was all that was required to determine his whereabouts. *M. Dubois is traveling,* Chapman was told. *He is on a buying trip with stops in many countries. He will return early next month.*

Chapman took the opportunity while he was in Europe to pay a visit to his lock box in Switzerland, where bank accounts were once again most sacrosanct. He took the opportunity also to renew his acquaintance with his bankers and modify his instructions and contingencies in the unlikely situation of an untimely demise. *One never knows, does one?*

Chapman returned to Paris and checked in as Mr. Johnson at the Hotel George V. He enjoyed a late dinner at Le Cinq, a very elegant dining room decorated in grey and gold. Chapman's table looked out on the hotel's courtyard and garden. He ordered the duck and soon the appropriateness of Le Cinq's Michelin awards became clear. The Crystal stemware, china and silver were all created specifically for this legendary hotel. The four poster bed in the Empire Suite would feel especially luxurious tonight. Chapman planned to sleep quite late.

It was not entirely a ruse for Chapman to take in a Formula One race before returning to Sanibel. He truly was a fan of the motorsport. It would be difficult trading the Hotel George V for the Bedford Hotel, but the Bedford was adjacent to the raceway. There was no more convenient place to stay in Brussels and their restaurant offered decent French cuisine. He would go in time to catch the qualifying races. These contests for the better grid positions were sometimes the deciding factor for points and podium. Going early and staying close to the track would also run him into drivers and celebrities. That could be amusing.

Travel to Brussels was uneventful, but Brussels itself was hard to take. The number of police required to keep the socialists out of the reserved spaces seemed to grow each time he visited. And the images of the poor, begging for money or food, was more disconcerting than ever, probably because the proximity seemed ever more proximate. If these social issues could not be managed better, Europe was in danger of losing the last of its tourism, and the most lucrative of that trade.

The race was a bit of a disappointment as well. Ferrari's better driver spun out when he was clipped on the first lap and was taken out solidly when the Mercedes driver broadsided him. Then Force India ran away with the numbers one and two spots. Ferrari didn't even finish in the points. Ah, well.

Chapman prepared for his return trip to Sanibel. He had orchids to tend.

Chapter Twelve

The gait was an unusual one for Beverly. Her strides were long and brisk in the direction of Jesse's sailboat. Her shoulders swung back and forth in a cocky circular sway and dip motion as she moved in his direction. Jesse saw her approaching, sat up straight and smiled.

From his perch on *Serenity*, Jesse called out, "I have company. This may not be the best time..." He was teasing her for showing up unannounced.

Beverly wasn't buying any of it. "I have a car," she said. "Tell your friend she'll have to go now."

"You don't have a car!"

"I have a *smart* car!" she came back. "And reservations for lunch at *Sweet Melissa's*."

Jesse was off of *Serenity* now, walking in her direction. "Where did you get..." They met without breaking strides, as if they stuck to one another, and kissed. Jesse held her to him with one arm around her waist. They kissed a second time and looked in each other's eyes. Smiling, Jesse pushed gently, leading Beverly as if they were dancing, and they began walking in the direction from which she had come. "...a *smart* car?"

"It's a loaner," she said, holding Jesse's arm with both hands and smiling up at him as they walked. "It's a prototype. Dr. Zugat has finished installing the radio transmitters along Periwinkle, Tarpon Bay, and Sanibel-Captiva roads. We are guinea pigs." She squealed softly, "Eeeek, eeeek."

"No steering wheel, right?"

"None."

"OK! I think I feel safer already!"

Beverly elbowed him sharply in the ribs.

"Ow," cried Jesse, and he meant it.

They approached the car and Jesse said, "This is small. Can we both get in this thing?"

The smart car consisted of two rather comfortable leather seats on a flat platform. The plastic and glass covering formed an arch similar in shape to the great arch in Saint Louis. Two arches on each flat side were connected by one curved piece of glass from bumper to the curved top and back to the other bumper. The sides filled the lower half of the arches with composite plastic material. The windows, three on each side, rose at the touch of corresponding buttons, or automatically if it rained.

In the easiest of steps, they swung open the lightweight doors and sat down in the surprisingly comfortable and supportive ergonomic chairs. The curved glass front revealed everything from the gravel in the parking lot to the clear blue sky overhead. The photosensitive tinting worked well to reduce glare. The glass along the roofline turned slate grey at its fullest tinting, and in that mode full advantage was made of the photovoltaic charging of the new super-dense compact lithium battery that powered the smart car. A holographic monitor appeared in response to their weight on the seats. It was positioned in the center of the small vehicle, accessible by passengers from either seat so that a solo "driver" could choose to sit on either side. The default position was at knee level with a slight upward tilt. Being holographic, of course, meant that the operator could position it elsewhere with an easy move.

Beverly touched the screen and a satellite-generated map revealed their location and a blinking green dot. She spoke the phrase, "Go to *Sweet Melissa's.*" The map expanded to show the entire island and a red dot flashed on the eastern half of Periwinkle, between Donax and Casa Ybel.

"Go!" said Beverly and the car began rolling with an eerie silence. On Sanibel-Captiva Road the car quickly obtained the full 35-mph speed that satisfied the posted speed limit. It seemed incredibly fast to passengers who were not in control of steering, stopping, or anything else. The small size of the smart car and its proximity to the gravel that whizzed by beneath them took some getting used to.

"Let go and let God," mumbled Jesse as he settled into the comfortable seat, now soothing with road vibration.

"Or let Dr. Zugat," said Beverly, as she placed her hand behind his neck and played with his hair with her fingers.

.   .   .   .   .

Marti Leinhart was working. As owner and sole beautician at *Marti's* she was in constant demand and had not accepted new customers in years. There was a waiting list. Marti was an artist; so if she suggested a style change, her clientele were more often than not eager to go along, even if they were delighted with their current hair style.

Alison Swanson was in the chair. Marti and Alison were best friends; not for the same number of years that Marti and Beverly had been friends, but long enough. They had met as beautician and client, but they evolved into confidants and a mutually assured support system. Marti was learning to craft jewelry in Alison's studio; Alison, in turn, was letting Marti instruct her in some of the finer nuances of wine appreciation. Marti had learned from some of the Island's best oenophiles. Conversely, Alison had always enjoyed only the best wines. She simply had done so with no analysis. Alison's enormous wealth did not appear to factor into the friendship equation. Given Marti's fame and prowess as a master – or rather mistress – of all things hair, it would be uncertain who would be voted off the island by the council – men who still had to go home to their wives – if push came to shove. Not that it ever would. The larger point to be made is: once you were *in* you were *in*, and Marti's status was *very* secure.

After the usual gossip and talk about their own situations, Alison got quiet, then said, "I need to run something by you."

"OK," Marti leaned to work on one side of Alison's head. She adopted a wry smile and said, "Shoot."

"You remember that I asked you to play the part of Desdemona in the production of *Othello* next summer at the Pirate Playhouse?"

"Sure. I can still do that."

"Well, I'm starting to have second thoughts."

"About me or the play?"

"You, I guess. I still want to mount the production."

"Mount. That's a good word."

"Head out of the gutter, please."

"So what's the problem?"

"It's just that Clyde Markowitz is slated to play the role of Othello…"

"Yeah, well that makes sense, what with him being so handsome and African-American and all. And I do mean *and all!*"

"Oh, Marti. This was what I was really concerned about. You don't know do you?"

"Know what, Alison? Spill it!"

"Clyde Markowitz has taken up with Jennifer Marin, the tennis pro?" Alison framed the statement as a question because she did not know how much Marti knew about Jennifer. "They are an item. They go everywhere together lately."

"How long has this been…"

"About a month as far as common knowledge is concerned. I spoke with a few of your clients and they were sure you didn't know and no one wanted to be the one to tell you."

"*The Beautician,* starring *Marti* as 'the last to know'!" Marti extended her hands, scissors in the right, to frame an imaginary theater marquis.

"Well," Marti paused, dropped her arms, and reflected. "That's just crappy."

Alison sat in silence as Marti worked with her hair.

"Thanks, I guess," Marti offered after a few moments. "You know, I was just talking to Beverly maybe two weeks ago about Clyde and Greg, and maybe Jeffrey someday, and commitment, and Beverly wasn't having any of it. We did drink the best bottle of wine on the island though."

"Life has its moments."

"The thing is," Marti felt the need to talk now, "that I wouldn't care about losing Clyde – Clyde and I never were really serious – but I really don't want to lose Greg. I do like Greg, maybe more than I realized. It's like the relationship meter of external validation has dipped from two to zero."

"What's going on between you and Greg? You've been with him off and on for years."

"Greg's talking about leaving Sanibel. He wants me to go with him."

"Going away!" cried Alison. "Why on Earth? And where?"

"He keeps talking about this place in Tennessee called *the Farm*. It's an old commune. "

"I've heard of it, but frankly it doesn't sound like you," said Alison.

"Yeah, that's what Beverly said, too; just not so polite as you," said Marti. "She also let me know that I'm not ready for commitment," Marti spoke as if she had used the words before. She was relaying the news, not discovering a conviction. "Well, you know. I do like him," Marti continued with the rote recitation. "He is a gentleman. He's a good person. He is always there for me." She smiled at the thought that she was inventorying her future losses.

.   .   .   .   .

It had been two weeks since the war games and the invasion of two of Sanibel's homes. The Widow MacIntyre was buried and vengeance was vowed. General Presswood had been fully briefed by Sheriff Cochran regarding the robbery of gold and jewelry from Dr. Müller's home in the sanctuary. A Nobel Prize laureate, Dr. Müller and his wife had been visiting friends and accepted their gracious invitation to spend the night. Sheriff Cochran considered that the decision probably saved their lives.

Captain Birch, despite the severity of his wounds, was among the survivors of the incursion. Privates Nichols and Lewis were the two who surrendered at the hopeless last moment. The other three were dead: two from the firefight and one had not survived the ongoing interrogation. Birch had been in the infirmary healing his gunshot wounds and having a series of cardiac arrhythmias stabilized with anti-arrhythmic medications. When Sergeant Russell heel-kicked Birch, Birch sustained a cardiac contusion severe enough to turn the anterior heart muscle to mush as it healed. The arrhythmias were a result of that injury.

Privates Nichols and Lewis were in worse shape if anything. It was a tribute to their loyalty that they had not revealed the former location of their headquarters, which seemed to be a focus of the interrogation. They were expressing the conviction that if they had known two weeks ago what they knew now, they would never have surrendered. Going out in a blaze of glory would have been much more preferable to the beatings and torture they had been forced to endure.

Yesterday, the three had been moved into the same small room for the first time. They had shared their stories, and Privates Nichols and Lewis were amazed about the similarities of the torture routine. Island Security was highly methodical.

This morning a contingent of Island Security soldiers had come in and placed tight restraints on all three men, not that Birch could get out of bed anyway. He was in traction in a long-leg cast that was elevated by the orthopedic ropes and pulleys attached to an overhead framework of metal bars. It was unclear why after placing Privates Nichols and Lewis in Posey vests and wrist restraints, they were provided with similar overhead frameworks. It would soon become all too clear.

A thin man with a thinner smile entered the room. He could not have appeared more sinister if he had been dressed in black leather rather than his Island Security Major's uniform.

"We have no more time or patience, gentlemen," he announced to the group rather than any individual. "You will talk now or die."

The three were quiet and apprehensive. They suspected that whatever was about to happen was not going to be pleasant. Only the major appeared to be at ease.

An assistant entered. It was Sergeant Russell. "I requested a temporary transfer," he explained. "I wouldn't want to miss this."

"You have heard of the Chinese water torture. Yes?" Major Cadman began. "We have improved upon it considerably."

As Cadman spoke, Russell made himself busy attaching an intravenous bottle to its hanger directly above Private Nichols' forehead. Nichols was thinking that it would take more than the incessant drip-drip-drip of water on his forehead to get him to break. The Chinese water torture was reputed to drive people to madness eventually, but that was an urban legend. The Chinese never did such a thing and those who *had* actually used venom from a live snake. The realization suddenly struck Nichols like a Taser. That was not water in that bottle!

"Start the drip at a slow rate, Sergeant," instructed Major Cadman. "We don't want to melt his entire face off just yet."

With those dire words as prologue, Russell said, "With pleasure, sir," and turned the valve to allow the first drop to fall.

Nichols watched the drop swell, burst its surface tension, and fall toward him, slowly at first then gathering speed and momentum until it crashed, burning and searing his forehead. He could hear the sizzle as the dilute acid dissolved his flesh. The second drop followed... too soon, too soon! Nichols started whimpering, then screaming with muffled high-pitched sounds that were intermittent as he hyperventilated. The third drop burned deeper into the subcutaneous tissue and the wound began to widen. The fourth drop ran out of the wound and into Nichols' right eye. Nichols was flailing and screaming at the top of his lungs now. "Jesus, take me now!" he begged. But the jerking around could not escape the drops, and the private's face was soon cratered with new acid burns.

"Finish the first minute, Sergeant," said Cadman, "then turn off the drip for five minutes before we resume."

"Do you expect him to talk?" yelled Birch, incredulous at the inhumanity.

"No, not really, Captain Birch," explained the major. "I rather expect him to die eventually. "I am hoping that it will be you who talks, in order to spare Private Lewis the same... *inconvenience*."

The interrogators left the room to the stunned silence of Birch and Lewis, the whimpering of Nichols, and the faint sizzling from the last few drops of acid.

"I'm not prepared to go through with this any further, Bill," Captain Birch said quietly to Private Lewis.

"I am very glad to hear that, sir," replied Lewis. "I'm done in. Do you think Nichols will make it."

"It might depend on whether he wants to survive at this point," Birch was guessing. "The burns may be superficial at this point, but he will be blind."

"I can hear you guys," Nichols whispered hoarsely. "Don't let them do another round on me, sir, if you can help it. I know now I never should have surrendered, but nobody deserves this."

"I'll do what I can, Jim," *but these assholes are enjoying themselves.*

Cadman and Russell returned to the scene and Russell positioned himself at Birch's bedside. Wordlessly Russell sneered as he punched Birch in the face, hard enough to daze him. He regained consciousness to the salty taste of his own blood and the screams from Private Nichols.

"I'll tell you what you want to know," said Birch weakly. He was defeated.

"We know that, *prick*," said Russell. "We heard you during the 'break'. Of course the room is monitored."

Of course, thought Birch. "So how do I stop this."

"Oh, we're stopping," said Russell as he reached up to turn off the valve. One last squirt fell onto Nichols, hitting his nostrils, acid fumes filling his lungs. "Oops," smiled Russell. "Too bad this wasn't you getting the drip," Russell glared at Birch. "Sergeant Bell was my friend. I will leave you to Major Cadman. Rest assured that if your story is shy of detail, or contradicts what we already know to be true, I will be back."

Nichols hyperventilation had turned to harsh uncontrollable coughing as the last dose of acid burned his trachea and bronchial tubes with its fumes. The coughing led to retching and emesis. Because he was restrained, unable to turn on his side, the vomitus was aspirated. Over the next few minutes, Nichols suffocated, his struggles becoming weaker. Birch and Lewis watched helplessly as his respirations became agonal: Cadman just watched.

"I'm thinking that is a blessing," said Lewis.

Two orderlies brought Major Cadman a chair as they rolled the bed containing Lewis out to another room. Nichols' body was moved to the corner – an ever present reminder. Lewis was separated from Birch and would be useful later to corroborate the information Birch provided. It was one more measure for keeping him honest. But these men were broken. They would tell Major Cadman everything he wanted to know. The human spirit can only take so much. The reason torture by civilized governments fell into such disfavor, thought Cadman, was that it never went far enough to truly break a man. Half measures produced half-truths. *Water boarding*, he thought. *Oh, please.* No wonder information derived through torture was so unreliable ten and fifteen years ago. No guts; no glory.

Cadman turned to face Captain Birch. "Tell me," he began, "about troop numbers, names and characteristics of officers, former locations of headquarters, and tell me, please, about your general's ambitions towards this island."

.   .   .   .   .

Beverly watched Chapman closely as he tended his orchids. He was removing the "scape" – the spikey flowering stem left from when the bloom has faded.

"This is necessary to encourage the orchid to bloom next season," he said.

He cut the stem at an angle about a half-inch from the base and said, "This stub will dry up and disappear."

Beverly pressed in closer to observe the technique with the sharp knife. Chapman smiled at her. "You really should know enough now to grow your own," he reassured her. "Don't you think?"

"Probably so," she agreed. "It's not like I can't get expert advice if I run into an issue."

"Exactly," he said. "So, in recognition of your outstanding achievements in the field of orchid tending, I present you with your very own phalaenopsis." Chapman held out a magenta orchid for her to take. Beverly accepted the gift with a broad smile.

"She's a beauty!" Beverly acknowledged.

"Phalaenopsis is a warm growing orchid," Chapman continued, "but it still needs to cool down to about sixty-five degrees at night. Phalaenopsis hybrids enjoy the light behind curtains and window blinds, in other words filtered, not direct. The sunburn will produce black blotches. When you water your orchids, take care to avoid wetting the leaves. If water gets trapped in between the leaves, dry them quickly by using a piece of tissue or a cotton ball. After watering, do not allow standing water to come in contact with the base of the orchid pot. And again, when the last flower drops, cut your flower spike at an angle about an inch from the base to hopefully generate a rebloom."

"Aye, aye, professor!" teased Beverly.

"Oh, I know you knew this stuff. I wouldn't trust my orchids to you when I am gone if I didn't." But he couldn't resist adding, "And let it dry out a bit between watering."

"I am really beginning to wonder if you trust me with this orchid after all," teased Beverly.

"You're right. I know. I'm sorry. I've said all I'm going to say on the subject."

"Speaking of being gone, did you hint earlier that you are going away again so soon?" asked Beverly, although she wanted to ask more.

"Yes, in a few days, but maybe not for as long this time."

Summoning her nerve she asked, despite knowing she shouldn't, "So what is it you do with yourself on all of these trips anyway?"

Chapman looked at her more with amusement than disapproval. "You know we don't talk about that," he chided gently, "but listen, there is one thing."

Beverly looked at him and waited.

"It *is* a dangerous world out there, you know."

"Which is why I question your trips," she said with genuine concern.

"I want to ask a favor of you," he said.

"Name it." She was sincere.

"If something happened and I did not return..."

"No. I don't want to have this conversation," she protested.

"If something happened and I did not return," Chapman persisted, "I want you to promise that you will take care of this place for me – the orchids especially"

"Brad..."

"Promise..." he pushed.

They stared at each other, one as tight lipped as the other. Finally Beverly acceded. "I promise," she said.

"Good." Brady Chapman turned back to inspecting his orchids: turning leaves to examine the hidden surfaces; checking the moisture of the soil; ignoring Beverly completely. At last he said, "There really are some rare species here. Did you know that?"

"Yes," she said softly as she stuck her finger into the soil of her new orchid. "Medium dry," she murmured.

"Yes," agreed Brady without looking up.

.   .   .   .   .

General Presswood was becoming impatient waiting for the Mayor's administrative council members to assemble. Sanibel Mayor Henry Farber and Ron Weber, the island's treasurer, were on time but their offices were just down the hall. They had projects they could work on while the three of them waited for the other dignitaries. Jeffrey Rodgers stuck his head in the door.

"Have I got time to get a sandwich?" he asked Henry.

Henry did not look up from his work. "Better not," he said. "As soon as Cochran and Wilson get here we will start. Alison can't make it."

An interminable five minutes passed before Dr. Wilson came in and sat down.

Henry asked him, "Have you seen Sheriff Cochran?"

"No," said Wilson. "Should I have?"

"No, it's just time to get started is all."

"Well, sorry I was late. Patients don't understand about meetings in the middle of the day, and frankly, neither do I," said the man with too much on his plate.

"OK, let's get started. The sheriff will join us when he gets here," said Henry, overstating the obvious. "General?"

The man in the uniform had the room's attention.

"We have made progress since our last meeting," began General Presswood. "For one – and I wish Cochran was here to share more details – it does appear that the crime spree originates off island. Paramilitary forces are probing our defenses to plan a combat mission and loot the island."

"Seriously?" asked Weber.

"There is no doubt what-so-ever," continued the general. "We have been interrogating enemy combatants since we captured them in conjunction with the home invasion and murder of the Widow MacIntyre. We have detailed and reliable intelligence that these home invasions are merely preliminary forays to gauge our defenses and study our deployment patterns.

We have studied our technology through a series of exercises and found ways to improve our computer algorithms to enhance detection of incursions. Our defenses are the best they have ever been, but they are only defenses and therefore a reactionary approach. My officers and I have another suggestion to place before you today."

"I appreciate the professionalism and seriousness that you bring to this matter, General," said Farber. "This sounds like the biggest problem we have faced."

"No shit," echoed Weber. "What's your idea?"

"I know some people," General Presswood began. "We can get one or two hundred more temporary troops to supplement the three hundred that we billet on the island."

"OK," said Weber. "Treasury is good with that."

"They can bivouac in several areas until we are at full force, then we strike the mainland to "send a message". If we fail to stop them now, they will probe and grow until we won't be able to keep them out. We need to let it be known to these warlords that Sanibel is off limits – plunder elsewhere. We need to put a bad taste in their mouth for messing with us. Put the fear of God in them. Send them packing."

"Metaphorically, of course," said Dr. Wilson, making light of the general's run-on string of metaphors.

The general misunderstood. "Hell, no," he said. "Send them packing for real!"

Wilson would have snickered if the news were not so serious and threatening. He decided to drop it.

Sheriff Cochran came in and sat with the others. "What did I miss?" he asked, trying to judge the atmosphere.

"Where have you been?" asked Farber.

"Doing my job!" Cochran went off on his friend. "Don't you fucking question me, Henry! I'll roll you around in the fucking dirt."

"Oooh, somebody's having a day," said Wilson, and Cochran just looked at him.

"So, what did I miss?" he asked again.

Farber filled him in on the findings and plans presented by the general.

Cochran was in agreement but expressed some trepidation, too. "Seems to me that we could be more secure maintaining our low profile. I mean I know mainlanders know about us, but we are not on their radar."

"Not until recently perhaps," countered Presswood. "These incursions represent a sea change, Sheriff. If we fail to take control, we are looking at more of the same, and maybe a lot worse. We can generate a response to neutralize these current forces. We can make this go away, gentlemen."

"Then do so," said Ron Weber. "Let's make things the way they were."

"How much firepower are you talking about, general?" asked Sheriff Cochran.

210

"Whatever it takes," replies General Presswood. "I don't mean to be cryptic, but if our intelligence is accurate – and I do believe it to be – then we have ample munitions and heavy equipment presently. The additional troops are more for show and to present the enemy with an overwhelming force. There will be fewer casualties on our side this way."

General Presswood paused for emphasis. "Gentlemen," he looked the council in the eyes. "Let's not forget that we are asking men to pay the ultimate price in the defense and for the security of Sanibel Island and your families."

"Sheriff," General Presswood continued. "I don't know if I totally satisfied you regarding your question about firepower. Please know that you are more than welcome to accompany us on the mission. We could embed you..."

"No thank you, General Presswood," said Cochran. "I would just be in the way. This is one instance where I think the less I know of the plans, the better."

"Well, if you change your mind..." the general couldn't help but feel a little smug.

"No, but thank you anyway, General," said Cochran.

Henry Farber rose to his feet. "General Presswood," said Henry. "Thank you for coming.

Let us know what we can do to support your mission."

The others had risen while Henry was addressing the general.

Now that's more like it, thought the general.

. . . . .

When Sheriff Cochran, Dr. Wilson, Jeffrey Rodgers, and Clyde Markowitz played poker, they studied the cards carefully. One of them said, "it's not life and death, it's much more serious than that." The Sanibel Think Tank was holding court once again in the bar of the Jacaranda, and all was right with the world.

It was not always the same four who were gathered at the table. "Check," said Cochran, and he took a sip of scotch – Johnny Walker Blue. The scotch with the expensive price point was not the usual for Cochran, but neither was the opportunity to engage the world in mortal combat – an opportunity that he recently passed on with a simple "No thanks".

"Check," said Wilson, and he took a sip of Irish whiskey – Jameson. He liked the Jameson best.

"Raise," declared Rogers, and he slid a short stack of red chips to the center of the table. The group had discussed local events for the last hour. Rogers had agreed with Cochran that it would be better not to draw attention to their island, but like Cochran, he saw no alternative. They had exhausted the topic and were looking for a chance to lighten the mood. "What is up between you and Jennifer Marin? Isn't she just a few notches out of your league, piano man?"

"See you and raise twenty," said Markowitz, and he slid the blue chips.

"I'm out."

"Me, too."

"Call," said Rodgers, gently topping his previous red chips with two blue ones. "Let's see what you have."

Markowitz turned over three cards. With the four that were already face up on the table, he could make a full house, king high. It was a pretty hand.

"You disrespected the game, Rogers," needled Markowitz, smiling at his winning hand.

"Hey, that's my line," protested Rogers. And the whole table seemed to enjoy it that the tables were turned on the unflappable Jeffrey Rogers.

"So what about you and Jennifer?" asked Cochran, following up on Rogers' question.

"Can't tell yet," confessed Markowitz, smiling at the attention he was getting.

"Jesus, you smile a lot," complained Rogers. "What about you and Marti, then?"

"No, I think that may be yesterday's news. Marti and I have never been all that serious."

Cochran was sorting the cards, preparing to deal. He said, "Greg's probably leaving Sanibel – maybe Fernando, too."

"Christ, I hope not," said Rogers, cigar in hand. He sipped from his glass of Ketel One. "Those guys are almost the only ones who know what they are doing around here. They know their labor crews, too. What's up with that anyway?"

"I'm not sure," said Cochran, or maybe he just didn't want to go into it. He understood why they no longer wanted to be here. "I hear different stories about it. It's a free world, I guess."

"It's a damn dangerous world is what it is," said Rogers, the former NSA agent.

Only Henry did not drink during the regular gatherings of the Think Tank, but Henry wasn't in attendance on *this* night. He said he wanted to be home with the missus. He and Mabel had some things to discuss. At any rate Henry was not here, and as if someone had taken the governor off the locomotive, *these* four were drinking like there was no tomorrow.

Cochran dealt two cards face down to each player and one common card face up. The men in turn examined their cards.

"Check," said Wilson, and Rogers tapped the table sharply with his middle finger.

Markowitz said, "Wusses," and slid a stack of blue chips to the center.

"Fifty dollar limit at this stage," reminded Wilson.

"Wusses," Markowitz reiterated. He removed all but one blue chip and the others matched his wager.

Cochran turned over another card.

Rogers asked the table, "Did anyone hear anything more on the North Irish Prime Minister assassination?"

"Why?" replied Markowitz. "Jealous because it wasn't you that took him out."

"Oooh, did I touch a nerve? What do you care anyway, Markowitz?" Rogers looked at him. "It's not like you are Irish."

"Clever boy," said Markowitz. "Maybe not, but it doesn't mean I can't recognize a bigot. That McMasters asshole was poised to make Ireland another hate crime scene. Good riddance."

The table had passed in turn. Cochran turned over another card.

"Anybody following Washington politics?" asked Wilson.

Rogers was the first to answer. "Fuck it!" he said. "Impeach her."

After a pause, Wilson observed, "You usually talk our ears off with the complex nuances of politics and Washington intrigue."

"Nothing complex about it, then is there?" Rogers added.

Markowitz called to the bartender, "Absinthe, my good man, and since my good friend Rogers here is blowing cigar smoke all over me, I may as well counterattack with some of that choice weed I know you have under the counter – assuming the good Sheriff has no objections."

Cochran looked at Markowitz and said, "You talk too much. It's to you," he added, referring to the game. "And any objection I might have depends entirely on how well you share."

It would be two hours yet before the bicycle taxis lined up outside the Jacaranda to take these four home.

.   .   .   .   .

Jesse felt the ship list to starboard. Beverly called out as she climbed aboard, "Anybody home?"

"Hello, you," said Jesse as he powered down his laptop.

"What are you doing there, sailor?" asked Beverly.

"Working on the novel that will never be finished, like you have reminded me a time or two before," said Jesse.

"What's it about?" Beverly asked for the umpteenth time.

"What brings you all the way out here, unannounced and all," asked Jesse as Beverly made her way into the cabin.

"What's it about?" Beverly asked again. "Really, I mean."

Jesse cocked his head to look at her. "It's an application of string theory to determine if the Chilean earthquake of 2010 was the actual – or merely catalytic – cause of the devolution of mankind these last thirteen years – thirteen is a significant Fibonacci number, by the way – when it sped up the Earth's rotation and increased the tilt as a result of the exosphere tsunami."

Beverly smiled at him, "No, I mean really."

"It blew a lot of energy into space at an angle, you know. It was a real KERS."

Beverly smiled at him patiently, "No, I mean really."

"Kinetic Energy Recovery System."

"I know what you are saying. It's an old horsepower kick from one year of Formula One racing when I was in graduate school. I also know why you are talking this way. Why won't you tell me about your book?"

"You can read it if you can guess the password."

"*Serenity!*" she said.

"No way!" he cried. How did you know?"

"You are so predictable."

"Maybe so, but that's not it."

"Ooh, "she said, and punched him.

His defensive move was to grab her arm and pull her to him. "You are too close to manage a good punch now," he said.

"I can still bite," she warned.

"Promises, promises," he whispered.

When they kissed, Beverly wriggled against him hard, pressing with all she had.

"*Beverly*," he said.

"Hmm?" she moaned.

"That's the password … *Beverly*."

"I'll read it later."

Chapter Thirteen

The sunrise was a spectacular culmination of the pink glow that formed over the horizon, framed by wisps of clouds above and the Florida mainland below. Supplies and mainland day workers were being off loaded at the bayside "Port of Sanibel" as the locals called it. Fernando Lopez and Greg Johnston were there to select familiar laborers. Alison Swanson was up early as well, awaiting the arrival of some art supplies.

The "Port of Sanibel" was a comfortable early morning gathering spot at a site where the causeway previously served as a motoring artery to the mainland. After the causeway's destruction, local workers removed the twisted rebar and massive concrete remnants to fashion a maritime loading dock. Island Security liked the location as well because it was nestled in the middle of a concave shoreline, with excellent line of site observation status from their post at the Sanibel lighthouse on Point Ybel to the lookout station on Woodrings Point. It was the station on Woodrings Point that had given Island Security such a clear picture of the activity of the former headquarters of the mainland militia.

Lopez and Johnston had abundant time to drink their morning coffee and discuss the relative risks and benefits of having a violent paramilitary integral to Sanibel's community. This topic had become particularly prevalent as war games, incursions, and imaginary threats suffused the conversations and thoughts of many islanders. The arguments of risk followed the same line as whether an individual was safer if he or she possessed a handgun and kept it in the house. The elements of risk, perceived changes in troops' attitudes, and an increased awareness of scrutiny on the part of the islanders combined to make an argument against paramilitary protection rather cogent; but what was the alternative?

The Processing Center at the "Port of Sanibel" seemed to require longer than it did in recent months even though most of the laborers were familiar hands. Lopez and Johnston had abundant time to discuss local politics, their personal lives – fortunes and failings – and paramilitary protection primarily because Island Security, which was at best your typically bureaucratic nightmare, was on high alert for some reason.

Alison walked over to where Johnston was refilling his coffee from an urn. He smiled upward at the former actress and producer. For an über-rich and still gorgeous woman of some significant power, Alison Swanson was widely known to be incredibly kind, sensitive and down-to-earth. Maybe she had internalized the abundant literature that formed her thespian development. There was wisdom to be gleaned from much of the world's classic literature.

"I can see my crate," she said to Greg, complaining conspiratorially to a fellow sufferer approaching the inconvenience threshold.

"They take too long to process men and women that we already know are trustworthy," agreed Greg. "The freight can't be off loaded until the men are cleared to handle it."

"Fernando..." she smiled reflexively in acknowledgement as Lopez approached the two. Alison filled her own cup. "Yes," she replied back to Greg with an exasperated sigh. "I know."

Fernando joined them in getting a refill. The three stood silently in the cool morning air, sipping their coffee. It would have made an excellent oil painting, Alison thought.

Greg looked toward Alison and asked, "If you couldn't be here – on Sanibel – where would you want to be?"

Alison smiled curiously. "I really haven't thought much about it. I don't know; maybe Montreal or Monaco...maybe another island." She was beginning to process it now. "Maybe Cuba... No one ever thinks of Cuba because it is so poor, but Cuba has always been poor. It was affected less than a lot of other places when the economy collapsed. The country was already fairly self-sufficient and the dictatorship didn't budge – no riots in Cuba. If you are looking for safety and a laid back lifestyle, you could do worse. What about you? Where would you want to be?"

"Have you heard of the Farm, in Tennessee?" asked Greg.

"Yes, of course. It was a legend when I was young. Is it still around?"

"So they say."

"Where would you want to be, Fernando?" asked Alison, inviting him to play in their parlor game.

"Oh, I like it here," he replied noncommittally.

222

"No one said you didn't," Alison persisted – he wasn't getting out of playing a hand in this game – "but what if?"

"OK. I hear Phuket is holding it together, much like we are here," Fernando shared.

"Phuket? In Thailand?" asked Greg. "How would you get there?"

"Well, that's not the issue is it?" Fernando came back. "If you are going to add conditions to the game, you need to establish some ground rules." The banter was picking up steam.

"OK," said Alison. "Why Phuket?"

"I think he just likes to say the word," Johnston chimes in.

"Well, like I said. It's a lot like it is here. They blew up the only bridge from the mainland…" Lopez began.

"I didn't know that!" said Alison, eyes wide.

"They have a strong police presence in a former resort community," continued Lopez. "They are overseen by a council of billionaires."

"I didn't know all of that!" repeated Alison, ignoring the reference to a council of billionaires. "Where did you hear this?"

"It's common knowledge," Fernando said defensively.

"Dude's an amateur radio operator," explained Greg, motioning to his friend and partner. "Talks to people all over the world the way we once used to blog and do all of the social networking online; you know, before the bandwidth got so outrageously expensive."

Greg spoke before he realized that the cost of bandwidth was not an issue for Alison. She was adept at ignoring references that did not apply to her. With her wide social circles – Alison was a bit of a maven – she was accustomed to filtering information that carried a reality variable, rather than a constant, across social strata.

"Gentlemen," she smiled – mavens knew how to smile – "I have certainly learned something this morning! Thank you for the coffee and conversation, but as you see, my supplies await." She spun toward the new activity on the dock as Lopez and Johnston wished her a good day. Her exit carried far less drama than that of which she was capable.

"Did we run her off?" asked Greg, always the naïve one.

"Yes and no. We made her a little uncomfortable discussing topics she would rather not hear, and we peppered that with some references that hit home with her, but mostly she was looking for an excuse to get what she came down here for," said Fernando. Then he added enigmatically, "I think I am about ready to go to that Farm with you."

"No shit," Greg grinned.

"*About* ready," Fernando emphasized.

The two walked over to greet their favorite workers. One, a young Haitian named Emmanuel, was smiling broadly, irrepressibly. He was always smiling. Fernando asked him, "How do you put up with it?"

"What choice do we have?" he asked earnestly. "At least my family has food on the table. So many do not."

"Are there still the food riots?" Lopez continued. He was exploring mainland conditions for a reason. Greg had gotten him thinking.

"Sure, some; but not like before. Not whole cities. People wore themselves out with that, or died. But there are still desperate people. Food and water stay scarce for those with nothing to barter. I am lucky to be on the transit list. I love the Sanibel!" Emmanuel smiles bigger than ever.

"What about the cavity searches?" asked Greg. "That's just wrong! It reminds me of South African diamond miners."

"Oh, they don't do that now. They speed things up with the body scanners like they have at all of the airports. It's much better now!" said Emmanuel.

"I am glad to hear that," said Greg Johnston. "Let's go have a good day's work in paradise."

"I heard that!" said Emmanuel, mimicking the local dialect and laughing.

Fernando drove and Greg rode shotgun. Emmanuel and three others rode in the back of the Toyota pickup truck as they drove west-northwest along Periwinkle. Greg turns to his friend: "So, are you really thinking about going to the Farm with me if I go?"

"What do you mean, 'if you go'?" Fernando asked. "Not a day goes by that you don't bring up *the Farm*. It's *the Farm* this and *the Farm* that."

"So, are you?" Greg persisted.

"Yes, *compañero*, I am really thinking about going to the Farm with you if you go."

"Let's do this!" Greg pushed for the next level.

"What's your hurry?"

"Call it a feeling."

"We can't just leave. The trip might get dangerous."

"Tell me about it!"

"I mean that this will take some planning. Who else do you think might go with us?"

"I've been talking to Marti, but I don't know. I don't think she can make the break."

"Well, keep it quiet. There are no rules about leaving, but things *are* getting a bit weird with Island Security. You never know when rules might change, and I don't want to attract any of their scrutiny," cautioned Fernando.

"I know; and isn't that exactly why it's time to leave – this burgeoning police state and all? Sanibel just feels different – not so relaxed and laid back."

"That is a lot of it. The place doesn't feel so real, you know, genuine."

"Did it ever?" asked Greg.

.   .   .   .   .

Alison Swanson selected a worker by the name of Delores Davenport to help her with transporting the crate to her studio. Delores was a large boned woman and appeared at least as strong as some of the men. They were afforded use of one of the community trucks and Delores loaded the crate with the kind assistance of one of the laborers who had not yet been chosen for activity today. Alison tipped the grateful worker and got behind the wheel of the delivery truck. It sported one of those continuous drive transmissions that made it easy to drive.

Delores told her story as they rode along. She was one of six children born to a working family in rural Florida. Mitch Davenport was a handsome suitor and when the opportunity arose, they eloped. They were young, she recounted, and had no awareness of what made things tick. The first they knew of the collapse was when food was not available anywhere, to anyone. There just wasn't any. The first of the waves of food riots found them in Orlando, caught between mobs and police forces. Mitch was shot in the thigh and managed to get to a hospital. They still had those open to the public then. The scene was so crowded that he was treated and released back to the streets. He kept his leg but infection set in. The wound drained for years. He would get the fever from time to time; sometimes he would talk out of his head, but he always got better. Delores would find work wherever she could, but Sanibel was the best situation she had seen – nice folks that never stiffed a person after a hard day's work. That's why she kept coming back despite the strip searches and cavity searches; she was so glad for the new body scanners. Mitch died about a year ago: one of his fevers wouldn't go away. He was better off now; gone to a better place to be with Jesus. Anyway, she was doing the best she could and life did seem a bit more dependable in its routines. She was thankful for her blessings and praised God every minute of every day.

Alison listened politely. She had heard many such stories. Some were obviously crafted to increase the payment for labor, but Delores seemed too simple and too sweet to deviate far from the truth. "We're here," Alison announced cheerily. "Let me give you a hand with the crate."

"Oh, I don't know ma'am," said Delores with concern. "It's mighty heavy. You could hurt yourself."

"I'm pretty strong, Delores," said Alison, realizing however that it had been a week since her last workout. "I tell you what, though," suggested Alison. "Let's open it here in the truck bed. We can take half of it inside piecemeal. Then the crate will be lighter when we go to move it." Alison was counting on the shipment of gold bullion being in the bottom of the container. She was not eager to advertise those contents to Delores or anyone else."

"Good thinking, ma'am," agreed Delores. She was not afraid of work but she *was* afraid of an injury that would start her life spiraling toward the starvation she had witnessed in so many others. It was vital to stay functional.

They were coming back to the truck after carrying in the first load when Sheriff Cochran drove up.

"Sheriff!" Alison greeted him warmly. "What a pleasant surprise. To what do we owe the honor?"

Alison's cheerful greeting and the sheriff's smile put Delores at ease. Police were just another gang of warlords with their own colors where she came from. Plus, she said *we*. Delores was feeling more like family by the minute.

"Just happened to be in the neighborhood," Cochran lied. "Thought you might have some coffee for a hard working constable."

"Why, yes, indeed," Alison lied back at him. "Come in and make yourself comfortable."

Being a member of the Council, Alison Swanson was well aware of the interest Sheriff Cochran had taken in the news of her bullion shipment. It was no coincidence that he arrived at her doorstep only moments after they had arrived with the gold. She was pleased for his concern and protection, however unnecessary it might be. She put coffee in the coffee maker and added water enough for three cups, turned it on and turned to Cochran. "You are too much," she said.

"What?" he protested. "You can't afford coffee all of a sudden?"

"You know what I'm talking about... above and beyond, mister," Alison said. "Above and beyond... I suppose you want to stay long enough for me to check my inventory," she said hopefully. "I need to talk with you about another matter anyway."

The coffee machine made gurgling noises. Delores was outside leaning against the truck, waiting. They could see her through the open studio doors. She lit a cigarette. She could afford them again now that she had a dependable income from her work on Sanibel. They tasted better than they ever had; a guilty pleasure that seemed like a luxury item to her.

"What about?" asked Cochran.

"Marti and Jeffrey," replied Alison.

"What?" said the puzzled sheriff. "What about Marti and Jeffrey?"

"Well, nothing yet, but what do you think? You know them both. Don't you think they would make a handsome couple?"

"You are so asking the wrong person. Yeah, they are both alright, but it's not about *handsome* is it? It's how they do together, isn't it? Why ask me?

"I want you to drag, if you have to, Jeffrey Rogers to a cocktail party – I know they are a dime a dozen – but this is one that I am throwing a few weeks from now, on a Friday night. I will see to it that Marti is there. That's all – nothing more sinister than that. We'll let fate handle the rest."

"Yeah, I can do that. Friday won't interfere with the Think Tank, so I have no problem with it."

"I had forgotten about you boys and your poker game."

"Well. It's not like you need to know, now is it?"

"You mean I couldn't buy my way in if I wanted to?"

The coffee machine made an electronic beeping. Delores extinguished her cigarette.

"That's exactly what I mean," said Cochran. "Some things are not available at any price."

"Huh!" Alison couldn't decide if she wanted to pick up that gauntlet or let it lie. "We'll see," she added finally, enigmatically. "We'll see."

Chapter Fourteen

"Welcome back to the Hotel Cinq Georges, Monsieur Johnson," said the clerk at the check in. *"Bienvenue à Paris."*

Festooned with rich woods, the traditional luxury of the Four Seasons Hotel George V did not understate its attraction: *une atmosphère unique, un équipement high tech... À deux pas des Champs-Elysées, le Four Seasons George V Paris définit la notion de raffinement et de service dans la Ville Lumière.*

Paris, more so than many places, had cordoned off its undesirables. The semblance of normalcy was not lost on the privileged who still called Paris their 'home away from home'.

Here there was safety. Here there was civilization, cuisine, art, and even romance. After the collapse, so much of the remaining wealth of the world's aristocracy, captains of industry, and robber barons of finance was poured into the city state, that it had survived after a fashion. No one burned the ancient architecture the way they did in Rome and Athens. No one torched the art in the museums like they did in Leningrad, or trashed the libraries like happened in New York. Why Paris escaped the wrath brought to bear by the masses of starving people, or the more orderly invasions of roving warlords, is a question that may never be answered.

Chapman felt lucky to have an assignment here. Targeting an art dealer should be a walk in the park after the numerous assassinations of heads of state that he had accomplished over the years. That was why as his reputation grew he could charge such outrageous fees. And that, in turn, is why he could afford to live on Sanibel Island.

The assignment was to assassinate a wealthy art collector, a man who never hurt anyone but declined to sell a masterpiece to a Kuwaiti financier. The job would put this masterpiece and other art on the market and send a public message to others who might defy the Kuwaiti.

Chapman would allow himself the luxury of time to discover the man's patterns. It is the nature of man to seek routines that promote comfort and a sense of security. It is ironic that the behaviors that promote this sense of security actually increase one's likelihood of being intercepted successfully. Chapman would go into surveillance mode. What a tragedy that he was having to spend his time walking the streets of Paris – and in the art districts at that! During periods when he could be assured that Monsieur *Art Dealer* was cloistered by his art dealer duties, Monsieur Johnson would work on his fitness routine at the gym, followed indulgently by some rewarding time at the spa. Why surround oneself with the traditional luxury of the Four Seasons Hotel George V and not take full advantage?

The art dealer's name was Jean-Pierre Fitzroy. He not only had routines, he had *strict* routines. He left his secure and guarded townhouse each Monday, Tuesday, and Thursday at 8:43 a.m., picked up by his driver and bodyguard, Arnaud and Tristan, respectively. A sixteen minute drive and one minute walk placed him inside his secure and guarded studio at 9:00 a.m. precisely. Lunch was catered. The delivery man was also apparently the chef, preparing his creations on site. At four in the afternoon, the pattern was reversed and Monsieur Jean-Pierre Fitzroy returned to his elegant townhouse. In addition to working three days a week, Jean-Pierre Fitzroy dined on the town twice each week, Thursdays and Saturdays, always at the best restaurants but with no clear pattern other than the time – eight o'clock. Townhouse departures varied to accommodate the distance and traffic, but restaurant arrival was always precisely at eight o'clock. Departures from the restaurants varied according to the complexity of the meal and the company, although it was not unusual for Monsieur Fitzroy to dine alone. Despite the well-earned reputation for slow food and the Parisian dining experience *as* an experience, Monsieur Fitzroy rarely arrived home after eleven o'clock.

Chapman followed Monsieur Fitzroy for two weeks before planning his encounter. Over the following two days he refined the plan extensively. He wanted, indeed he was requested, to make the murder appear to be a random mugging. It would be so much more complicated than a sniper shot, but he was being paid quite well. He could not imagine what amount Monsieur Fitzroy had turned down for the *Renoir*.

The restaurant chosen by Monsieur Fitzroy on this particular Thursday was located on the Isle Saint Louis, undoubtedly one of the prettiest neighborhoods in Paris with its views of Notre Dame and its narrow quaint streets and interesting shops. The Brasserie de l' Isle Saint Louis offered Monsieur Fitzroy marvelous views as he dined on the Alsatian-style food. More importantly for Chapman was the view that Chapman had of Monsieur Fitzroy as the art dealer dined sumptuously on Cassoulet and Charcroute Alsatian, a bit of beer, and an onion tart.

Chapman had chosen the Thursday meal over the Saturday night out because he suspected that the streets would be less crowded, Monsieur Fitzroy would be more fatigued after a day at work than he would be after a day at the townhouse, and Chapman was ready and eager – he didn't need more time to plan his move. All that remained was for Monsieur Fitzroy to choose a restaurant that allowed Chapman to observe him eating, and Fitzroy had been most accommodating.

Monsieur Fitzroy brought his napkin to his lips and rose from the table. He never paid or went through any obvious transaction when he dined out – that would be too vulgar. Other arrangements were clearly made and understood. The maître d's were always excited to have him as their patron, so the arrangements were clearly generous.

The timing would have to be precise. The window of opportunity – the time from the restaurant door to the car door – was fifteen seconds at best. Chapman was walking now from the corner where he had loitered to the restaurant door which was midblock. The chauffer, Arnaud, brought the luxury sedan curbside and Tristan, the bodyguard, jumped out of the vehicle and strode purposely to the large red double doors of the Brasserie de l' Isle Saint Louis. He opened one door and held it widely as his employer stepped out into the cool Parisian air. Tristan looked up and down the street and appeared to take no particular notice of Chapman, now closing to within thirty feet.

Chapman's next strides were longer and graceful – one, two – followed by a pirouette that allowed him to pull his favorite 9 mm Ruger, complete with silencer, from its concealed holster. To the casual observer the pirouette was just a manifestation of a slightly inebriated man dancing in the streets of Paris. To Tristan it was more. As Chapman raised his weapons and squeezed off the first of three rounds, Tristan lurched sideways; the protector throwing his body in front of his protectorate, Monsieur Fitzroy. The driver, and as it turned out second bodyguard, Arnaud, reacted just as quickly. As Tristan was being struck by rounds from Chapman's weapon, Arnaud stood beside the open driver's door and leveled his own handgun on the roof of the car. As instantly as the aim was achieved – a matter of one second, not two – Arnaud squeezed off two rounds. Chapman had no time to react to the new threat. He was struck in the chest and spun viciously counter-clockwise by the impact. He was fighting to breathe while

Arnaud hurried Monsieur Fitzroy, unhurt, into the car and sped away.

Chapman was writhing in pain, helpless on the ground when several staff emerged from the Brasserie. It was all he could do to manage to conceal his Ruger once more in its holster. Two men stopped to assist Tristan and two more walked the distance to Chapman.

"I was attacked! That man," he pointed to Tristan, "That man," he repeated for emphasis, "saved my life!" Chapman knew the staff would recognize Tristan as Fitzroy's trusted bodyguard. He was trying to concoct a plausible story on the fly. *So far, so good*, he thought.

"*Monsieur Fitzroy's homme est mort! Sacré bleu!*" cried one of the staff.

So far, so good, thought Chapman again. "Take me to…" Chapman paused and reconsidered. "*Pardon! Prends-moi à un hôpital, s'il vous plaît*"

"*Hôpital Hôtel-Dieu est étroit, Monsieur.*"

Chapman understood that the man was telling him that the hospital was close. More importantly Chapman was recovering his breath and his senses. He might have a fractured rib – the tenth? – but he thought the vest had protected him from a penetrating wound. The next concern was the police. He was sure that a phone call from Monsieur Jean-Pierre Fitzroy would have them mobilized and on their way. Time was of the essence.

"*Oui. Bon. Merci. Mais rapidement, s'il vous plaît*" Chapman was again out of options and dependent on the tender mercies of the French. He tried to rise and was helped by the Frenchman. He thought, *the man doesn't know the first thing about casualty triage or he would never allow a person to be moved.* About that time another of the staff pulled up in an old Citroën. And he was off.

On the adjacent island in the middle of the River Seine, a nun assisted as Chapman was transferred to a wheelchair. She rolled him toward the emergency entrance of *Hôpital Hôtel-Dieu* as the young man from the restaurant pulled away. He surprised her by stepping out of the chair near the taxi-stand and announcing that he was feeling much better now, thank you. He placated her objections with a gold coin: "For charity," he insisted.

"*Merci, Monsieur.*"

"*Vous êtes bienvenu, Souer.*"

Chapman took the taxi only three blocks before overpaying the driver and sending him to *Jardin du Luxembourg* to wait for him. Chapman asked him to turn off his radio so as to not be tempted by other fares. Chapman had paid him well enough to expect this consideration. The driver took the gold and departed.

Chapman walked two blocks before hailing another cab. He felt surprisingly good under the circumstances. He hurt like hell, but he could push through that. He was increasingly functional: that was what mattered. Chapman hailed a third cab, then a fourth, in much the same manner before asking the driver to take him to the airport. The police were searching earnestly by now. They would discover the first cab with its radio silenced at *Jardin du Luxembourg*, but it would take considerable time to find the succession of cabs. By then he would be on the first plane out of Paris. He was leaving valuables at the Hotel George V, but it could not be helped. He was leaving Paris with his life: that was what mattered.

Chapter Fifteen

Alison Swanson was never known for elaborate parties. She considered it enough to announce the event to some people who might spread the word further, or not. She provided some food to eat and a reasonable mixture of alcoholic beverages and fruit juices. People could show up, mix, mingle, watch the sunset from her beachfront lawn, talk, share, hug, smile, dance, sing, or get silly; or not. It was not typical of Alison, however, to miss her own party.

When Alison did show – nearly one hour late – she was still wearing her smock from her studio. She apologized to the thirty-some people gathered on her lawn, and explained that she had gotten "caught up" with an art project and didn't notice the time. No one doubted her for an instant.

Mrs. Davenport, as Alison now called Delores, her sometimes stay-over domestic, had everything prepared. Large gulf shrimp lounged nonchalantly on beds of crushed ice, surrounded by a visual cacophony of colorful fruits. There were bacon-wrapped scallops, baked salmon roulade on a potato galette, wonton purses, and of course Mrs. Davenport at the carving table offering beef tenderloin with horseradish sauce, Creole mustard, or with a Bordelaise-style red wine sauce. In other words, it was everyday fare for Sanibel – nothing special. But *tasty*!

When Alison *did* show, festivities were in full swing. Doctor Wilson was holding court on the virtues of the discredited theory that says man's consciousness, his self-aware thoughtfulness, arose from the merging of experience, memories and hallucinations to form metaphorical thought. She needed to warn Mrs. Davenport not to put out the better wines so early; not if Dr. Wilson was expected.

Sheriff Cochran and Jeffrey Rogers were discussing deep sea fishing with Marti Leinhart, Lucy Cochran, and Thelma Coggins. *Good job, sheriff!* They were talking about going out after red snapper this weekend. *Good job, indeed!*

The various members of the council were gathered discussing security issues; but Allison had had enough of that for one week. *Stay at it boys. Let me know when you come up with a better plan.* Their wives – Alison was the only woman on the council – were all gathered at the white wicker settee, sipping champagne or cosmos. They were absentmindedly helping themselves to the spiced toasted pecans in the bowl on the table. *Those would not last long.* The women were joined by Lucy Cochran, the sheriff's wife. That area was becoming a full-fledged hen party.

Clyde Markowitz was here with Jennifer Marin. They were over by the bar. Alison had deliberately not invited Clyde, and by extension Jennifer, but word got out and lawn parties are fair game. It might be for the best. The visual reminder might be the catalyst for something (or someone) new for Marti. Clyde and Jennifer were such fun people that it was actually for the best on several levels. Alison was feeling guilty for not extending the invitation personally at this point. She would ask him to play the Steinway a bit later. Clyde always enjoyed that and it would make Alison feel better.

Jesse was here! That was a nice surprise. Jesse rarely came to this end of the island unless it was on business or someone needed help. He was down by the shoreline with someone... *Beverly!* Well,

244

there was no mistaking *that* body language. *Get a room you two!*

After taking a quick inventory, Alison began the obligatory hostess role of making the rounds, contributing to the conversations where she could (Dr. Wilson was a lost cause), and seeing to it that everyone had everything that they could possibly want. Dr. Wilson was a lost cause again. He requested a Bordeaux that had not been available for years.

Alison lingered longest at Marti's grouping. Alison was at her most charming. She flirted with Jeffrey despite being at least 15 years his senior. She was poised and beautiful and rich in the best of Hollywood traditions. The aftermath of her attention toward him was to put Marti into action. As Alison moved gracefully to another cluster of guests, she couldn't help but notice Marti laughing and coming out with some zinger that others thought was uproarious. Marti was clearly enjoying herself and she looked more beautiful than ever. She was having a great time and stoking others to do the same. If nothing further came of the evening, it was at least becoming one hell of a party.

Sharon Welker and Liz Forbes were enjoying themselves a little too much. Alison glanced back over toward John Cochran, who was now interrogating Thelma Coggins, and Jeffrey

Rogers who was discussing something apparently quite interesting with Marti Leinhart, and she decided that she was free to move on. She saddled up to her friends, Sharon and Liz. They looked at each other with tightening smirks until all three broke out laughing. "Don't think that we don't know what you are up to," said Sharon.

"Why, Sharon," Alison drawled. "I am sure that I have no idea what you might be referring to." Alison's disclaimer was met with silence, smirks, and the kind of spewing laugh that happens when you know from the onset that you can't suppress it for very long.

"Bubbles in the nostrils!" Liz complained, lamenting the loss of champagne.

Alison took the golden time to linger with best friends, telling stories, telling lies, having fun. It was the opportunity she needed to relax and unwind. After a time she made the transition from hostess to partier, and she was grateful to her friends for the transition.

Alison wandered into the space occupied by Dr. Wilson, who appeared to be gazing idly at the gulf's horizon.

"Michael?" she said softly, startling him not only out of his reverie, but also by using his oft neglected given name.

"Best party in years, Alison," Michael assured her.

"Everything copacetic, then?"

"Never better." Michael reassured her.

"You are a trained observer," she continued. "Tell me what you see."

He looked at her to gauge her meaning and replied, "Well, I would say that if your intent was to get Marti and Jeffrey noticed, one by the other, then you have worked your wily ways. That's the only new dynamic I see right now."

"What have you found to drink?" Alison asked, nodding toward his wine glass.

Michael leaned toward her conspiratorially and almost whispered, "It is a first rate first growth Bordeaux that Mrs. Davenport found especially for me. I think I like her. She is keeping the bottle under the table so the riff-raff won't swill it like it was two buck chuck; but if you want I can get some for you."

"Why, yes, please. That would be nice," she smiled, not only to be gracious but also out of amusement that he would offer her some of her own best wine and not be totally able to hide his disappointment when she accepted.

Michael Wilson returned with a generous pour of the Bordeaux. Alison swirled and stuck her nose in the glass and swirled again. They watched quietly as Jeffrey and Marti walked slowly, swaying a little, toward the beach.

"They are joining Beverly and Jesse," Michael observed.

"Mm," Alison grunted in agreement and took her first sip. "Mmm. That will be with me in the morning – on my palate. Good choice, doctor."

Michael smiled, taking the credit that was not his. He was thinking it was becoming one very nice party. He put his arm around Alison's shoulder like the old friend that he was. "You may be my platonic lover just now," he said as if granting her the ultimate privilege.

"Careful," she cautioned. "It might lead to more than that," she said to the wise and funny man who just happened to be the same age as she. As Alison rested her head against Michael's chest she swirled her wine again. "It's opening up nicely," she said referring to the wine.

"I'll say!" agreed Michael, referring to something else altogether.

.   .   .   .   .

Across the island on West Gulf Drive, the Webers were hosting a party of their own – invitation only, formal attire requested. This was no casual bash. Attendees included three retired U.S. Senators and five Congressmen, their wives or mistresses, and a number of celebrities. No one but no one left their egos at the door.

A dozen oriental women – each approximately five feet two inches; each sporting the same hair style (rounded, with bangs); and each dressed identically in a white silk blouse, white pearls, black skirt and black shoes – were positioned on both sides of the path between the circular drive and the Webers' front door. Their function was to bow as the guests arrived.

Inside, butlers in tuxedos and maids in "little black dresses" greeted arriving guests with a variety of potent cocktails. The dining room table was a rich walnut. On it were six oval mirrors. Each mirror was decorated with generous lines of cocaine. Short plastic straws were situated in silver holders. In the kitchen and on the terrace that overlooked the Gulf of Mexico with its enormous rising full moon, there were three stations of master chefs and their sous chefs, each group vying to outdo the other with outrageous gourmet selections. The wine was rare and its price was subject to debate and auction.

Chef Katherine offered blackened seared sesame Ono that had been swimming near Hawaii only seventeen hours before the Webers' gathering. Packed fresh on ice, the privileged fish merited its own special flight accompanied by the freshest pineapple and a troupe of Luau dancers and fresh foods appropriate to the beach party: poi, kalua pig, poke, lomi salmon, opihi, haupia, and beer.

Chef Katherine was stationed on the beach near the fire pit. On the terrace Chef Valentino was preparing Italian cuisine paired with Super Tuscan wines, the cabernet dominant non-traditional wines that everyone seemed to want and almost no one could obtain.

In the kitchen Brazilian Master Chef Gabriel was kicking his cuisine to a new level with moqueca capixaba, which is made of fish and tomato; and *chouriço*, a mildly spicy sausage. Root vegetables such as cassava, and fruits like açaí, cupuaçu, mango, papaya, guava, orange, passionfruit, pineapple, and hog plum were arranged throughout the kitchen. There was nowhere a guest could stand and not be within reach of one delicacy or another. Salgadinhos, cheese bread, pastéis and coxinha were common finger foods. Cachaça, a popular Brazilian liquor, was used to make the chic Caipirinha cocktails. The event was exotic to say the least.

Although several bedrooms were made available for discrete sexual encounters, there were other areas of the estate that became sites for group sex. Considering the enormity of cocaine and opiates, it should not have been a surprise to anyone that things got out of hand with drugs, sex, and hurt feelings. The Webers themselves were too strung out to leave their bedroom. There was no mention of their absence. Perhaps the guests thought they were around but had just missed them for the moment. At least no one got killed this time.

.   .   .   .   .

Fernando Lopez, Greg Johnston, and Jennifer Marin were the only three who ultimately decided to risk the uncertain journey to the Farm – the commune in middle Tennessee that everyone had now idealized in terms of expectations. Marti was in, then out, then back in again, then finally out. She did care deeply for Greg, but her good life on Sanibel had gotten even better after Alison Swanson had matched her with Jeffrey recently. That relationship seemed to be going somewhere; and Marti's fantasies were focused somewhere other than Tennessee just now. Jennifer Marin was the real surprise. No one had her on their radar as wanting to leave Sanibel. Her relationship with Clyde was smooth as far as anyone knew. She was so beautiful and athletic that she seemed relatively unapproachable, more like a supermodel that one only dared to glance at and not look too closely lest one fell hopelessly in unrequited love. Everyone thought Clyde hit it lucky mostly because he was funny and superficial. No one thought, and rightly so, that Clyde and Jennifer were a serious match.

That was how they each would want it to be. That was why they worked as a couple – minimum commitment, maximum fun.

So it *was* that when Jennifer approached Fernando about the rumors of the group's eminent departure, he was shocked beyond words. He felt like the ugly duckling that had just become a swan when *she* approached *him*. As they talked and he got to know her better, he cringed inside as he recognized a reverse discrimination on his part. She seemed down-to-earth in a level headed sense. Her native good lucks had taken her further from her roots than she had wanted. Her intelligence had allowed her to stay comfortable with any social setting, but her comfort level did not assuage her integrity, and she simply had had it with the superficial schemes, the conceit, and frankly the loose morality of the rich and famous. She was a world class tennis star who had easy inroads to Sanibel society, but she wanted no more of it. It was time to leave and get to something a bit more reality oriented. She was not looking for hardship – none of them were – but she did desire a place where the people were more real. She also wanted someplace relatively safe, and she wasn't afraid to work. She had a strong work ethic. The Farm seemed worth a look.

The three travelers met at Castaway's marina. Jesse was there and so was Captain Bill, a long time Captiva native and rum guzzler, whose Catalina sailboat was usually docked at Tarpon Bay. Tonight they had other plans for the 35-foot beauty.

Jesse spoke first. "The place sure won't be the same without you. You will be sorely missed. You know that."

"We'll miss you and a bunch of others, Jesse, but it's time to be moving on," said Fernando.

"I know that's right," said Jesse. "You wouldn't be going anywhere with this old rummy if you didn't have fierce convictions. You must be desperate," Jesse continued, teasing his old friend Captain Bill.

"Hell, I'll get 'em there! Sail 'em all the way to Tennessee if they want," Bill protested. The Captain looked his passengers up and down as if he were seeing them for the first time. "Aye, they're a fit group. I'll have 'em turned into master sailors before we reach Tampa."

"Just how are you going?" asked Jesse.

"We thought about an overland route, but it's just too dangerous," Greg jumped in, "what with all the road jackals, as Lopez calls them. There is no way on God's green Earth I would try to go through Atlanta. Talk about your urban jungles!"

"We've talked it over a bunch for the last week or two," added Fernando. "It was Captain

Bill who suggested that we take the Intracoastal Waterway to Mobile, then up the Mobile river, the Tombigbee River and waterway, all the way to the Tennessee river. We can work our way over land from there. It definitely seemed the safest route, and probably quicker, too."

"I wouldn't have thought of it, Bill," said Jesse admiring the old sea Captain. "And you guys," he added focusing now on the group, "are damn lucky to have somebody like Bill offer to run you up there."

"Oh, I'm charging them. Don't worry about me," Bill chimed in.

"He's not charging hardly anything," protested Greg. "Barely enough for food and gas."

"Not planning on needing much gas," Bill justified his generosity.

"Getting what you pay for with that one," Jesse teased again. "He'll probably get you lost for sure."

Captain Bill had had enough of teasing and flattery and wasting time. He was ready to get this show on the road. "Load the gear in the cabin," he told his group. "If you don't need it, don't weigh us down. You'll have to carry it on your back later."

"We are packing light, Bill. Just carrying the sum total of our lives and the essence of our souls and being," Greg surmised.

Jennifer had remained quiet, smiling at the banter, but serious at the thought of exchanging one life for another. She had packed two pair of shoes – one for tennis, another for walking – and a pair of Timberline boots for working. All six were stuffed with gold and a few diamonds: the hard asset fortune of one who was better off. She knew to stay quiet about her largess. She knew, too, to carry her own load. She trusted her companions but she didn't want to burden them with knowledge of her risky payload. They were as likely to run across road bandits as not. They would be relatively secure while they were on the boat, but even that setting was vulnerable to raids by pirate ships. Her upper body strength allowed her to carry her backpack as if it were stuffed with laundry.

Jennifer swung lightly over the rail and onto the Catalina 320MKII. She scurried down into the spacious cabin. Being the fairer sex, she was assigned the V-shaped forward berth with its hanging locker. She tossed her backpack onto her V-berth and climbed back into the night air. Back on the dock she turned to Jesse and said, "You and I never had a chance, did we?"

"But not for any reason," he reassured her. "We just didn't have anything in the way of *chance* encounters," he grinned a crooked grin. "I guess we hung with different crowds, mostly."

She hugged him briefly, but well enough for him to feel what he had missed. "Too bad," she said.

"Yeah," he agreed too readily. "May-*be*."

Captain Bill was in the cockpit now, starting the Yanmar engine. He would not hoist sail until they were underway with a fair wind at their back. "All ashore that's going ashore," he called out as if he were the captain of a cruise liner.

Eagerness mixed with trepidation was the heady brew that had their collective adrenaline flowing. The adrenometer would have pegged into the red if they had known Island Security was tracking them by geosynchronous satellite.

.　　.　　.　　.　　.

At the Sundial headquarters Captain Rodriguez was on duty scanning satellite images for activities of all types. He had followed Captain Bill's short journey from Tarpon Bay to Castaway's. He had attended to the small group as they mingled. He thought it was an unusual time to go for a sail but the tide charts were favorable and the idol lifestyle on Sanibel lent itself to odd schedules. It was pitch black with the new moon, and that bothered the Afghani veteran more than the timing. A nautical accident might happen and Island Security might be called on to mount a rescue mission. "They think we're the damn Coast Guard," Rodriguez muttered under his breath.

He tracked the larger of the two crafts as it pulled into Pine Island Sound and headed north-northwest. *The fool must be spotlighting the islands,* thought Rodriguez. He couldn't conceive of the skill that it would take to navigate the islands otherwise. He did not know Captain Bill. Rodriguez went back to other tasks. He had expected Jesse to sail out with the larger yacht, but none of this behavior was as Rodriguez expected. Still, there was nothing threatening about the launch. They were going for a midnight sail in pitch dark blackness. "Maybe it was a candlelight cruise," he snickered to himself. *Bunch of rich fools,* he thought. Maybe they were going on an extended trip. *Good, then,* he thought. *That's one less sniveling parasite to pick up after.* Rodriguez was not overly fond of his protectorates. He was becoming a resentful Doberman.

.   .   .   .   .

Michael Wilson visited Brady Chapman. "Thanks for coming, Dr. Wilson," said Chapman. "I have been surprised at how slow this injury has been to heal."

"Tell me how it happened," said Dr. Wilson as he examined Chapman's chest wall.

257

"Well, as I said, I was driving the Gator and looking the other way when I ran into a branch rather straight on. It knocked me off the little tractor. I felt like I had lost a jousting match," he said smiling.

Wilson was compressing the chest now with two hands. "Does it hurt when I do this?" he asked.

"Yes. A bit, but not where you are pressing; more here," Chapman indicated the area where the bullet had impacted the Kevlar vest.

"How about now?" asked Wilson.

Chapman winced before he smiled this time. "Yes, that hurts," he said.

"Let me listen to your lungs," requested Wilson. He spent considerable time listening to the different regions of Chapman's lungs with his stethoscope.

"What's the verdict?"

"I would say you have cracked a rib," suggested Dr. Wilson. "Would you be able to come in for x-rays."

"Is that necessary?" asked Chapman. "I agree with your diagnosis, but it's just a matter of time, at this point, until it heals, isn't it?"

"No, it's not necessary. You will be fine without x-rays," Wilson reassured him. "I can give you some hydrocodone to take as needed for pain."

"Did you find any other problems or issues? You seemed to check me in places I wouldn't have thought to look."

"Just trying to be thorough," assured Dr. Wilson. "No, again. I think you are good to go. The chest wound is minor – a cracked rib and some overlying contusions. There is no evidence of a pneumothorax; no jagged rib causing a punctured lung. You can do whatever you feel like doing," assured Dr. Wilson again. "Go back to Europe, if that's what you are wondering."

"I just might, doctor. Thank you."

Chapter Sixteen

Several days later Beverly and Jesse were at Castaways Marina cleaning *Serenity* in anticipation of taking Marti Leinhart and Jeffrey Rodgers on a day sail. The itinerary included a visit to a friend's beach house on North Captiva. It was still early, but there was a fair wind, and Jesse was growing impatient to cast off. Beverly disappeared into the cabin while Jesse was rubbing the cabin door with teak oil. He was sitting in the cockpit with the door on his lap when Beverly returned with a cup of coffee. He took it and smiled. Beverly sat across from him with her own cup, balancing the boat. She was pensive, but without the melancholy part that sometimes accompanies being seriously thoughtful.

"Do you ever think about us?" she asked.

"All the time," Jesse replied.

It was not what she had meant, but it was a damn good answer. She was wondering whether she and Jesse had a future; whether their love would grow, persisting into eternity; whether they would take their relationship to the next level. He was either ensconced in the here and now, or cleverly and deliberately avoiding the bigger questions. *Men!* She thought with exasperation. She sighed audibly.

"You OK?" he asked.

"Oh, *hell* yes," she replied sweetly. And she meant it.

An hour later *Serenity* was about as clean as she could be. The breakfast dishes were clean and stowed.

"I think I hear them," said Beverly.

"Yes," confirmed Jesse.

Jeffrey and Marti arrived in Jeffrey's electric Porsche. It was a beautifully designed very high-tech vehicle. No one was certain where Jeffrey got his money. It was not from the civil service position of being an NSA agent. That salary started at about fifty thousand dollars and rarely rose higher than seventy thousand. You do not get to Sanibel on a civil servant's salary. Of course those positions disappeared a decade ago with the collapse. Working counterterrorism for the National Security Agency would obviously place an agent in a world of highly connected, wealthy, and powerful individuals. When the oaths of office disappeared, much opportunity was presented. That is at the same time clear and vague. Jeffrey Rogers wanted to keep it that way.

Marti was a far more straight-forward person. She and Beverly first met at the University of South Florida in Tampa. She was a sophomore and Beverly was research assistant working on her doctoral thesis in marine biology. Beverly had graduated in biology from Centre College and moved to Tampa to pursue her doctorate. Marti followed Beverly to Sanibel, where Beverly had grown up, after the university closed for the last time. The causeway was still intact and there was not yet a means test. It wasn't until then that Marti discovered a talent for hair styling. She could make people look perky or pretty; but more importantly she could make people feel good about the way they looked. She had an easy conversational style and she was smart; she could listen empathetically or she could motivate. Often the encounter was exactly what her client needed. She was a therapist of sorts, without the stilted baggage or any expectations on anyone's part. The energy could flow more freely that way. Women who had the means to go anywhere in the world would go to no one other than Marti for their hair. Of the four people going sailing, ironically Marti was the only one with any serious income.

Jesse O'Connell was giving Jeffrey Rodgers a crash course in sailing: rigging terms, navigation, safety (including how to duck for a swinging boom), how to read the wind by its patterns on the water and in the tell-tales, and how to tack. The rest he could learn as they went.

Both gasoline tanks were full. Jesse started the small outboard motor, untied the lines, and tossed them onto the dock. The four were moving into Pine Island Sound at the beginning a lovely day's sailing trip. The wind was light but the C&C 27 was adept in light winds. The wind would pick up dramatically once they maneuvered into the gulf.

Jesse handed Jeffrey the halyard and Jeffrey hoisted the main sail. There was sufficient wind that Jesse could shut off the little engine. The resultant quiet showered them with peace.

Jeffrey was a quick study, but the real surprise was Marti. She took to sailing as if it were natural. Beverly was a patient instructor, and it was an opportunity for her to articulate all that she had learned from Jesse. Jesse, of course, was the master – more comfortable on his sailing yacht than he was on land.

They were navigating the many small islands bayside of Cayo Costa when they came into the open waters of Charlotte Harbor. Marti hoisted the jib and the watercraft moved swiftly between the land masses of Gasparilla Island and Cayo Costa on its way out to the open sea. Smiles abounded.

The day was sunny without being hot; the sea breeze helped in that regard. Jeffrey and Marti were having ice cold beer in long neck bottles. Jesse and Beverly were sticking to water for the moment. The day was young.

They sailed back and forth to the west of the barrier islands, going as far south as the southern edge of Sanibel before turning around the first time. Their northern extent was the far end of Gasparilla Island. They never went so far out that they couldn't see land, but they could have sailed to Mexico if they so desired.

What they desired, however, was lunch. They put in at the North Captiva beach house of a friend – Professor Isaac Zugat, the inventor of the holographic computer screen. Professor Zugat spent his days in highly secure research enclaves, usually in North Carolina, Colorado, or Massachusetts. When he took time for himself, he had this place and a Swiss villa among his choices. Recently, however, he was consumed with his dabbling into smart car technology. Jesse had carte blanche to visit and use the beach house whenever he wished – very convenient for an inveterate sailor.

They secured *Serenity* to the private dock and went up to the massive redwood and glass dwelling that used the term *beach house* euphemistically. Jesse had come here yesterday while he was sailing alone. He had stocked the refrigerator with manchego (his favorite cheese), grapes, spinach, and portabella mushrooms among other items.

While Beverly negotiated with a bottle of Rioja concerning the issue of the surrender of its cork, Jesse heated the grill to high, brushed the mushroom caps on both sides with olive oil and grilled them, cap side down, until they were lightly charred. On these he would pile a slice of manchego cheese, some sautéed spinach, and a drizzle of sherry vinaigrette; then another mushroom cap, more vinaigrette, spinach, another slice of cheese, and a third mushroom cap on top. More drizzling and garnishing with chopped chives, then *voila!* Awesomesauce!

After lunch they lounged in the brightly lit dayroom. Jesse was fixated on the highly polished spruce of the cathedral ceiling. Beverly was reading. The music on the sound system was smooth jazz. A sleepy couple was cuddling in an oversized chaise lounge.

Beverly turned to Marti and suggested, "You poor babies look like you could use a nap."

"We were up kind of late," she perked up at the thought of some afternoon delight with Jeffrey.

Jeffrey took the hint and ran with it. "Yeah," he exaggerated a stretch and yawn. "Sounds good to me, too."

Marti stumbled to her feet acting too sleepy to walk straight and Jeffrey played along again by pushing her weaving body up the stairs, slow fun foreplay, one foot after the other. In an upstairs bedroom, Marti was out of her clothes and between the sheets first. Jeffrey wasted no time, but at a gentleman's pace. He climbed into bed and held her close. He rolled on top of her and she opened to him, as natural as life gets. Deliberate deep and slow thrusts yielded to energetic acts of desperate need until they collapsed, thrilled and laughing – until they fell asleep.

Beverly checked on them for the second time. "They are still sleeping. What do you think?"

"We might better wake them," suggested Jesse. "We want to make Castaways before dark."

"Right," agreed Beverly as she turned and headed back upstairs.

On the sail homeward, Jesse kept the speed down and the course straight. Jeffrey and Marti were cuddled in comfort on the cabin cushions and that was fine with him. If he and Beverly were trying to add support for their fledgling relationship, today's trip had exceeded their expectations. Meanwhile he and Beverly had never been better. She was cuddling to Jesse in the cockpit as they sailed, and a more comfortable warmth was never known. He could no longer imagine his life without her.

.	.	.	.	.

Another group of sailors was making its way along the Intracoastal Waterway toward the Tombigbee system of rivers and canals. Captain William Fitzpatrick, Fernando Lopez, Greg Johnston, and Jennifer Marin had made good progress in the 35-foot Catalina sailing yacht. They were passing Dauphin Island and approaching Mobile Bay. Captain Bill was scrutinizing his charts to determine how far up the Mobile River he could safely navigate.

One danger to navigation that Captain Bill had not anticipated was sunken pilings and marine debris that, when the economy had functioned, would have been cleared as a matter of proper maintenance. Storms produced dangers that had not been set right, and there was no upgrade to the NOAA navigational charts on which sailors of all stripes depended. The point was driven home when a bone jarring *thud* caused the sailing vessel to lurch and list as the *screech* of rusty iron against her hull suggested that they had struck a sunken ship.

"I am afraid that I have taken you about as far as I can, young wayfarers," said Bill. "I will set you ashore if we stay afloat that long."

"Damn, Bill. I hope your ship is not seriously damaged," said Greg.

"She'll be fine, son. Don't you worry. We've been through worse. Still, if you would, take a peek in the bilge and make sure that it's dry," Captain Bill requested of his crewman.

"There's a little water, Bill," Greg called up to him a minute later.

"Just a little?" Bill asked.

"No more," Greg confirmed.

"That's normal enough. We'll keep an eye on her," Captain Bill reassured them. "What are your plans after you get off?" They were passing the Mobile Bay Lighthouse. It was a dilapidated structure supported by seven legs, one in the middle and six more in a hexagonal pattern, sitting (rotting) in the middle of the bay. Bill muttered as an aside, "That thing should have been demolished years ago – nothing but another hazard now."

"Same as if we had made it a distance upriver," said Fernando. "Try to find somebody trustworthy to let us hitch a ride with them. Either that or pay somebody. Guess we can walk if we have to, but you know that wouldn't be smart."

Bill muttered to himself, "Need to stay in the channel. The bay is shallow; needs dredging."

"I am guessing that we all brought some money. I know I have some I can contribute," Jennifer added. She was trying to reassure the other two that she would be contributing her fair share.

Mobile had devolved into a frontier harbor town. You could get anything and everything for a price, but mostly you could get dead. "People would kill you as soon as they'd look at you," one old timer told them. Prostitutes, thieves, and murders *were* the rule of law. If you didn't like it, you might want to move on. That being the case, it was with some sense of relief when Captain Bill, after traversing the remainder of the harbor smoothly, decided that he could indeed go a few miles up the Mobile River – "just to check it out". The Captain was a good man: they could never repay him for the risk he was taking.

At the northern extent of Mobile Bay, the alarm on the depth gauge sounded, confirming the Captain's fears. "She'll go no further, mates. The river is silted in and getting more shallow by the second." Bill was hurrying to drop the mainsail before the wind impacted the centerboard into the riverbed. Fernando was feeding out the halyard on the jib. With both sails down Greg and Jennifer worked to fold the sails and stow them in their zippered covers. Captain Bill had started the Yanmar engine and the crew could feel the tension in the revving of the motor as Bill threw it into reverse and willed his ship to slow down and back up. The centerboard did hit bottom – they could feel it – but lightly, and the great ship did begin to reverse course. They had dodged a narrow one.

"What's your pleasure?" asked Bill. "Would you rather swim to shore or have me drop you off in Mobile?"

"Swim, I suppose," said Fernando hoping to avoid trouble.

Greg nodded, but Jennifer looked concerned. Her pack weighed a lot with the gold coins in it.

"How about that private dock we spotted a short distance back?" she asked. "Would that be a reasonable alternative?"

"Sure, I think so. I don't know what or who you will run into there or anywhere else, but you will be finding out soon enough in any case," said Bill.

The men nodded in agreement.

Book Three

Chapter Seventeen

RESOLVED, that Constance M. Pollard, President of the United States, is impeached for high crimes and misdemeanors, and that the following articles of impeachment to be exhibited to the Senate:

ARTICLES OF IMPEACHMENT EXHIBITED BY THE HOUSE OF REPRESENTATIVES OF THE UNITED STATES OF AMERICA IN THE NAME OF ITSELF AND OF ALL OF THE PEOPLE OF THE UNITED STATES OF AMERICA, AGAINST CONSTANCE M. POLLARD, PRESIDENT OF THE UNITED STATES OF AMERICA, IN MAINTENANCE AND SUPPORT OF ITS IMPEACHMENT AGAINST HER FOR HIGH CRIMES AND MISDEMEANOURS.

ARTICLE 1

*In her conduct of the office of President of the United
States, Constance M. Pollard, in violation of her
constitutional oath faithfully to execute the office of
President of the United States and, to the best of her
ability, preserve, protect, and defend the Constitution of
the United States, and in violation of her constitutional
duty to take care that the laws be faithfully executed, has
prevented, obstructed, and impeded the administration
of justice, in that:*

*On June 17, 2022, and prior thereto, agents of the
Committee for Patriotism committed unlawful entry of
the headquarters of the United States Attorney General,
for the purpose of removing documents pertinent to her
valid conduct of high office. Subsequent thereto,
Constance M. Pollard, using the powers of her high
office, engaged personally and through her close
subordinates and agents, in a course of conduct or plan
designed to delay, impede, and obstruct the investigation
of such illegal entry; to cover up, conceal and protect
those responsible; to conceal the existence and scope of
other unlawful covert activities; and to commit murder
against the person of the Unites States Attorney
General, Alfred B. Sloan.*

*The means used to implement this course of conduct or
plan included one or more of the following:*

1.   *making false or misleading statements to lawfully authorized investigative officers and employees of the United States;*

2.   *withholding relevant and material evidence or information from lawfully authorized investigative officers and employees of the United States;*

3.   *approving, condoning, acquiescing in, and counseling witnesses with respect to the giving of false or misleading statements to lawfully authorized investigative officers and employees of the United States and false or misleading testimony in duly instituted judicial and congressional proceedings;*

4.   *interfering or endeavoring to interfere with the conduct of investigations by the Department of Justice of the United States, the Federal Bureau of Investigation, the office of the Committee for Patriotism Special Prosecution Force, and Congressional Committees;*

5.   *approving, condoning, and acquiescing in, the surreptitious payment of substantial sums of money for the purpose of obtaining the silence or influencing the testimony of witnesses, potential witnesses or individuals who participated in such unlawful entry and other illegal activities;*

6.   *endeavoring to misuse the Central Intelligence Agency, an agency of the United States;*

7.   *disseminating information received from officers of the Department of Justice of the United States to subjects of investigations conducted by lawfully authorized investigative officers and employees of the*

United States, for the purpose of aiding and assisting such subjects in their attempts to avoid criminal liability;

8.   making or causing to be made false or misleading public statements for the purpose of deceiving the people of the United States into believing that a thorough and complete investigation had been conducted with respect to allegations of misconduct and murder on the part of personnel of the executive branch of the United States and personnel of the Committee for Patriotism, and that there was no involvement of such personnel in such misconduct: or

9.   endeavoring to cause prospective defendants, and individuals duly tried and convicted, to expect favored treatment and consideration in return for their silence or false testimony, or rewarding individuals for their silence or false testimony.

In all of this, Constance M. Pollard has acted in a manner contrary to her trust as President and subversive of constitutional government, to the great prejudice of the cause of law and justice and to the manifest injury of the people of the United States.

Wherefore Constance M. Pollard, by such conduct, warrants impeachment and trial, and removal from office.

Additional articles of impeachment went on to detail the personal involvement in the murder of the attorney general who, along with key paperwork and evidence against President Pollard, simply disappeared from the face of the Earth. After an extensive search, he was thought to have been cremated or vaporized – but among the *Disappeared* he was.

The articles of impeachment detailed additionally the failure of President Pollard to execute the office of President of the United States that called on her to preserve, protect, and defend the Constitution of the United States, in order to ensure that the laws be faithfully executed: specifically, a failure to provide for the common defense as the citizens of Mexico overwhelmed the U.S.A./Mexico common border; a failure to promote the common welfare as food riots resumed and law enforcement disintegrated; and, well, there were so many treasonous "failures", their enumeration became an overwhelming indictment.

Whether the motion for impeachment would lead to the processes required to remove a sitting president from office remained to be determined. At one time the presidency was considered among the most powerful offices in the world; even now it was still powerful. How much so is what remained to be seen.

President Pollard vehemently denied the allegations and decried the witch hunt. She spoke to the American people using streaming Internet video, making her case in her lovable folksy way. She evoked her Christian supporters – her special ones who could see she was chosen in a miraculous act that stupefied the pollsters and other detractors – to cast aside the lies of Satan that were everywhere in these end times. Surrounded by flags and family, she appealed to patriots and lovers of freedom to not be swayed by the political forces of evil.

To many of the American people, she was right as always – America's last, best hope, as her campaign slogan said. It was she, after all, who moved the country back to the gold standard (after the necessities of the collapse did so first). To many others of the American people, she was as insane as always; not *clinically* insane, but delusional, anti-scientific, irrational, coldly conniving and deceptive to be sure. She had her *mendacity* on, and it was in high gear.

To *most* of the American people, it was merely Washington as usual. How *was* that last shipment of cocaine, Senator?

.   .   .   .   .

Forewarned is forearmed was a maxim in which General Douglas firmly believed. His intel regarding Island Security was scant however. The team led by Robinson had returned safely and undetected, but without any high value intel. Douglas could have guessed that the sanctuary landing would fare better than the one at the populated site chosen for Birch. Douglas did not know the fate of Birch and his men, and that concerned him. It was clear that they were dead or captured. Either way was not good.

. . . . .

General Presswood had many advantages: professional troops, gung-ho and pumped on steroids; the element of surprise – Island Security had never left Sanibel in force, and no one would anticipate the brazen move; detailed intelligence about troop strength, leadership caliber, headquarters location, barracks locations, and more gleaned from the acid drip incident; and last, but not at all least, the latest in high-tech weaponry. He had new toys he was eager to test under combat conditions. The most highly anticipated were the powerful Fükkrrand guns – more like high speed cannons – that were capable of rending men and earth so severely that testing on Sanibel was not possible.

The resultant combat was a massacre. Two days prior to the mainland invasion, General Presswood gathered and briefed his officers, and introduced them to the officers of the new battalion, approximately 320 men in two companies who would more than double their ranks. The officers then briefed their troops and staged the marine craft for deployment.

One day prior to deployment, the men were rested and fed, encouraged to work out or go for a run, and were reminded frequently of the Widow MacIntyre and of Sergeant Bell. The men wanted payback. They wanted to rip those mainland-bastards' heads off!

General Presswood's forces assembled before dawn. They were planning a direct frontal assault – overwhelming force to "send a message". They were primed and pumped and ready. On the beach beside the rafts, they were bouncing around like a boxer in the corner of the ring, waiting for the bell.

The first wave of troops was nearly to the mouth of the Caloosahatchee River when the volley of rocket fire from the mainland took out two rafts. *Bad mistake*, thought Rodriguez at Island Security headquarters. *Couldn't hold it in your pants any longer, could you?* he thought as he transferred satellite generated coordinates into the computer's launch codes. Moments later the first of several missile strikes took out the mainland's missile systems. Moments after that he launched the prearranged missile strikes that would take out the mainland's headquarters and barracks. *If the attack troops don't hurry, they are not going to have much to do,* thought Rodriguez.

By ten a.m. General Douglas and 350 of his followers were surrounded by Island Security troopers as they were camped in defensive positions along the Caloosahatchee River. A small number of the mainland forces had been dispatched and were on their way to Fort Myers, in hopes of persuading others to serve as reinforcements, but they were intercepted and killed. During the first hour more of Presswood's soldiers arrived at the site and began to set up their new electronics guided artillery: four powerful Fükkrrand guns capable of rapid fire, gyro-stabilization, and satellite guidance. These were placed along the south and west regions surrounding the mainland forces' camp.

At noon, Colonel Forsyth, the onsite ranking officer of the combined Island Security forces, ordered the surrender of weapons and the immediate removal and transportation of the mainland forces from the "zone of military operations" to awaiting rafts. Angered by the demands of the enemy, the mainland forces officers urged their troops to put on their courage and defy the demands of Island Security forces. At that moment a young mainland soldier raised his gun in protest screaming that he had paid good money for his weapon and was not going to just give it to anyone.

Forsyth's troops had surrounded the mainland forces. Douglas saw how hopeless it would be to fight, but he wanted to extract some modicum of revenge for LaFerla. He considered surrender as the only prudent course, but his hesitation was all that it took. Shots rang out. With the sounding of gun shots, the Island Security troopers began shooting at the mainland forces, many of whom were unarmed. The powerful Fükkrrand guns ripped the hapless mainland forces apart.

Island Security troopers rushed the encampment. At first the struggle was fought at close range; fully half the mainland forces' men were killed or wounded before they had a chance to get off any shots. Some of the mainlanders grabbed rifles from fallen comrades and opened fire on the soldiers. With no cover, and with many of the mainland forces unarmed, this phase of the fighting lasted a few minutes at most. While the infantry soldiers were shooting at close range, the artillery soldiers turned to use the powerful Fükkrrand guns against the encampment of women and children nearby. The women and children – the wives, lovers, sons, and daughters of the men now being slaughtered – tried to flee their camp, seeking shelter in a nearby creek bed. Forsyth's officers had lost all control of their men. Some of the soldiers fanned out to run across the battlefield and finish off wounded civilians. By the end of the fighting, which lasted less than an hour, at least 250 mainland soldiers had been killed and 50 mortally wounded. Island Security troop casualties numbered 25 dead, some from friendly fire due to the difficult logistics of close quarter combat. Thirteen were wounded.

Following the massacre that day, Island Security soldiers left the wounded mainlanders to die in a three-day process of slow exsanguinations, semitropical heat, and dehydration. They later hired civilians to remove the bodies and bury them in a mass grave. A message had certainly been sent.

.   .   .   .   .

Things were not much more civilized in Ireland – never had been. This was a nation of warriors from time immemorial. The devolutionary forces in Ireland appeared to be getting the upper hand over the Republicans. On the current trajectory, there would be no attempts at building an island nation anytime soon. Powerful chieftains were backed by armies of men whose goal was to secure and defend territory. The regions of conflict were separated roughly into the four historical provinces of Leinster, Ulster, Munster and Connaught. The clans in the counties of these regions were at war. The fighting was not between these ancient and venerable provinces. That blood sport would come later – after the Great Chieftains of all four provinces were selected.

The men of Liam O'Neill wore face paint identifying them as such, so unafraid were they of reprisals. Liam O'Neill was the undisputed leader of the Ulster province. The well-timed assassination of McMasters assured his ascendance as the forces of provincial unification were emboldened and the British influence was swept away. The form that the unification would adopt was inchoate. The key players, however, were becoming clearer – *more* obvious – and their relationships, one to another, better structured.

O'Neill came from a line of the O'Neill clan derbfine – a power structure based on kinship – that was widely recognized as the legitimate successors to the chieftainship of the O'Neills, the ancient historical line of Ulster kings dating back fourteen centuries if not more. Hugh O'Neill was of this same lineage, ruling this same region over four hundred years previously. Liam O'Neill was Hugh's great-great-great-great-great-great-great-great-great-great-great-great-great-great-great-

great-great-great-grandson. Going back twenty generations would have kept the ancient bards busy recalling such an impressive legacy.

Liam O'Neill's career was marked by unceasing power politics. At one time he appeared to submit to British authority, and at another he intrigued against the Dublin government in conjunction with lesser Irish lords. It was he who did the most to revive the remnants of the Irish Republican Guard, enveloping them within his clans. It was he who supported the latest wave of bombings, including the one that rocked Belfast this year at the British military headquarters where Oliver Cromwell Nielson, the conservative Tory member of the House of Lords, drew his last breath. It was he who was most widely presumed to have directed the assassination of Prime Minister McMasters.

Liam O'Neill had bribed officials both in Ireland and in London for years. Though initially supported by the Dublin administration, he seemed to grow increasingly uncertain whether his position as head of the O'Neills was best advanced by alliance with the Dublin-based Irish government or by rebellion against them in advance of his own provincial government in Ulster. Until he became more certain, he could play the role either way as the situation demanded, and still gain.

O'Neill gradually fell into a barely concealed opposition to the national governments of both England and Ireland, especially as they weakened dramatically in the aftermath of the *Great Collapse*, as it was known in Ireland. The Dublin-based Irish government especially irked the chieftain, and he, *the O'Neill*, proclaimed that it was just as unctuous and vile as the genocidal English from which it sprang. Liam O'Neill was proclaimed a traitor by the Dublin-based Irish government, but they had neither the political will nor the military resources to pursue the notion further. A proclamation by the Houses of the Oireachtas – both the Dáil Éireann (House of Deputies) and Seanad Éireann (Senate) – was the most that they could afford and concoct.

Liam O'Neill had no plans to bomb or invade the capital of Ireland as he had Belfast. No, he would be content to rule Ulster. He would leave Dublin to the descendants of Úgaine Mor (Hugony, the Great), and Finn Mac Cool. The tribes of Leinster were united by several minor chieftains. They were not as far along as the tribes of Ulster, but they were getting there.

It was clearly Liam O'Neill, if not Ireland herself, who gained dramatically from the rebalancing of power. The British had *not* the popular desire, the political means, nor the military resources to pursue the Irish "troubles" further.

After so many centuries of occupation and genocide, the British and their minions were inexorably being expunged from Irish soil.

Although the aphorism is often attributed to Thomas Jefferson, it was actually Henry David Thoreau who said: *That government is best which governs least.* If this is so, then planet Earth was becoming an increasingly better governed place in the aftermath of the collapse.

.   .   .   .   .

Major Kipling Alderman was comfortable. He had nowhere he needed to be, and no issues requiring his attention at just this moment. He was considering calling Captain Damien Lincoln, Captain Ephraim Kimsey, and Lieutenant R.H. "Jack" Jackman to see if these fine officers were up for bowling. "Kip", as his closer comrades-in-arms called him, had become increasingly enthralled with the sport since they took over a bowling lanes business on the outskirts of Atlanta. Abandoned years ago along with most enterprises after the collapse, the facility was still more or less functional when they explored it, as long as one brought some newly enlisted troops to fetch the balls and set up the pins. The grunts would roll the balls back up the gutter to the awaiting officers. They had even found an old dust broom with which to sweep the lanes. Now after some mechanical repairs, even the automatic pin setters were functioning. Alderman was not sure he didn't like it better when his men had to do the work manually, the way it was done in the early days of bowling.

Before Kip could make any calls, however, Lincoln was on the horn with a more urgent matter.

"I already know about the police helicopter that was brought down yesterday by our guys," Kip began.

"This has nothing to do with that, Boss," said Captain Lincoln. "I think you need to get over here," Lincoln apprised the commander of the Southeast Alliance. "We have an issue."

"Ten-four," Major Alderman replied. His relaxed paramilitary style often mixed and combined catch phrases, and he could shift between being buddies or being commander-in-chief. But when he was in military mode, he was no-nonsense. He had spent too many years in too many wars.

Alderman arrived at headquarters in the old Lenox Square shopping center. With its parking garages and empty spaces (former retailers) he had abundant room for military command and control operations.

He walked into the offices of high command with the adjacent communications center. He spotted Lincoln and asked, "So what's with bringing down a police helicopter? I didn't think there were any left, or anyone left who could fly one for that matter."

"It's too bizarre to go into. Basically three of our men were intoxicated and needed some fresh weapons training with out of date technology. They took it upon themselves to appropriate an old Stinger missile from some stockpile or another. They were on the roof when a police helicopter flew over. I agree; I didn't think the remnants of Atlanta's Metro had anyone who could fly. I think the sucker was stolen! Anyway, these three blew them out of the sky. I'm just glad it wasn't any of our men up there."

"Where are these geniuses now?" asked Alderman.

"In the brig, still sobering up," replied Lincoln. "They could hardly walk when we found them on the roof. One was sitting on the tar with the Stinger in his lap, bent over the tube and sound asleep."

"What are you going to do with them?" asked Alderman. He already knew the answer.

"We are going to give them a fair trial and line them up and shoot them," said Lincoln with an odd grin.

"Good man," said Alderman. "We can't be wasting missiles, even old ones. Now what do you have for me that couldn't wait?"

"You better have a look at this!" said Lincoln, and he handed the major a collection of print outs from recent encrypted Internet communiqués. "We have a major development in South Florida."

"The first one is from Douglas," said Captain Kimsey as he approached the two, "alerting the region to an imminent invasion from some mercs who call themselves 'Island Security' and hold sway over anyone who might want to crash the garden parties on Sanibel Island."

"Sanibel?" says Alderman. "I hope we don't have to mess that place up. I've thought about moving there myself someday."

"The next series of messages is from Blaylock, the captain of the division in Fort Myers," Kimsey continued, ignoring his commander's retirement dreams. "He confirms that Island Security came in hard and heavy, basically massacred Douglas and his men. Killed their families, too. Left them to rot; left the wounded to die slow – *real* slow."

"No shit!" exclaimed Alderman. They had his undivided attention now.

"No shit. And there's more," Kimsey paused. "Blaylock thinks Island Security is sending a message to mainland forces: *Don't mess with us or else...*"

"No shit!" scoffed Alderman. "We'll see about that. Won't we?"

"Blaylock is afraid that he and his men might be their next targets. He's asking for reinforcements, just like Douglas did; but it was too late for Douglas."

"I am way ahead of Blaylock," declared Major Alderman. "Saddle up, men. Lincoln, you take the lead on this. Jackman!" Alderman called to the lieutenant who immediate strode to his side. "You get with the quartermaster and muster the troops. We leave at 0800 hours. Leave a thousand here in Atlanta; the locals will never miss us. Have the men increase their visibility here; patrol the streets a little. The locals might wonder what we are up to but they won't know we've deployed in substantial numbers. We'll take a dozen different routes out of town and converge in Macon. Notify General Williams in Macon. Brief him on the mission and have him gather several battalions. We will pick up others from population centers along the way. I want to be in Tampa this time tomorrow with invasion plans completed, Captain Lincoln. Remember Captain, you are from central command. You outrank all of these self-proclaimed "generals" that we are going to be coordinating."

"Yes, sir. I know."

"You, too, Lieutenant," Alderman nodded toward his officer. "Don't take any grief from anyone. Clear?"

"Clear, sir."

At dawn the first eighteen-wheeler carrying food, medical supplies, ammunition, and a MASH compound rolled out of the lower parking garage staging area of Lenox Square. The second had similar cargo but no field hospital, mostly large mess tents. A total of six of these tractor-trailer rigs left before the first of their military escorts joined them. These were followed by a squadron of urban tanks, the new army's cavalry, and these were followed by troop carriers. Major Alderman when he deployed was driven in an armor-reinforced Cadillac Escalade. Captain Lincoln rode with the major. They had plans to make and maps to review. At 0800 hours the last of the military vehicles left Lenox Square. Major Alderman's departure time meant the time at which the last vehicle leaves; not the first.

By 0930 they were approaching Macon. General Williams was ready and waiting. He joined Lincoln and Alderman in the Escalade. By 1000 hours the convoy was rolling south again. It stretched over one mile on the interstate. They would be in Tampa before dark, even with the other planned stops to gather the Army of the Association.

President Pollard's chief of staff, Madeline DeLorme, made some telephone calls and called in some favors. As a result, beginning next week the major television, cable, and Internet providers would be showing re-runs of the popular *Left Behind* series. The downloads would be offered at deep discounts also. It was a simple enough action plan, and the president's approval ratings always jumped higher whenever the association was foisted on the public. Seventy-two percent of the public were certain or very certain that mankind was currently in the *end days,* and that the rapture was at hand. Sixteen percent were not certain, and twelve percent did not know.

Chapter Eighteen

Chapman returned to Paris the day after Doctor Wilson cleared him physically; too bad he couldn't clear him mentally. Chapman had never had such a close call. He felt lucky to be alive. He was beginning to realize that this could be his last assignment. His orchids might need his full attention. He would have enough saved for a lifetime retirement, even on Sanibel, after this last job. *Last job!* Did that ever sound appealing! He could travel. He could even risk finding another companion – someone with whom he could share his life and someone with whom he could grow old gracefully. He did know someone – someone with whom he could share his love of orchids and cooking. Maybe he would stop by Key West on the way back to Sanibel.

Chapman had called the Hotel Georges V a second time as soon as he returned stateside. *No*, he was reassured; no one came around asking questions. *Yes*, they did pack up his belongings as requested. He had called them initially from the airport while waiting for his plane to Morocco – it was the first flight out. From there he had gone to Brazil, then Atlanta, then Fort Myers. It was all rather convoluted. He was gratified that he felt better with each successive flight. The wound, even with a rib fracture, was proving to be superficial.

Chapman called the Hotel Georges V a third time as soon as Dr. Wilson left. The staff was so pleased to hear from him. *Yes*, his items were in storage. *No*, everything was perfectly alright. *Yes*, his clothes would be laid out in his suite the day he arrived: everything would be in perfect order. *Fly safely, Monsieur!*

Brady Chapman arrived at the Hotel Georges V for the second time in recent weeks. He was greeted with the attention usually reserved for royalty. "We were so afraid we had displeased you, Monsieur Chapman. You left so abruptly," they said. "We are so glad that you could resolve your personal matter quickly."

In the following days Chapman took his time doing surveillance. He planned each and every detail of the next encounter and choreographed his moves in his hotel suite. *Tomorrow was Thursday night,* he thought. Wherever Monsieur Fitzroy, the art dealer, planned to dine, Chapman would be there. If the opportunity presented itself, this last job would be done.

It was an easy matter to watch the townhouse and follow the large black sedan undetected. It was easy also, because of the great amount of time the Parisian culture dedicates to the evening meal, to plan the final encounter to a finely honed mechanism—much like a Swiss watch with its finely integrated movements.

Monsieur Jean-Pierre Fitzroy was picked up at his townhouse at precisely 7:42. That meant a seventeen minute ride to the restaurant to accommodate his eight o'clock reservations. He would be easy to follow as always.

Jean-Pierre Fitzroy on this night had chosen Fellini: great Italian dishes with a film theater atmosphere. The sleek sedan pulled curbside at 47, rue de l'Arbre Sec, and Monsieur Fitzroy stepped out unassisted. He was a minute early so he loitered on the street for a moment, stretching his torso and looking around at the neighborhood. Chapman would never have expected such nonchalance; if he had, he would have made his move at this precise time. It was an opportunity lost, but there would be others.

There were cars parked on the street. Monsieur Jean-Pierre Fitzroy was lucky to have been able to find a spot near the door. He would not be so lucky when he came out. Chapman would borrow a few vehicles from the neighborhoods and park them advantageously. Monsieur Jean-Pierre Fitzroy would be forced to walk a short distance to his car. It was then that Chapman would make his long anticipated move.

At 9:45 p.m. Monsieur Fitzroy was greeted at Fellini's front door by his body guards. *They both walked with him now* thought Chapman. Smart, but not sufficient. Chapman approached them from the direction of their car, but paid them no unusual attention. Chapman was wearing a discrete disguise and his hair was dyed grey. His hat was a Mizen Head Irish tweed driving cap. His hands were in his coat pockets cuddling two Taser guns – one for each hand: one for each body guard. He would not be fired on again. Not this time!

They were narrowing the distance rapidly. Chapman looked up as they approached. Monsieur Fitzroy was boasting about his meal, especially the black truffle ravioli. His guards were unduly attentive to his story: they were probably hungry and thinking of when they would be off duty and could eat. They might even come back to Fellini. It was among Paris's best and still it was surprisingly affordable; and even if it were not, Fitzroy paid very well.

Chapman made his move. The body guards were *off* guard. Chapman, quick as anything, pulled the Tasers out of his pockets with both hands. He leveled the stun guns at each guard and pulled the trigger before they could react. The darts flew into the flesh of their targets and both guards began the writhing motions of someone being electrocuted. They were falling to the ground with no control of their skeletal muscle when the next surprise surfaced. Brady Chapman, with Tasers in each hand, watched helplessly as Monsieur Fitzroy produced his *own* gun. Chapman felt like an imbecile for not anticipating that Monsieur Fitzroy himself might be armed. He did not have to feel like an idiot for very long. As Chapman dropped the Tasers and reached for his hand gun, the 9 mm Ruger with a silencer, Monsieur Fitzroy took aim from six feet away and put a series of bullets into the erstwhile assassin – two in the head and two in the chest. Monsieur Fitzroy's body guards, who had suggested this extra measure of safety, would be so proud of him when they came to.

. . . . .

Fernando Lopez and Jennifer Marin were waiting for Greg Johnston to return. Captain Bill had gotten them to shore safely without getting stuck himself, so everyone was thankful for the way things had gone so far. By being cautious, or actually *circumspect*, maybe they could maintain their good fortune. They could not help but feel like characters in Cormac McCarthy's post apocalyptic novel, *The Road*. Perhaps the trek through Alabama, Mississippi, and Tennessee would not be as perilous as one might imagine, but this was one of the poorest areas of the country even before things got so bad. People would do what they needed to do to survive. The back roads were not safe, especially for outsiders. The Deep South was historically xenophobic and racist. None of these issues bode well for the three travelers. That is why Greg went alone to ask about transportation up the Tombigbee. He left his gold with Fernando, but took his gun.

He seemed overdue to the others when he appeared, rounding a corner a quarter mile down the dirt road. Greg waved and Jennifer left her cover of bushes, followed by Fernando. They met at a half-way point, and Greg seemed pleased.

"Good news," he said. "I think we are in luck. There is a marina. We can rent a pilot or buy an old boat."

"I vote for renting the pilot and his boat," said Fernando.

"*Her* boat," corrected Greg. "And I agree. Everybody seemed OK at the marina, but it might all be a big front. I think we can all go back there; just keep your eyes and ears open."

"For all *they* know, *we're* the ones who are armed and dangerous," said Jennifer.

"Yeah. I heard that," Greg agreed. "Just stay cautious. That's our by-word."

The trio approached the marina warily. The off-white paint was peeling from the wood and areas of the decking were missing. The boats appeared old but serviceable. They entered into the one room office area. A youngish woman was behind the low counter. She did not get up, but she did look up at them.

"Welcome back," she said pleasantly enough. "Are these your friends?"

"Jennifer and Fernando," Greg offered.

"Pleased to meet you, Jennifer and Fernando," she said. "My name's Marci."

"Greg says you might be able to take us up river," said Fernando. "Is that so, Marci?"

"That would be the case if we can come to terms." Marci was an old hand at negotiating and not getting taken; they could tell. "Tell you what though," she added. "You do not want to get caught on these back roads at night. And if you don't know the people along the river, well some of them pirates will kidnap you for the ransom, and kill you if they don't get it. It's a tough run, too, if you don't know the locks and who to pay and who to negotiate with."

Greg was feeling less easy, as if he were being set up for a scam, or at best an overpriced service.

"You make it sound like there aren't too many other options," observed Fernando.

"Honestly, if you are determined to go north from here, you got lucky finding me and this place," said Marci. "I'm about the best you are going to find. I admit I could use the money, but my daddy raised me right. People know me around here. I serve a purpose and they can trust me, so they look out for me. If you can believe half of what you hear, I'm doing pretty well. So, what's your pleasure? Want to fish or cut bait?"

"What is this safe passage going to cost us?" asked Fernando. "We aren't rich; just looking to start over."

Marci looked them over. They seemed sincere, maybe honest, too. She liked them enough. "I can take you for four ounces of gold...," she said. "Each...," she added; "plus gas."

"Ouch," said Greg, "Twelve ounces."

"Plus gas," Marci reminded him. "And I could have charged more, but that's it. Take it or leave it."

"A Hobson's choice," said Jennifer."

"What's that," asked Greg.

"I'll tell you later," she said.

"Y'all need to talk about it some?" asked Marci.

"It's not that. I'm just not sure if we have it. We sure won't have anything when we get where we are going," said Greg.

"Where are you going, if I might ask?" asked Marci.

"Place called *the Farm* in Tennessee," said Greg. He appeared to be the only one still talking. "You know it?"

"I've heard of it," replied Marci. "I kind of think of it as some kind of place where people with no direction go to find somebody who will tell them what to do. We do that farming and self-sufficiency stuff on our own around here."

It was clear Marci was on home turf. She was showing more self-esteem than one might have thought at first, Fernando was judging.

"But if you feel the call, then by all means, get yourself there. I'm here to help," Marci continued.

"For a price," said Jennifer.

"For a price," said Marci, staring her down.

"So, if we came up with twelve ounces," Fernando began.

"Plus gas," said Marci, staring *him* down now.

"…when exactly could we be leaving?" Fernando completed his question.

"For good money like that – half now: half on arrival upriver – I can be ready whenever you are."

"Enough talk," Jennifer said rather forcefully. "Let's do this."

"If we have the money," said Greg. They hadn't discussed each other's circumstances.

"We have the money," said Jennifer. "We may not have any when we get there, but first we have to get there," she said rather philosophically.

"I take it you are ready to leave today?" asked Marci.

"That would be best, I think," replied Greg as Fernando nodded his approval.

"I'll gas up the tank then," offered Marci. "While you cheapskates pool your resources, I'll need six ounces plus gas money upfront."

After Marci left for the dock, Fernando said, "Spoken like a woman who's been stiffed before."

"I don't know how she does it," Jennifer joined in. "It can't be easy working this place, living out here. Not knowing who or what might show up."

"I guess it's all she knows, Jennifer," offered Greg. "She's lived here her entire life. She can live here…"

Greg was startled into silence by the appearance in the doorway of a large black man in overalls and work boots, blocking the available light. "Where's Marci?" he demanded, looking them up and down.

"I'm down here, Sam," called Marci from the docks.

"You OK, Miss Marci?" Sam called back to her.

"I'm fine, Sam, but wait there a minute for me, can you?"

"Yes, ma'am, Miss Marci. I'm not goin' anywhere." Sam came into the small office and looked the three over a tad more deliberately this time. He had nothing to add to the conversation.

Marci came back into the office and had to twist to work her way through the bodies. Back in her chair behind the counter, she said, "Gas came to four tenths of an ounce, so your down payment is six-point-two ounces of gold."

Sam let out a low whistle. "No wonder you needed me to stay, Miss Marci. Sounds like there's a regular Fort Knox in here."

"Greg, I've got some baby Krugers," offered Jennifer. "Let me get the gas." She was searching her backpack and came up with two one-ounce coins and two one-tenth ounce coins. She handed them to Marci, who smiled at her.

Fernando and Greg produced two ounces each and the deal was done.

"Sam," said Marci.

"Yes ma'am," Sam responded.

"Sam," repeated Marci, "I'm going to take these three up river. I'll be gone a few days. Can you look after the place for me until I get back?"

"You know I can, Miss Marci. After all you've done for me, you know I can." Sam turned to Fernando because he was the oldest. "If Miss Marci doesn't come back safe and sound, I will find you and I will kill you."

"Oh, Sam!" Marci punched him. "These folks are OK. If they weren't, I would know, and I wouldn't try to help them get to that Farm in Tennessee, would I?"

"No ma'am I 'spect you wouldn't." He turned to the travelers. "What do y'all want to get to that Farm for? Nothin' there but old hippies."

"Guess we just need to see for ourselves, Sam," said Greg. He was starting to appreciate Sam. He was protective of Marci and because of Sam, Greg was more confident than before that she wouldn't sell them to the highest bidder upriver. But Sam had put doubts in his head about the Farm. Had he idealized the place beyond reasonable expectations? Time would tell.

Marci called out, "Let's get on the river. Anybody need to use the facilities before we go?"

There were three takers on the offer. As they filed out of the crude concrete block "facilities", Marci said to them, "There's some homemade ham and biscuits over there. Since I had to overcharge you on the gas, you can help yourself to them." There were three takers on that offer, too.

The journey upriver was uneventful, except it was remarkable for its beauty, the abundant wildlife, and the charm and friendliness of the people they met. When Fernando complimented Marci on knowing all the best people and the best places to stop and eat, she said to him that he was a silly fool. She told him that everybody in these parts was like that – kind and helpful. "Things haven't changed much for us," she told him. "Poor is a way of life, but so is helping each other make it. It's been that way since reconstruction: a hundred and fifty years of making do with what you've got. That collapse didn't change any of that for us. People label us any way they want to. That doesn't mean anything to us. We know who we are, and who our neighbors are. Folks around here are good to each other – a bit wary of strangers like you folks – but ready to help the good ones we see."

Fernando rode in silence for awhile as the boat churned against the current. When he spoke, it was to apologize. "I really want to say that I am sorry I stereotyped you and this region. The shame of it is that it happens to me all of the time. People look at Hispanics and right away they think of gangs and drugs, lazy workers, and ignorance. Hispanics are just as diverse as the next group. It's a shame people judge someone before they get to know them, but I see that I am just as guilty as the next one."

"That is not a problem, Fernando," she said. "It kind of reminds me about that joke where somebody thinks that a Southern intellectual is an oxymoron."

They looked at her uncomprehending.

"Never mind," she said. "It's not much of a joke.

"What did you do before you took on 'boat charters'?" asked Jennifer.

"I worked as a social worker around this area. I got my Masters degree at the Mississippi University for Women. It was a very good school. I still try to do what I can for people. The calling doesn't go away just because the system crashes down around you."

They rode in silence for much of the morning on the last day of their trip. Marci had taken them onto the Tennessee River and was studying her charts to determine the best place to drop them off for the last leg of their journey.

"I think the best course for you to take from here is for me to let you off at Cyprus Creek near Perryville," she said looking up at the others.

"From there you need to walk along highway 412 – same thing as state road 20 – and stay on it until you get to Hohenwald. That's about thirty miles. Then stay on 20 for maybe another twenty miles to Summertown. You might even get to the Farm before you get to Summertown. It's not exactly like it's on my charts, you understand."

The group put together the last six-point-two ounces of gold before Marci had anchored. By the time the boat came to a rest, the group was ready to finish their journey. Jennifer hugged Marci and said *thank you* more than once. Each of the three felt like they had been on a voyage of personal discovery, like an Outward Bound experience. "Thanks, again," they called from the bank as they waved good-bye.

"You're welcome. Stop in to see me if you get back down near Mobile," she called back. "And watch out for the elephants!"

"What did she mean by that?" Fernando asked Greg.

"I have no idea," said Greg.

"There was a large elephant preserve near Hohenwald. It lost support about ten years ago, so the elephants kind of run free between here and the Farm," said Jennifer. "Don't you guys read the paper?" she teased.

"Oh, great!" said Fernando. "And I thought all we had to worry about now was road jackals."

"Jackals and elephants," reflected Greg. "It's sounding more like a safari all the time."

The group was in good spirits when they put on their backpacks and headed east. "Let's see if we can make it as far as Hohenwald by night," said Fernando. Their chances for success rose immensely when a farm truck loaded with two round bales stopped and the driver, a bearded man in his sixties, asked them if they needed a ride into town. *What a nice place*, thought Jennifer, as she noticed the honest-to-goodness twinkle in his eye.

Chapter Nineteen

The travelers *did* see elephants. It turned out that the farmer who picked them up was delivering round bales of hay to a field where the elephants frequented. The locals chipped in to help keep the elephants fed. "It is astounding how much those creatures can consume," said the farmer with the twinkle in his eye. "It used to cost $125,000 a year for each elephant. You can't measure it that way now, but we do what we can around here. There are still a few donors, but mostly it falls to us around Hohenwald."

The three got out of the truck to help push the round bales over the side of the flat-bed Ford and onto the ground. "They trample half of it," he shrugged, and they stood back while an old cow ran over, head swaying and trunk swinging, to sample the offering. "That one's Minnie – Minnie the Mooch. They all have names. They stay pretty much to the original land from the original elephant sanctuary – it's about 2700 acres, so they are not cramped. They got used to it. As long as we take care of them, they have no place they would rather be. We kind of like having them here."

With each successive sentence, the farmer paused longer and longer before the next, until finally it was as if the engine just died. The group stood in rapt silence amazed by the giant gentle creature, and the two that wandered in afterwards.

Fernando asked the man, "How long have they been here?"

"This started sometime around 1995, I think," he paused. "I was in my thirties, so that sounds about right."

"How many elephants are there?" asked Jennifer.

"Can't rightly say for sure," admitted the farmer. "If the numbers have stayed steady, then there's probably about a hundred."

"That many!" exclaimed Greg. "That's more than I would have thought."

"We took on quite a few when so many of the zoos closed," the man said. "Where else could they have gone?"

Greg didn't want to offer him the obvious answer.

"You say you are heading for the Farm?" asked the farmer.

"Sure are," said Greg. "Can you give us directions? We don't really know which way to go from here."

"I can do better than that. Climb in. I'll take you there. It's just down the road."

"That is so kind of you," said Jennifer. "Let us at least buy you some gas."

"Well, OK! I won't turn down some gasoline."

As it turned out, a baby Krugerrand – one-tenth ounce of gold – in Hohenwald, Tennessee, was exactly the right amount to fill the nearly empty tank of a ten year old Ford F-350.

.   .   .   .   .

The Farm was a beehive of activity. The three of them, led by Greg, found their way to a central area of activity and introduced themselves as people who had traveled far to get there. They were greeted warmly and soon a young woman was chosen to show them around. She had lived on the commune – *intentional community*, they now called it – all of her life. Her name was Stacey.

Stacey began with the story of the place. "The Farm is a 1,750 acre commune that was founded by Stephen Gaskin, a former English professor at San Francisco State University. The Farm would be considered a 'service' or 'intentional' commune because of its social structure. People pool resources and agree to live a certain way with a motivating philosophy. Membership is more closed than it would be in an 'anarchistic,' or 'retreat' commune. Residents must commit to the commune's purpose and social organization, with leaders and rules."

Stacey went on to explain concepts like anti-materialism, not having any more than is needed in order for there to be enough to go around the world. "On the Farm," she said, "we are committed to strict vegetarianism because we believe there would be more food to go around the world if people ate soybeans instead of cattle." *She has a point,* thought Jennifer. *We might not have had food riots and starvation if the rest of the country and the world was even a little more like Stacey and her friends.*

"The primary purpose of communal living initially was to repersonalize a society," Stacey continued, "to make person to person relations the core of existence in order to promote greater intimacy and fuller human development." Stacey had said all of this before; she was well rehearsed.

"By rejecting the established order," she continued, "on which capitalism rests, competitiveness and production is replaced by unity and cooperative work. In communes people pool their resources and work together instead of against one another because an emphasis is no longer placed on competing for material goods, but instead on friendship and family. The Farm, for example, was economically based on the Book of Acts where it says: 'Those who believed shared all things in common; they would sell their property and goods, dividing everything on the basis of each one's needs.' There is no greater hypocrisy," said Stacey, "than a wealthy Christian; except the preachers who promote the idea of Christians getting rich."

Fernando touched Greg to get him to lean in toward him. He whispered, "If you were trying to find an antidote to all that Sanibel stands for, I think you just found it."

Stacey continued for another hour explaining concepts like permaculture and communal economics. She showed them their unique buildings and sustainable organic techniques for growing crops. She introduced them around as they explored the grounds.

The Farm seemed like a utopian society that was actually sustainable. It seemed to be about justice, sincerity, honesty, humanity, and peace. Greg and his friends felt like they had found their new home.

.   .   .   .   .

Major Kip Alderman, commander of the Southeast Alliance, was leaving Tampa with the largest force he had ever assembled. General Williams of the Macon division was impressed that the Army of the Alliance was as large as it was, and so well equipped from the years of collecting abandoned or captured equipment from the police stations, Army posts, and National Guard armories – ready and waiting to be put to good use. He joined Lincoln and Alderman in the Escalade SUV. With them now also was General Newton from the Orlando division. They were mid-position in the two mile long caravan, now less than two hours from Fort Myers, where Captain Blaylock was gearing up with his troops. As far as anyone knew, Sanibel would not see this coming.

The attack would have to be coordinated. The heavy equipment would do them no good except for the early bombardment from Punta Rassa and Pine Island. Island Security would return fire with missile launches of their own to be

315

sure, but Alderman's missiles were on eighteen-wheelers. He could move them after each volley from the island if necessary. Sanibel would be wasting missile strikes hitting targets where the trucks *had* been only minutes before. Stringfellow Road, down the center of Pine Island, would lend itself perfectly to that strategy. It was straight enough, and flat, that the truck could actually build up speed when needed.

After taking out their key positions with missile strikes, it would come down to what wars always came down to: boots on the ground. Here again the advantage was Alderman's. True, Sanibel was surrounded by a great natural defense system with its water barriers of the bay and the gulf, but armies have mounted amphibious invasions since time immemorial. This invasion would follow the military textbooks with minor exceptions. For one thing there would be no beachhead; no storming of entrenched defenses. For another, the water that began as an advantage should quickly become a liability for the island defenders. The water meant they would have no place to run and hide. *These rent-a-geardos better learn to embrace the suck, because they were going to wish they had never gone all Blackwater,* thought Alderman as he continued to come up with details and tactics for his overwhelming force.

The most devastating strategy of all, one that would make this escapade complete, was the plan to replace the gap in the causeway with the modern equivalent of the old pontoon bridge. A short gap like the one in the causeway could be filled with the new rolls of tubular steel rods, each nearly the length of a truck's trailer. The rods were bound into one massive roll by polymer sheets, and supported on the water surface by two giant attached airbags that would explode open and fill with air upon deployment. It should take two; anyway that is how many Alderman brought. If they don't span the gap, his men would have to fall back on barges to get the heavier equipment onto the island. He might not need the causeway if his men could capture what they need from the enemy combatants on the island. He didn't want to expend good foot soldiers by throwing them against tanks, though. He wanted them to have the right tools for the job. An open road from the mainland would see to that.

At Port Charlotte, Alderman dropped off General Newton and his Orlando division so that they could be commandeering an armada of boats for the gulf sided amphibious landing. "Get some barges, Jake," said Alderman. "Bring their pilots and crew, too, if you can," he added.

Alderman dropped off other officers and their men at North Fort Myers and Cape Coral.

317

"Commandeer everything that floats," he told them "We hit the beach at "0-dawn-thirty". His next stop was at Captain Blaylock's headquarters. He left the convoy on the interstate – out of sight, out of range.

Their deployment would be timed such that they would arrive two hours after the early morning shelling and missile strikes had done what they could to disrupt their command and control centers at the Sundial condominiums. *Oh, yes. Our intelligence information is that good.* The daily commutes of day laborers provided ample opportunities for Captain Blaylock to reconnoiter the island second hand. The details of information were confirmed several times over by independent sources. The games would begin at 0440 and would continue until the last player had gone home.

At Captain Blaylock's headquarters in Fort Myers, Major Alderman heard first-hand accounts of the aftermath of the Caloosahatchee massacre. Alderman was welcomed as a savior. He did not need additional inspiration, however. Indeed, what he *did* need was freedom from such distractions. Blaylock understood this and immediately set out to focus on the task at hand. They reviewed coordinates of targets and well suited initial shelling locations. They would deploy to Pine Island and Punta Rassa simultaneously at 0330 – just enough time to set up and program the launch codes into the computers to match the global positioning satellite data from the launch point to the coordinates on the map. At that hour there would be enough hesitation, once they were noticed, to debate whether to wake the commanding officers. After all, what's the big deal about a few trucks? Maybe they were moving vans coming back to pick up the dead soldiers' possessions. The sides on the trucks would not be dropped until moments before the first missile launches. The tops were hard shell, but split down the middle to fold over with each side, like a big transformer toy. They would then be detached completely for mobilization purposes. Those first missiles would be coordinated to take out their eyes and ears at the Sundial headquarters. *Oh, yes. We know about your geosynchronous satellite. It will still be there. You just won't be able to see its transmissions.* Additional strikes would be directed at barracks and outposts, and especially at the cluster of tanks in the motor pool. This circus could be over before it begins. Captain Blaylock was trying hard not to act as giddy as he was feeling.

Chapter Twenty

"What a marvelous idea this was! What an exquisitely marvelous idea!" exclaimed Michael Wilson as he pulled his Jeep Rubicon onto the gravel parking lot of the Mad Hatter Restaurant at the west end of Sanibel Island. "Whose idea was it for a wine dinner here?" he asked his dinner companion.

"It was Jeffrey's," replied Alison. "He is even paying for the whole thing since he and Marti are hosting it."

"Well, I for one am expecting some mighty fine wines," proclaimed the doctor. He stopped the engine, slid to the ground from the high seat, and joined Alison who was already waiting for him on the sidewalk beneath the canopied entrance to the small restaurant.

"I am certain you will have some *mighty fine wines* tonight," she reassured him, mimicking his earlier phrase. "Why don't you trade that big thing for something I don't have to climb down out of?" she asked him.

"I *like* my Rubicon," he said pathetically.

"I *know* you do, Sweetie," she mocked him with pursed and puckered lips, speaking in exaggerated sympathetic tones – almost in baby talk. "I *know* you do."

Wilson took it for a sign of affection and let it slide. *Always the actress*, he thought. When they went in, two of the couples were there already. The Mad Hatter was closed otherwise because of this private dinner party.

Jeffrey approached them with glasses of champagne. "Welcome," he said, playing the host.

Marti came up on his side. She had a champagne flute in one hand and an appetizer in the other. "You must get one of these," she indicated. It's some sort of smoked char with chopped veggies on an almond cracker. It's yummy."

Chef Kurt joined the group to top off Jeffrey's champagne. He was both chef and wait staff tonight because the affair was so small – only five couples. As Chef Kurt poured, Michael Wilson noted that the bottle was a 2010 Louis Roederer Cristal! *Incredible! Simply amazing*, he thought. *This is going to be an evening to remember.* He couldn't have been more prescient.

Alison walked over to where Jesse and Beverly were watching the preliminary activities with detached amusement. "Hello, you two," she said.

"It looks like Dr, Wilson has discovered the Cristal," said Jesse. Holding his own glass up to the light, he added, "It *is* amazingly effervescent."

"Must be dusty flutes," suggested Alison.

Beverly smiled at the explanation. She said, "Check out the appetizers."

"What do we have?" asked Alison. They moved toward a center table, arrayed with finger foods.

"These skewers of chicken with some kind of green sauce are my favorite, but the bruschetta is to die for!" Beverly said.

"Oh don't say 'to die for'" Alison requested.

"It's just a saying," Beverly protested.

"Honey, at my age, flowers scare me," she laughed, nearly losing a mouthful of Cristal.

"Oh, hush! You're not old, Alison. And *oh my God* you are beautiful!" Beverly went beyond reassurance all the way to admiration.

After a pause the women hugged briefly and each gave out a short giggle. They were drawn by a pick-up in the conversation level. They turned to Jeffrey who told them that John Cochran and his wife Lucy wouldn't be joining them tonight. Apparently he is needed elsewhere to coordinate some activity with Island Security. Clyde Markowitz and Jennifer Marin would not be coming either. It seemed that she had gone missing. No one has seen her for nearly a week.

"My God!" said Allison. "I hope nothing has happened to her."

"Me, too," echoed Marti, but not with the same conviction.

The six milled about smartly for another half-hour, taking full advantage of the appetizer table. Chef Kurt had reset the round dining table to accommodate only six. The place settings were his personal antique china, brought from his house, not his usual restaurant fare. The centerpiece was made from fresh topical flowers that his friend had arranged only this afternoon. "First course," he announced.

The three couples sat boy-girl-boy-girl and oohed-and-aahed as Chef Kurt presented them with a shrimp ceviche in a martini glass. The rim on the glass had a fine crust of a reddish peppery spice.

"Fire & Ice Shrimp Ceviche & Cilantro Sorbet," announced Chef Kurt as he presented the dishes. I will be right back with the wine pairing.

"Oh my goodness," Alison swooned and gasped. "This cilantro sorbet is to die for!"

Marti looked at her and they broke out laughing.

Chef Kurt returned with a German Riesling. He poured the ladies first, then the gentlemen.

"What are we drinking?" asked Michael, sandwiched between two girls with the giggles.

"This would be a German Riesling," began the chef, who doubled quite well as the sommelier. "In fact this might be *the* quintessential German Riesling. It is from the Mosel region, of course. It is an ultra concentrated wine. I find it to be quite complex and *très elegant*.

"Oh. It is truly marvelous," offered Alison as she sipped.

"It's good. I like it," said Jesse who was enjoying the evening and the company even though he was not saying much.

"Me, too," said Beverly, suddenly realizing how quiet she had been.

The group ate in comfortable silence or talked in hushed tones now. They continued to chat about personal issues mostly. Alison indicated that the plans for her jewelry design classes were complete and she would be starting those soon.

"It got so quiet in here I thought you had left," quipped Chef Kurt as he exited the kitchen with a tray containing soup dishes.

"No way," Jeffrey reassured him. "We were all busy enjoying the shrimp dish."

"Yes, you should put that on your menu," said Michael.

"I just might," Chef Kurt beamed at the compliments. "Next," he said, we have an "Apple Cheese Soup". The wine selection is from New Zealand. He left and returned with a recent vintage of a Kim Crawford sauvignon blanc.

They ate and talked some more. Jesse considered whether to tell them that Jennifer Marin left with Captain Bill, Fernando Lopez, and Greg Johnston. He decided that *that* information was on a need-to-know basis and he could keep a secret.

The door from the kitchen swung open again and the six friends metaphorically salivated like a pack of Ivan Petrovich Pavlov's dog. Chef Kurt beamed for the remainder of the evening over the appreciation for his creations. "What compliments!" he said. "You honor me."

"It is you who does us the honor," offered Alison.

"Next," he said, "we have a 'Seared Duck Breast'. This is my personal favorite. I have garnished it with a blueberry barbeque sauce, and on the side we have a peppercorn grit cake. Enjoy!"

325

The chef's presentation was beautiful. The duck breast was carved into even slices and spread in a fan shape across the plate. The sauce was drizzled artistically and contained whole blueberries. The gritcake sported a golden crispy crust. He returned with a Rued zinfandel from Sonoma County – a marvelous selection under any circumstance – but especially well suited to the duck.

They continued to eat and talk. Jeffrey asked Alison about the council's recent proposal to increase the annual fee assessment for the defense contract.

"Oh, not tonight, Jeffrey. We can talk about that another time," pleaded Alison.

"Well, I don't know when I will just happen to run into you. I was just wondering if you went along with hiking everybody's taxes, that's all." Jeffrey spoke his piece.

Michael frowned at him, but Alison replied, "Jeffrey, you ought to have some idea of what it costs to administrate this island. As a councilwoman, I pay approximately ten times what each of you registered islanders pay, and you don't see me complaining. There is an issue we had to resolve, and even though we didn't all agree with the tactics, we felt we had little choice. You just need to be thankful that someone is watching your back."

The ensuing silence reflected tension.

"Well, that was fun," Jesse said sarcastically to lighten things up. "Anyone for a midnight sail?"

"Well, Popeye the sailor man, there are two problems with that," suggested Marti, eager to change the subject.

"Only two?" laughed Beverly.

"First," Marti continued, "It's nowhere near midnight. And *B*," she paused for effect, then repeated the non-sequitur, "*B*, there's the next course."

Right on cue, Chef Kurt entered with an announcement of a "Red Wine Braised Short Rib of Bison, sautéed Swiss Chard and Cauliflower Puree". He added, "The wine is so amazing that I cannot share it with you."

"No," protested Michael. "Tell us!"

"No," seriously said Chef Kurt. "It is such a good wine that I am keeping it all for myself. I am not sharing it with you." Chef snorted at his joke, but returned with a bottle of Screaming Eagle, the legendary cult cabernet sauvignon from Napa Valley.

Michael slid off of his chair and onto his knees. "I have waited my entire life for this moment."

The laughter grew louder when Alison pretended not to understand the oenophile's meaning. "Michael, I didn't know you cared so. Are you proposing marriage?" she asked.

Michael looked around, and like a comedian on the stage – in fact with his best Groucho Marx imitation – he wiggled his eyebrows, rolled his eyes and said, "*I might be!*"

Uproarious laughter swelled from the inebriates. But *damn!* The cab was *good*.

Dessert was a bittersweet chocolate & raspberry pot de crème with wafer cookies. It was complimented by a 1994 Sandeman Vintage Port – nearly thirty years old and delicious.

Chef Kurt grazed against the door jamb as he entered and Alison observed, "Chef Kurt! I do believe you have been drinking a wee bit yourself as the evening has progressed."

"Well," the chef offered in his own defense, "I originally procured food for ten, as you know. So, yes, I have been having my own little party back in the kitchen. You couldn't blame me now could you?"

"Not at all," reassured Jeffrey, as he handed the chef a small coin purse presumed by all to contain a prearranged number of gold coins.

"Jeffrey, this was very generous of you," said Beverly.

"Hear, hear," agreed Michael, swaying and pounding the table with his fist.

There were smiles all around until Jeffrey indiscreetly mentioned the source of his fortune being related to arms dealers with whom he had made contact during his years as an NSA agent. A hush came over the room as Jeffrey tried to enact damage control by saying that he was merely trying to show the contrast, the yin and yang of it all – how out of misery and death there could come such vivacity and life.

"Oh, come *on*," Jeffrey protested, but it was a hard sell. "You can't have a light without a dark to put it in. You can't have love in your heart unless somebody else has hate. One extreme can't exist without the other. Everything would be grey and mediocre. The world has to have balance."

"But Jeffrey," Alison expressed her disappointment, trying not to let it stretch to disdain, "you may have contributed to the world's deepest misery. Gun running is one thing, but to trade with Somalia, knowing that the resurgence in their genocide was escalating. I just don't know what to say. It's been a lovely night for the most part, but we really must be going now." Michael rose to assist her with her chair.

"Well, the things that I may or may not have done are certainly no worse than other people around here – Ron Weber or that Brady Chapman. Hell, *he's* still active!"

"We all know about Brady, Jeffrey," said Alison, deflecting the tension. "Even I considered hiring him once – to take care of my philandering bastard husband – but the *piece-o-sheet* gave me a divorce before I could do anything drastic."

Several at the table laughed, but not Beverly. *We hadn't all known about Brady.* She just smiled sweetly at the new revelation. He was her friend and always so nice to her. Marti wasn't laughing either.

Others began to get up as well. Jeffrey was the last; he appeared tired, and not just from the wine. It became clear that the evening was coming to its awkward conclusion. Everyone said their fond good-byes and profusely thanked Chef Kurt for his culinary miracles.

Alison drove Wilson's Jeep Rubicon while the good doctor struggled to stay awake. She disliked the heavy bouncy tank almost as much as Michael loved it. She suspected that he liked it so much because he thought it was named for one of his favorite wines.

"Marry me," Michael slurred his words. "Marry me. I love you," he said.

"OK," Alison agreed. They rode in silence. He snored for a short time. *After all*, she thought, *it was a good evening.*

Jeffrey and Marti rode in silence, too, but for a different reason. They each knew it was over between them. Jeffrey had shared things that no one should have to live with. He had blurted out secrets of criminal deeds, beyond criminal really. It was his *MOAS* – his mother of all secrets – the one you never share because, if you do, you lose. You lose the important things: friends, trust, even the last vestiges of self respect. It was a fatal flaw in the relationship as of tonight. *What is wrong with me?* thought Marti. *Why can I not find somebody too?*

Jesse and Beverly retired to *Serenity*. It was moored across the street at Castaways marina, only a few hundred yards from the night's sumptuous feast.

"Come here you," demanded Jesse when they reached the ship's cabin.

"Woman on top!" Beverly countered aggressively.

Chapter Twenty-one

Beverly and Jesse were sleeping soundly, locked in a lover's embrace with their thighs pressed to each other's genitals as if there were no satiating them. The blast caused Jesse to awaken. He was careful of his entwined companion, but he hurried to his feet and slipped on underwear followed by his Carhartt shorts, worn soft and pliable by years of favoritism. Another report sounded in the distance, then another. They needed to slip their moorings and now – right now. Jesse moved quickly to the cockpit and could see flashes on the horizon. There was the glow of a fire from the middle of Sanibel. He could not pin-point where exactly.

"What's going on, Jesse?" Beverly called out from below.

"Get dressed quickly, Beverly. We're leaving," he told her.

"What's happening, Jesse?" she repeated.

"Get dressed, Babe. It's the end of the world. We're going on a little trip. Get dressed and come up. I could use a hand. Quickly now."

Jesse sounded calm enough – that's what confused her – but the message sounded urgent and he was moving quickly around the sailboat to release the lines. By the time she could throw on shorts and a T-shirt, he had shoved off from the dock and was running the small outboard at a low revolution. He was taking *Serenity* out into the bay. He could see well enough even though it was a few hours before the sun would rise. Plus – this was a big plus right about now – Jesse knew these waters better than anyone. He also knew where the mines were, which was important because he suspected that they had been switched on by Island Security by this time. The mast prevented him from entering the gulf through Blind Pass. Redfish Pass, between Captiva and North Captiva was narrow and too heavily mined. He would have to go past North Captiva Island and take Captiva Pass. As the shelling faded into the background to an extent, he felt secure in increasing the motor noise. Eventually they reached Captiva Pass and the wind became favorable. Jesse pulled at the halyard. When the sail was hoisted fully, he locked the line. He gave Beverly the rudder and the mainsail and he went to hoist the jib by its halyard. Speed seemed like a good idea at just this moment. It just so happened that the wind offered them a southwestern trajectory as their best inducement for speed. *Southwest will be fine, please,* and Jesse accepted the offer from Aeolus.

Jesse's heart skipped a beat when he became able to make out row upon row of boats and ships of all descriptions. It was as if the harbors had been emptied. In fact, as he now realized, that is exactly what had happened. Too late to turn back now. He was in full sail and at an even trim. As they approached the armada, he could see that they were laden with armed men in uniform – soldiers! It was clear as never before that they planned to invade Sanibel. He had a radio. Should he alert anyone? There was no Coast Guard to notify – none of *those* sailors had been willing to serve for free after Fort Knox was depleted by all of the foreign debt. He could still hear explosions coming from the island and maybe Pine Island, too. Every one that needed to know already knew. How could they not?

They were closing in on the armada rapidly. He would have to slow and straighten his course to avoid hitting one or more of the floating watercraft. He lowered his jib and sailed exclusively powered by the mainsail. He picked a lane between some boats that seemed wider than the other possibilities. He would be among them any moment. It was surely clear that he was not among their ranks. For one thing, he was bare chested, he hadn't taken the time to pull on a shirt. For another he seemed to be going the wrong way. *Hey, friend, which way is the island?* And third, he had this girl with him. *Girl?*

"Beverly, get inside, please."

"No!"

"Please?"

"No!"

Smile and wave, boys. Smile and wave. They both tried to act friendly as they passed silently between and among the boats. One soldier put his rifle to his shoulder, resting it on his shoulder in the new style. He sighted down the barrel and centered his aim on Jesse's temple. He followed the target for a brief second and then said *pow*. A brief moment of onomatopoeia and then he refocused on the task before him.

Beverly and Jesse were almost through the maze when the engines exploded to life at the same moment. Beverly nearly had a heart attack and

Jesse was startled almost as badly. The roar of hundreds of engines all revving at once was deafening. It was a tactic to energize the troops as they began to move toward Sanibel. They looked at each other not knowing whether to cry or laugh, but they had open seas ahead. They trimmed the sails and got away as quickly as *Serenity* could go. That racing yacht was finding her stride when the sunrise began.

.   .   .   .   .

The onslaught went off essentially as Major Alderman had planned it. Some of the lead boats struck mines, but that just told the others where it was safe to pass now as it was understood that there was not another mine in that vicinity. The mines were spread about evenly and with each detonation, headquarters back at Fort Myers marked the coordinates and radioed the information to those who could use it.

Island Security forces fought gallantly, but they each must have felt like one of William Travis's two hundred men at the Alamo facing Santa Anna's army of several thousand – except the odds were better at the Alamo. Rodriquez was in the satellite room of command and communications when the first missile struck that building. All of the high-tech surveillance disappeared within the first minute of the attack. General Presswood's Spanish Hacienda-style palace was also among the first structures destroyed by an hour's worth of missile strikes on the island. It was rendered more burnt than orange. Entire residential neighborhoods were destroyed – so was a motor pool full of pristine urban tanks.

No one within Island Security could get a handle on the situation. No one knew for sure that the General was killed when his home exploded. If he was dead, no one seemed to know who *was* in charge. A captain did assume command briefly, but he was unrealistic in his demands and he fell victim to friendly fire.

At just the precise moment the shelling stopped, it became eerily quiet in a few areas of the island, near its center. At the same time the beaches were filling with motor craft of every description. While thousands were swarming the beaches from every direction, the temporary fabricated bridge worked like a charm. The Army of the Alliance had not had time to swarm the entire island before the heavy tanks and troop carriers and other military vehicles and hardware were streaming over the causeway from the mainland.

Snipers and pockets of resistance from well equipped and better trained forces could slow but not turn the advance. They were very badly outnumbered. Still the *Battle for Sanibel*, as it was to be called, was closer than could have been imagined. What one would have thought would have been a two hour mop up operation was surprisingly prolonged. After two days of going door-to-door there were still pockets of resistance.

After the Caloosahatchee massacre the Island Security forces did not expect mercy. They did not get it either. This was a no holds barred, take no prisoners slugfest. The mainland forces did not yield even to Island Security's attempts to use citizens as shields. Many civilians were killed.

Sanibel was plundered. The looting began in a systematic fashion even before a cease fire was called. In fact the Army of the Alliance hoped that they could provoke an Island Security trooper to reveal himself with a gunshot. The Army of the Alliance was all over that action.

Alderman's men were highly experienced at neighborhood invasions – but this was an entire island, and a wealthy one. The causeway repair also brought the eighteen-wheelers that were then loaded with prize possessions. No house was neglected. Exploded beach houses were picked over as meticulously as were mansions full of fine art.

Medical care was provided for wounded civilians after Alderman's troops were taken care of. Wounded Island Security troops were executed on the spot. There was no attempt to feed or shelter the civilians and soon after a cessation of hostilities seemed apparent, many disappeared – some left the island, others went into hiding.

After Sanibel was stripped of everything of value – and that took several days, even for an army – Alderman and his troops left. They took their temporary bridge with them. They left some sea shells.

Chapter Twenty-two

When they approached Sanibel from the northwest, Jesse and Beverly circled the island twice before docking *Serenity* at the Tarpon Bay marina. Captain Bill was sitting at a table with Barefoot Chuck watching the sleek craft drop her sails and motor slowly to the wooden pier. They looked tired and neither spoke nor so much as waved to the approaching sailboat.

"You did right to leave," Captain Bill said somberly as the two disembarked and made their way up the pier toward the covered deck. "It got bad."

Jesse noted the drying blood and stench of the marina's tour guide boat as they walked past the large pontoon craft. Captain Bill saw his reaction and explained, "We hosed it down, but we've been using the tour boat as a water hearse. There were so many dead bodies; we couldn't let them rot in the sun. We wrapped them up in some kind of shrouds and took 'em pretty far out so they wouldn't wash back to us. We figured some kind of burial at sea was the right thing to do. We said words over the ones we knew and tried to be respectful of the others."

"You did good, Bill," said Jesse. "I'm sorry I wasn't here to help."

"Don't be sorry mate. You did right. You probably couldn't have hidden for long, and if they had found you they would have killed you. As for a pretty white girl..." he glanced at Beverly and then cast his eyes down, "well, you don't want to know. "

Bill paused for a moment while Jesse and Beverly joined him and Chuck at their table. "They left us old farts alone," he continued, "They knew we couldn't hurt them, I guess.

After Island Security headquarters was breeched and *they* were all killed, the gangs just had their way with us. The island is all messed up. Craters from shelling, condo complexes were set on fire; it's bad. The only good to say about it is they won't be back for a long while. There's nothin' left for 'em here anymore. They looted the place proper."

Beverly's eyes welled with tears as her distorted face reflected the loss of so many friends. "Who's left on the island?" she asked Bill.

"Can't say for certain. Some folks are still holed up – shell shocked or some such. I've run into some I wouldn't have expected to make it. Dr. Wilson is still here, probably because he put on an armband when the fighting was bad and started running around like a battlefield medic. Didn't matter to him whose side a fellow was on as long as he had a dose of morphine to give. I saw Alison, but she didn't look too good. Cochran's gone," he paused. "Do you know if they hit Captiva?"

"Yeah," said Jesse, nodding, "it looked that way from the gulf and the bay. North Captiva, too, had some apparent shelling, but I don't know any details."

"Damn shame, but I'm not surprised. There were thousands of them."

Everyone sat quietly reflecting on life as it had been, was now, and would be – the extreme turns that can happen. It was Chuck who finally broke the silence. "Forgive that old bearded sea Captain," he glanced over at his friend. "He's more demented than I am. Is anyone besides me hungry?"

"Do you have enough?" asked Beverly. They would be alright until they could find something of their own.

"We have redfish and snook. I recommend the redfish, with a side order of fresh Sanibel well water. It's a good thing that plant is computerized and hasn't kicked off line recently," he looked at Jesse knowingly.

"I'll look in on the gauges later this week." Jesse took the hint. "Yes, a bit of lunch sounds good. Thanks."

.   .   .   .   .

They left the marina in one of the rickshaw-style bicycle taxis. Jesse wanted the exercise and Beverly was in a mood to just observe her beloved island as he peddled while she rode. Sad scenes of upturned palm trees, cratered landscaping, shattered store fronts, charred buildings, and trash everywhere told her Sanibel would never be the same, and her despondency deepened. They came to a beach access and Jesse pulled the taxi under the shade of an Australian pine and climbed off the bicycle.

"Time to let the horse rest," he said with a sweet smile.

She rarely saw him acting tired, but the aftermath of the violence had to be having an impact on his emotions as well. *Oh, Jesse,* she thought. *What would I do without you now?*

Beverly walked over the shallow dunes and looked out over the deserted beach. The beauty was unchanged. There was no blemish at all, and no people. The white sands stretched in both directions and the surf lapped and caressed the shore. There were shorebirds everywhere, and shells.

Beverly ran the short distance to the wet sand where the waves visited and left. Sandpipers darted from her path and a flow of gulls filled the sky with a temporary cloud before settling once more a safe distance up the shoreline. Pelicans floated on the gentle waves of surf a few hundred yards out and other pelicans tucked in their flight wings and dove for fish. She looked at her feet as she walked. Soon she saw a prize. She bent over in the classic Sanibel stoop and retrieved a shell to inspect. It was an apple murex with more than a little coral coloring. Its original occupant, a hermit crab, had moved on. Beverly bent again to rinse the shell in the surf, shaking off the sand.

The shell had a small break in its edges. It was broken and therefore imperfect. *Like my island,* she thought. *Broken and definitely not perfect, but still beautiful.* She tucked the shell in her pocket and turned to walk back to where Jesse was waiting, in the shade of the pine tree.

She came up to Jesse and sat beside him. She took hold of his knee for balance as she turned to face him, then she scooted herself away slightly so she could face him more directly. When she had his full attention she said, "I want us to stay on the island, Jesse. I want to move into the house Chapman left me when he died, if it's still intact. And I want to build something else there if that one was destroyed. I did most of that landscaping and I want to be near my old familiar projects. Mostly though, I want to be with you, if not there then you choose."

"I've been thinking, too," said Jesse.

He didn't say 'yes'; he didn't say 'no', thought Beverly. "What?" she asked.

Jesse looked into her eyes. "I want us to have children," he said softly.

Beverly did not see *that* coming. A bombshell is still a bombshell, even if it mellows sweetly over the next moments. Beverly's open mouth turned upwards into a smile that caused her eyes to crinkle at the outer edges and fill with tears.

So many emotions of such extremes – how could she process it all? Where had Jesse found the ultimate expression of optimism in the wake of the island's destruction?

Beverly's gaze had not left Jesse's eyes. She saw sincerity and she felt love. "I want that, too," she said at last. She straddled him and he fell back on the pine needles and sand. She was lying fully on him and took each of his hands in hers, palm to palm. They lay there fully clothed, breathing deeper. She added, "before Doc Wilson gets too old to catch the baby without dropping it."

"Let's go for another ride," said Jesse as they sat up. He was acquiescing to Beverly's request to move into Chapman's former house if it still stood.

They took the bike taxi along Middle Gulf toward East Gulf. Some dwellings appeared intact; others like the general's hacienda, across from the Sundial, were destroyed utterly. They stopped to talk with a couple who were walking toward them. The man was vaguely familiar in a common way – medium build, brown hair, late thirties. The woman was Marti Leinhart. Beverly climbed out of the seat and hugged her friend.

"I am so happy to see you," they each said in so many words. They each told their particular tale of survival. Marti introduced Antonio.

"Tony and I met in the wildlife refuge. Quite a few of us hid out there," said Marti.

"Only *now* are some of us feeling safe enough to venture out," said Antonio with what Beverly thought was a charming Italian accent. "Marti and I actually represent a sort of scouting party. Provisions are starting to, um, dwindle – is that the word? To grow smaller? And we are headed back to "Ding" Darling – I just love saying that – to give the others the 'all clear'. Do you think that would be OK now?" Antonio looked at Jesse.

"Yes. They are gone and I doubt they will be back," said Jesse. "How many are hiding out?"

"Hundreds," said Marti.

"How does the island look to you? We haven't seen the east-half for ourselves yet. We know it can't be good," added Beverly.

"Right. Some blocks are gone. Some of the crops are gone, but a lot seems fairly much intact. The bridge over the canal on Periwinkle is gone; apparently an antitank device took it out because there is a large burned out urban tank off to the side. No bodies, thank God! I don't think I could handle finding people that way," declared Marti.

"Thank Captain Bill and Barefoot Chuck for that," said Jesse. "They have been conducting burials at sea and bringing back plenty of fish to eat. Some of you might want to swing by Tarpon Bay marina and give them a hand cleaning the fish. The haul will not last and they would be happy to see so many survivors. They thought that not many people were left alive."

"No, we've seen more than just our groups," assured Marti. "We didn't take a head count but I would guess there are over a thousand left on Sanibel, maybe twice that. The real blood bath seemed to be directed at Island Security. No one has seen any trace of any of them."

"Not surprising," said Jesse. "This was more about showing the region, and maybe the country, that there is a new order – just like what happened with metropolitan police and National Guard units a few years ago. Anyway, it sure is good to see you two and to hear some encouraging news."

"Any word you want to send back with us, Jesse?" asked Marti.

"Not so much," said Jesse. "Just give everyone a week or so to settle back in and we will all get together soon enough – maybe at the library." With that he climbed back onto the bicycle seat.

Beverly and Marti hugged as Antonio shook Jesse's hand.

"Good luck, you two."

"Same."

As he peddled, he said loudly enough for Beverly to hear over the road noise, "I was just wondering…"

"What?" she asked.

"With the bridge out along the canal, we might be able to bring *Serenity* down the canal to the new house – if it's still intact."

The Chapman house *was* still intact. The doors were open and many items were missing, but the abandoned house had offered no resistance and had taken on no firepower. Even the glass on the greenhouse was still intact. The keypad outside the safe room had been removed and the safe room had been breached. The looters must have had a real "WTF" moment when they discovered the high tech communications equipment and their holographic monitors. Surprisingly, the wine cellar was largely intact. They appeared to have taken several hundred bottles for personal consumption, but wine cellars were common on Sanibel. The looters were probably saturated with that particular liquid asset.

Beverly turned to Jesse. "What do you think, Jesse? Can we make it here?"

"It's good," he replies. "It's a good place to start."

"I hadn't told you," said Beverly. "But when Chapman left me this house in his will, he left me a bank account in the Cayman Islands. I may be richer than you; not that it matters."

"Not that it matters at all," he said philosophically. "Still, I would doubt that seriously," he grinned. "*Quite* seriously."

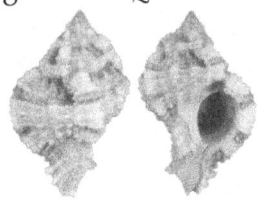

Only the Beginning